SAM ASTRAC

AN END TO DYING

A NOVEL

FARRAR, STRAUS AND CUDAHY

NEW YORK

Library of Congress catalog card number: 56-6161
First printing, 1956
Manufactured in the U. S. A. by H. Wolff, New York
Published simultaneously in Canada by Ambassador Books, Ltd., Toronto
Design: Klaus M. Gemming

CONTENTS

THE KAGAN-COHEN FAMILY

The progenitor of the Kagan family was Yitzhoc Kagan, a pedlar in Tsarist Russia.

Yitzhoc had two sons, Eleazar, who emigrated to America and became Louis Cohen, and Abraham.

Abraham Kagan stayed in Russia and married Heika Starobinetz. Their eleven sons and one daughter were named:

Jacob, Mendel, Samuel, Laban, David, Mordecai, Joshua, Elihu, Reuben, Solomon, Esther, Benjamin.

Five of the brothers—Mendel, Laban, Samuel, Solomon and Benjamin—emigrated to America. Mendel and Laban changed their first names to Morris and Larry and all five brothers changed their last name to Cohen.

Jacob, David, Mordecai, Joshua and Elihu Kagan stayed in Russia, but Jacob's two sons, David and Yitzhoc, emigrated to America and became David and Jack Cohen.

Esther Kagan married Dr. Isaac Starobinetz, a distant relation of Esther's mother Heika. They emigrated to America, shortened their family name to Star, and had one child, Sam, the narrator of this story.

A FULLNESS IN DEATH

There is an end to dying and a fullness in death. For a few months that were eternity, I awaited my mother's death. When I sat close to her bed while she slept, when I rode on the subway and everything faded into the roaring monotony of the train's powerful rhythm, when the vacuum I was living in crystallized into a moment of consciousness, I hoped, but knew there could be no reprieve. I had watched my father die and had prayed and cursed God; now I felt numb. While this eternity was rushing by, there were only rare moments of understanding, and though I was aware my mother was going to die, I knew it as a fact only after the brother she loved most, my uncle Larry, visited her for the last time. He told her he would be away for a month. My mother tried to hold back, but then cried hysterically, convulsively; small, wasted, turning the yellowish color she was to die with, she threw herself into his arms. They stood several feet from where I was sitting, he clasping her tightly, both crying.

Every day during the three months she was in the nursing home in Brooklyn, I would awake, go to school, then to work, and, at about eight in the evening, visit with her for several hours until she was given an injection of something that might permit her to sleep. I would leave and go home by subway: my eyes would close and I would watch the intruding electric lights play on an infinite black background. I knew always that if I were to open my eyes, then close them, I could see this infinity I felt so much a part of. In the morning, when the alarm went off, I awoke to know that she was in the heavy pain of morphined, dull agony. Hearing myself cough, wanting to lie down again, to cover myself and sink almost into sleep, I shivered, and still in pajamas, went to the kitchen. I prepared hot chocolate milk and then, going back to my bedroom, I stood next to the phonograph, and played *The Rites of Spring*. Impatient, I placed the needle near the climax, at the point on the record where the drums and brass become a crescendo that rises and falls in a steadily quickening beat; my arms were extended, my fingers pressed hard against the hot metal sides of the phonograph. The power that I felt manipulated me with deft, urgent hands, finally exhausting me as I gasped with the last upswing of strings and the extended, short, downbeats of drums and brass.

The chocolate milk was too hot; I sat at the dining room table and, sipping it, forgot the day before me, the fever in my body. Everything during those months, everything was distinct from this world—how different from now! I walk by the river, thinking of nothing, halting to stare at ships or at the barely moving, caressing water. A sudden shiver and I sense and then drown deep in the history of my love. Watching the approaching spotlight of a train coming into a station, hypnotized by the brilliance and finally by the lines within the core of light, staying up through the night, trying to sleep on hard, uncomfortable benches, smoking incessantly; and then the moment before sleep: an intangible but grasped moment. It is that split second before drowning when time and death are words without meaning and there can be only life.

One year after my father's death, my mother and I were driven to the cemetery in Long Island where he was buried, to unveil a stone and to say some prayers. At the rear of the crowd, made up mainly of my relatives, I saw my father's good friend, Doctor Deutschman. He was standing alone and he moved very slowly. Retired from medical practice because of a heart condition, all the pains of a friendless and nearly inactive existence had descended on him in this one year. When my father was alive, Deutschman visited him several times every week. They played pinochle and invariably Deutschman was the loser. They talked animatedly of the displaced persons, of Palestine, and said *olavasholom,* may his soul rest in peace, each time one of them mentioned the name of Franklin Delano Roosevelt. My father could sometimes make Deutschman laugh at himself; certainly he teased him enough about his abominable memory for cards. I never saw him without a jacket and vest; he was a very proper and serious man who wore dark suits and whose brow was creased a hundred times. After the unveiling, at our apartment, he took me aside and told me that my mother was sick, that he could tell by just looking at her.

"But she's been crying," I said.

"Never mind. I say she's sick."

Her first operation was performed three months later. Deutschman was in surgery during each operation. After the first, an exploratory, he came down to the lobby of the hospital; there must have been fifty members of my family around him and he said that there was definitely something growing there. Two weeks later he watched the surgeon and his assistants for four hours and when he came into the lobby he was wiping his forehead with an already moist handkerchief. "He's a master," Deutschman said. "I've never seen such perfection, like magic. He did more than anyone alive could have done." He padded his handkerchief and wiped his thick lips and said, "We still don't know."

After the third operation, they did know, and they told us she might live a year. We moved her back home, to the apartment in the East Bronx and we—the family—searched. Some of the numerous acquaintances of my relatives told of places they had heard of: a doctor in Missouri, a rest farm in Pennsylvania, a clinic in Texas. I wrote letters and tried to get more than second-hand, non-professional opinions. I spoke to Deutschman and several other doctors who had been friends of my father, and I was told that these places were not recognized, that some of them had even been exposed by the American Medical Association. "But how can we be sure unless we try?" my uncle Ben said. "We'll never forgive ourselves if we don't do everything."

We decided to send my mother to the clinic in Texas, but we did not tell her until all the arrangements had been made. David, the orphaned unmarried son of Jacob, the eldest of my mother's eleven brothers, would accompany her. On the evening before they were to leave, my uncles Ben, Sol and Larry, my cousin David and his brother Jack and I drove in one car to the Bronx and discussed how we could tell her why we wanted her to go without making her think of the immediacy. My mother had known from the beginning, had suspected for months previous to the first accurate diagnosis that she had the same disease that had killed my father, but after the last operation we never spoke of it. She suffered a great deal, more then, when she still felt the pain in each part of her body, than later, when her ravaged body and drugged mind made her incapable of feeling that kind of extreme pain. So solitary in her suffering, in her sleepless nights and drugged sleep, she drew courage with her every breath. Unable to enjoy her former pleasures, her life itself—cooking and eating, reading her newspaper, walking, visiting with her favorite nieces—she had not given up hope, had not accepted the fact of death. Before we went in to see her, I went next door and asked Doctor Weiss, who had taken over my father's office, to come in with us to give us backing.

"Texas?" my mother repeated. "There's no hospital in New York?"

"Eshka, I've heard from a customer, they've a new method," Ben said.

"It's the truth," Sol said in Yiddish and nodded his head.

"Do you think it's a good idea?" Jack asked Doctor Weiss.

"You can't lose," he said.

She nodded her head very seriously and said, "So? So I've never been in an airplane and I ought to fly maybe once before I die."

My mother and David stayed in Texas two days. We met them at LaGuardia Airfield and drove across the Triborough Bridge to the East Bronx. The stewardess had given my mother an injection of demarol a short time before the plane had landed, and in the automobile she was silent, her eyes open but sightless. Looking at her, her face and her body so wasted and drawn, I thought for a moment, forgetting the hope and anxiety I had felt during the two months she had had three operations, forgetting the gradual decay, that she was not my mother, that she was an absolute stranger, a dying woman but not my mother. David had brought back a bag full of medicines and an opinion that he delivered when we arrived at the apartment.

"They're fakers."

"How are you sure?"

"While she's being examined I go into town. There's a liquor store; the owner's name is Katzman and I go in and look around. He asks me do I want something. I buy a bottle of Dewars—it's forty cents less in Texas—and as I'm paying I say '*Lansman,* what about the cancer clinic?'

" 'What about it?' he says.

" 'Is it any good?'

" 'My friend,' he says, 'they're fakers.'

" 'So many are waiting to see the doctor.'

" 'All hicks,' he says."

My mother never took any of the medicines, but not because of David's report. The first time her nurse brought her the pills, my mother said, "Give it to the cows," and when the nurse asked her why she would not take them, she answered, "The *goy* told me I have cancer because I eat too many tomatoes. I wanted to spit in his face."

Doctor Deutschman had not approved of our sending my mother to Texas and he did not approve of our moving her to the nursing home in Brooklyn. Each time he visited her there, I felt as though he were asking me, "Why do you put her through this torture of hope?" We were living a lie, my mother, my family and I; we had hope and we tried not to think of death. In this nursing home, affiliated with a cancer research group, my mother received treatments described as experimental by the physicians who had developed them. She was used as a test case—a guinea pig in the cause of human suffering; her reactions to various treatments were recorded in nurses' day books and analyzed by physicians in weekly reports. She was kept to a rigid schedule that to a great extent deprived her of the narcotics she needed, and though there were rare moments when she felt better, and for all I know the treatments did lengthen her life, her condition grew steadily worse. She suffered incredibly when she was not given an injection because it was not yet four hours or five hours since she had had her last injection of exactly fifty cubic centimeters of demarol.

Up to the day we brought her from the apartment to the nursing home, she had been receiving as many injections as it was safe to give. The morning that we moved her, Doctor Weiss gave her a dose he thought would last for several hours. I sat in the tall armchair by the dining room window, waiting for Gloria, my cousin Jack's wife, who was to drive us to Brooklyn. It was raining, the room was dark; when I looked at the large clock on the wall I could barely make out the time. When Gloria came, the nurse woke my mother, and dressed her in a red and white print dress that hung straight down on her shapeless body. I helped her into a black broadtail coat she had had for fifteen years and that she could now wrap around herself twice. We had packed a small, overnight bag for her: her favorite perfumes, some other cosmetics, tooth paste and bed clothes. There was nothing more; we left the apartment. The nurse said good-bye and wished us the best of luck. With my hand I swept newspapers on the back seat of the car onto the floor, then I helped my mother in. I put a blanket over her legs. She was not fully awake; she looked at the apartment with its closed Venetian blinds, and pulled the collar of her coat tight around her neck. We drove down Lafayette Street, past the high walled monastery. For a short while Gloria talked as she drove, but when my mother began to moan, to bite her lips, and then relax, pale and colorless, Gloria stopped talking and stared straight ahead. I held my mother's burning hand, and each time I looked at her face, I quickly averted my eyes and watched the raindrops course down the side window.

We left her at the nursing home in the afternoon; she was sleeping. When we had taken her to her room, when she had seen how plain and ugly it was, when she had looked out the window and seen the dirty brick wall of a building not ten feet away, when she had heard the hideous screams of a partially paralyzed woman in the room next door, she had turned to me and had asked, "Where did you bring me?" She had been undressed and put to bed by a nurse, and when the pains had come again, not the steady gnawing she always felt, but the sharp lasting thrusts, she had begun to cry. "Why couldn't you just let me die at home?"

The last few weeks that my mother was alive, I lived in my uncle Ben's house in Long Island. Late at night, driving from the nursing home, he would tell me stories of my mother, of their life in Russia. And motionless in his fast, powerful automobile, the car's headlights illumining only a stretch of blank road ahead of us, and everything dark behind and above us, I listened and grew warm. He told me of their eldest brother, Jacob, a lumberman, the wealthiest Jew in all of Russia. He told me of Jacob's death and his own marvelous escape from Russia. Like his four brothers who had emigrated to America, Ben had gone immediately upon arrival in New York City, into the garment industry, had worked hard and, when he had made enough money, had bought his house and regained some of that sense of land and property, of solidly rooted wealth he had had in the old country. Here, with his own house—not an apartment in the city—with land and trees of his own, no matter how little, every night, before he went to bed, he would walk down the street he lived on, a block of houses like his own, and look at the stars and breathe deeply. His next door neighbor was my uncle Sol; they had bought the houses at the same time a year before. On the Sunday following their purchase, my mother and I went with Ben, Sol, and their wives to see the not yet completed homes. My mother pictured the trees and grass, knew not the names but the colors of the flowers she would plant, knew with just what kind of big furniture she would fill each room. "Maybe if I'm lucky, some rich man'll marry me and buy me a house."

"You need a house even less than we," Anna said.

"You want to live in the stinking Bronx till you die?" Ben said without looking at his wife. "In the summer it's cool; breathe the air, just breathe it, and tell me if it isn't different. It'll add ten years to your life."

"I won't last ten years," Anna said.

My mother nodded her head and said, "Annalle, if you die, God forbid, I'll come here and look after your husband."

Sol had not been as enthusiastically convinced as his brother that he had done the smart thing in buying his house. He had been worried, though, that he might be left out of the family group which had moved almost *en masse* to Long Island. Also, and certainly his wife reminded him of this enough, his daughter should meet nice Jewish boys and not Bronx hoodlums. He surveyed his property with his hands in his overcoat pockets. He placed a cigarette in a holder, stamped his feet and said to me, "Come on Sam, we'll go behind the house." He looked to see if anyone was watching and said, smiling, "Otherwise it isn't a house."

They were attractive seven-room ranch homes that had been furnished by the same interior decorator, a woman who had made both homes, inside as well as outside, absolutely identical. The favorite room was the knotty-pine-panelled, cork-floored den; here was the television set. In Sol's den there was also a canary whose singing, my aunt Gertie said, added beauty to her and her husband's lives. During the day, Gertie would sit in a deep cushioned armchair and work on crossword puzzles, forcing her short and huge body out of the chair only by remarkable effort of will, to answer a phone or to satisfy an overpowering desire for some bread and jam. While my mother was in the nursing home, Gertie and Anna, Ben's wife, visited her several times a week, and once Gertie asked her permission to give a sweet sixteen party for her daughter Edith. My mother said, "Yes, if it's not the same day as my funeral," and Gertie said that she shouldn't think like that, and later made plans for a surprise party.

Every evening, the man of each house, after a heavy dinner, retired to the den where he unfastened the top button of his trousers, took off his shoes, stretched his legs onto a hassock, and watched television or read the Yiddish newspaper until he fell asleep. If, one day, Anna forgot or was unable to get Ben his newspaper, he would telephone his brothers until he found one who had a copy and promised to save it for him. The newspaper had many features; often it carried interviews or accounts of famous Jewish Americans, and there was always the *roman,* the fiction installment that ran day after day for a year. In my family, while the *roman* was being published, everybody characterized everyone else by giving him the name of someone in the *roman*—Beckele, the girl with a broken heart; Motke, the butcher with a heart of gold; Alfred, the college boy who broke Beckele's heart and married a Gentile, a *shiksa.* Sometimes the newspaper republished stories by the great author, Shmyola Bernstein. In Russia he had been a friend and constant companion of my uncle Jacob; after the revolution when Bernstein went to Paris to live, he corresponded with my father and Jacob's son, David. On my *Bar-mitzvah,* the celebration of my coming into manhood on my thirteenth birthday, he sent me a book of his stories. In my opinion, he was a great writer, not because of his style, which was quite plain, but because of the philosophy that permeated everything he wrote. He always seemed to be making a plea for gentleness, generosity and decency, and many of his stories read just like fairy tales. When his stories appeared in the newspaper, why then my uncle Ben would read them with enjoyment and say, "Ah, Shmyola is as good as ever! You know," he would continue, "he was one of the ugliest and most peculiar men I ever knew, but about him there was a beauty."

While I lived in my uncle Ben's home, I was occupied from six in the morning, when I was awakened, till about midnight, going to school, working in the liquor store, and visiting my mother. On Sundays, I spent the entire day at the nursing home. Never alone with my mother for more than a few minutes, standing up to let visitors sit, leaving the room when there was a crowd, I never felt the passing of time, only the rush toward the single event I knew was almost imminent. There were moments when I thought that my mother was conscious of this rush, that, like me, she had surrendered to the disease.

Early one morning, the telephone rang, waking us. In a flat voice, the nurse told me that my mother had tried to commit suicide. Barely able to leave her bed, my mother had climbed three flights of stairs before she had been discovered. Ben and I immediately dressed and went to see her. We drove on parkways in the gray of the winter dawn. The sun was up when we got to her room. She was asleep and we waited for her to awaken. When she opened her eyes and saw us, she said, "I made them promise not to tell you," and began to cry. Ben and I were rooted to where we stood. We just stood and watched, and I wanted to cry but did not.

Only a few days later, she asked me to get her chop suey. She ate only a little but she relished it. Afterwards, she asked me to write down the names of the foods she wanted: frankfurters, broiled chicken, sturgeon, potato salad, lox and pumpernickel. Sarah brought her chicken but my mother did not eat it. Day by day, her spirit, her desire for life, her love of stories and imitations, everything began to lose its value, cheated by cancer.

Three weeks before she died, we moved her to a hospital in Manhattan; we wanted everything to be clean and proper.

Often, when my uncles and I drove to the hospital, we met other relatives and then all went out to dinner. We ate in expensive restaurants; sometimes we were a party of ten or more. After the first drink, we might forget my mother, what she had looked like, and then we could talk and laugh; but later, during the long drive to Ben's home, sleepy and so very tired, we had nothing to say. In the mornings, driving into the city, Ben and Sol would sometimes talk of business, of the price of this or that material, of the styles my uncle Larry had brought back from Paris on his last trip. One morning, Ben, who always drove, took his eyes from the road and glanced angrily at Sol, then he looked back at the road. At the entrance to the Queens Mid-Town Tunnel, we were moving slowly in heavy traffic when Ben suddenly applied the brakes, barely avoiding a collision with the car in front of us. Sol was thrown forward and hit his elbow hard against the door. "What's the matter with you?" he asked sharply.

Ben looked at his brother and said, "I'm upset. Do you know that Gertie's giving a party for Edith?"

"A party?" Sol repeated.

"Yes, a party! It's supposed to be a surprise for you and Edith."

"I need no surprises," Sol said.

That evening, after Sol had been served at dinner, he asked his wife, "When's the party?"

"Who told you?"

"What difference who told me?"

"Ben did, I know. Anna told him."

"Are you making a party?" Sol insisted.

"I was going to surprise Edith and you."

"You should make a party while Eshka's dying?"

Gertie's voice rose. "I asked her and she said it was all right. Besides, I've invited all Edith's classmates. A girl's sixteen only once and even if your sister's sick, it doesn't mean that Edith can't have a party."

"Enough!" Sol exclaimed.

"There's too much sickness in your family, anyway. All the

time there's someone dying. We don't always have to have sad faces."

Sol got up from the table and left the room.

The party was kept secret from Edith, and on the Saturday night, when she entered the house and all the lights went on and everybody screamed, "Happy Birthday!" Edith was shocked, and then laughed at the happy surprise. Everybody thought that the party was a great success. Sol came home late (he had visited my mother and had not wanted to go home at all), and entered the house filled with music and dancing and laughter. He was introduced to some of the young guests and later, standing alone, smoking a cigarette in a holder, he said as if he were speaking to someone, "You know it's no good. You live such a short life, in general, it should be better."

During the last few days, Ben and I spent all our time with my mother and Anna became our intermediary with the rest of the family. All day long, with secretarial efficiency, she received and answered phone calls: "They've been feeding her intravenously. She didn't say a word today; she recognized Ben but only for a second. No, we have no idea."

A pigeon landed on the ledge outside the room. It strutted for a moment, then, its beak down, walked back and forth, pecking at the ledge. It flew away and, joining a number of pigeons, swooped out of sight. Only in the corridor was there the occasional sound of a person walking or an attendant wheeling trays for afternoon tea. The room was light and clean, sunlight seeping through partially open bamboo blinds. There were wall closets with sliding doors and there was a bureau and two leather upholstered chairs made of white pine. The single large window overlooked Central Park; across the park I could see the twin towers of The Eldorado. A Seurat reproduction hung on the wall behind the bed; the diminished green of the grass and the static introspection of the woman at the right were a kind of mirror. Everything was happening outside of me, and though I could not deny I was sitting in a chair, hearing the sharp breathing noises of my mother, nothing seemed real. If it were real, if this were not a dream, I would hear sounds from the streets; there would be something moving quickly, a bus to run to catch. No. A tightrope walker standing a mile above the valley of a canyon on an inch-thick rope, suddenly forgetting who he is, what he's doing, where he's going, balanced and waiting, attendant to the wind. I tried to focus on my mother, and for a second she was transformed into the full, heavy woman she had been, but the picture was blurred and did not last. She lay on the double-jointed hospital bed, her head and shoulders higher than the rest of her body, her skin and the whites of her eyes jaundiced bright, deep yellow. Her flesh was empty and dry, sapped of fluids. Once I thought that her eyes had focused on me and I leaned towards her. Her open eyes stared straight out; perhaps she had seen me for a second. No. I knew it was almost all over, that except for her heart, which refused to stop beating, she was dead.

I went to the Bronx and said good-bye to the apartment I had lived in all my life. There was a wind from the East River blowing up Hunts Point Avenue. I walked unshaven, without a hat, wearing a T-shirt beneath my jacket, feeling all at the same time the wind and the sun and the city haze. There were women shopping and old men standing idly in front of stores or apartment building entrances. As I passed the vegetable store, I saw Horowitz bending to pick up a head of lettuce from a wooden crate on the floor. There were several women inside and I did not want to go in to say hello; he would only look at me sadly.

The apartment was dark. A few light wooden slats of the closed Venetian blinds hung one on the other, permitting a little light to pass through, and the ribbons hanging on both sides of the blinds were, in many places, half-torn. The window screens from the summer before were still attached. The rooms were in disorder; there were packed cardboard boxes all over and the furniture was piled one piece on top of another. I checked the number of boxes, expecting the storage people at any time. Then I lay down on the bare mattress of my bed. I heard the noise of the streets: the talk, the yelling children, the roar of the cars and the trucks, the powerful pick-up of the bus that stopped on the corner twenty feet away from my bedroom window. Nothing had changed and everything was the same.

The storage men were a little late and just after they arrived and started to move out the furniture, my mother's sister-in-law, Fanny, came. We stood together and watched them take out the furniture, the cardboard boxes filled with linens, dishes and silverware, and the two boxes of personal papers and photographs. My aunt saw one of my mother's shawls, dust covered, on the floor. She picked it up, shook it out, and said that she was keeping it. "Everything here means so much to me. To stand here and watch them move, it hurts my heart."

She looked at me sideways. "It's wonderful to be so strong and hard. I can never be."

We watched them take everything out, and a neighbor came in and said, "Such a wonderful woman. I'll never forget her." She turned to me. "You should never have another sorrow." When my aunt and the neighbor were leaving, I said that I would see if anything important had been forgotten, but when I heard the door close behind them, I walked back to it and locked it.

There were tufts of dust on the linoleum floor where some furniture had been. The Venetian blinds and three pieces of the dining room set had been left behind, too large or damaged to be stored or sold. The inch-thick marble top of the long mahogany-stained bureau was cracked in three places; one small triangular chip was lying on the floor.

The table was in the center of the room. Heavy and solid, it was about ten feet long and four feet wide. It was covered by a glass top, under which there had been a lace cloth that had hung several inches down on the four sides of the table. Between the glass and the lace, for the whole length and width of the table, had been photographs. Pictures of members of my family whose relationship to me I never fully understood were mixed with those of living, known, close and distant relatives. There were pictures from the old country of bearded men wearing heavy overcoats and derbies, men I perhaps had never met, but whose stories I had heard many times. These photographs, brownish, with yellowed cracking edges, printed on cardboard, were the most impressive to me. The subjects in these pictures do not smile but simply face the camera; in one photograph my mother, wearing a gaily embroidered peasant skirt and blouse, is standing with her brother Jacob and holding in her arms Jacob's infant son, David. She is wearing a kerchief, earrings, and several bracelets; it seems as if she had prepared herself at least one whole day before taking this photograph. Jacob is standing next to her, a giant towering a foot above her. In another photograph, my father and his brother Grisha are standing on either side of their father, Chaim Eliah Starobinetz. Chaim Eliah is seated and pulling at his ear in an abstracted way, as if he were listening to music. My father is wearing a student's plain uniform; he is standing absolutely erect. Grisha, ten years his junior, is wearing a sailor suit and trying to look as serious and stand as straight as my father.

Certainly these photographs were not the work of an amateur; great care was taken in the arrangement of the subjects, and I have had the sense that the members of my family posed for these photographs and later carried them through their migration, supremely conscious of the importance and irreplaceability of each photograph. As a member of a resettled segment of a family in which the members all had their roots, their upbringing, in the same small community—my parents and closest relatives, all immigrants, many dead—with only faded letters and photographs to recall any memory of them, this consciousness has affected me and these photographs have been my key to the past. There has always been someone whose photograph was necessary to me, whose story I have been told, who was either in Europe or dead. Strange that the one person, my father's brother Grisha, who, like a dead man risen, came to this country after the war, having been hidden from the Nazis for the duration, was not recognizable to me from any of his photographs. I know that now, so shortly after my mother's death, not one of her pictures catches her for more than a fraction of a second and that is all; but this fraction of a second can evoke, can jolt my mind until photographs merge, until the present becomes a memory in the past.

I stood for a long while by the table, knowing where each of the photographs had been. This was someone's baby, and that a four-year-old cousin; my father's sisters, all of them dead, were here. All the confusion of the placing of the photographs, of the family—the intermarriages, the physical distances, the unresolved silence of death, the myths, the stories of the old country, of Russia, the river Berezina—it was all here.

PART ONE

KAGAN

I heard my bedroom door close. My grandfather Abraham, already dressed, pulled gently with his right hand the watch chain looped across the front of his black vest so that the watch just dropped out of the vest pocket into his left hand. He turned it over with his long, hairy, bony fingers. He squinted, read it, inserted the watch into his pocket, shook his head from side to side, and then placed his cold hand on my forehead. "It's still early, Sam. We'll take a walk."

"I'll be dressed in a minute, *Zadeh*."

"Don't make noise. Mama and papa are sleeping."

He left the room and I got out of bed and barefoot walked to the window, yawned, and lifted one of the slats of the Venetian blind. It was just becoming gray; the street lights had been switched off. I dropped the slat and shivered. January 4, 1946. Today I am a man; a new white shirt. I stood, cold, and pulled out and crumpled the tissue paper, impatiently picked out the pins. Then we stood together outside: he, tall and straight, in a black overcoat with a black Persian lamb fur collar and a soft black velvet hat; I in a light blue woolen coat and boy's earmuffed cap. An almost empty trolley came up Hunts Point Avenue, swaying, and passed us.

We were quiet and I put my uncovered hands in my coat pockets and began to move my feet up and down. "Do you want to walk, *Zadeh?*" We crossed the cobbled avenue and walked on Lafayette Street. As we passed Faile Street, Abraham stopped and said, "Look, you see? Two synagogues here, but one," he said pointing, "is a temple. A fine building with trees and grass, much finer than the other. How small it is! It's made of orange bricks. We put our hearts into it, though, we who came from the other side; when we pray there, we pray with our hearts."

We stood together on the hard-soiled embankment of the Bronx River. There were cars crossing the small bridge at Bruckner Boulevard. Oil slick and refuse floated on the river and not far on the other side, sanitation trucks had already dumped garbage that at the end of the day would be burned in huge smouldering pyres.

"The sun!" I exclaimed.

My father, Doctor Isaac Star, felt a pain in his chest. Not much. No more, no less. Coronary thrombosis. On September 16, 1945, Dr. Isaac Star suffered a severe heart attack. On the basis of my repeated examinations and observations, I believe the patient to be permanently disabled. Morris W. Shellin, M.D. Forever. He sat up on the edge of his bed and looked at his sleeping wife. Five-thirty in the morning and I should be dead—a widow's greatest drawback. Sam's Bar-mitzvah. He was a small man, short and thin, and his hair was gray. He put his feet into his slippers and, standing up, put on his robe and walked to the bathroom. Cold water, then hot—plenty of soap. He felt his beard, rinsed out his razor, and began to shave.

My mother slept.

My uncle Larry turned over on his side. He pulled the covers up to his nose and rubbed his neck. No different. Every day for three years the neck's stiff like a board, and injections and baths and pills and diets, and nothing helps. The young ones have it; maybe should write letter with bond. Wealth is not all, you need health. Signed uncle Larry. Isaac 'ud laugh. Better get up. An hour's ride to Bronx.

My father opened my door and, not seeing me, he felt my bed to see if it had been slept in. He woke my mother. "At six in the morning on his Bar-mitzvah day, where could he be?"

My uncle Sam could not move. He wanted to get up but no muscle worked. His hands began to tremble violently and he put them under his body and tried to relax. "Fanny," he called. His wife turned over, her huge body making the bed springs squeak noisily. "Help me up." She got out of bed and came around to his side. She put a hand on his shoulder and he felt it pressing on him, turning him around so that his legs hung over the side of the bed. No power in fingers, hands; heart skips, can only eat and smile. Up. "Morris's coming for us at seven-thirty," Fanny said.

My father sat by the window in the tall, straight armchair and thought that it must have been Abraham. To wake him up so early, this morning above all other mornings, when the least little thing could upset him. He picked up yesterday's New York *Times* and reread the editorials and the obituaries.

My uncle Morris took a plain blue tie from his closet and placed it against his double-breasted jacket. "All right?" he asked his wife.

"If you've nothing better."

He adjusted the knot of the tie until it was just between the two points of his collar. Then he put on his jacket and, taking out his wallet, he asked, "Have you an envelope?" Rebecca pointed to a drawer, and he found an envelope and put a crisp hundred dollar bill inside.

"So much?" she asked. "For my nephews you only give bonds."

He shook his head and said, "He'll need it more." No children of his own, one child born dead. At least for Eshka. "We'll be late, we have to pick up Sam and Fanny."

My father saw my grandfather and me crossing the street and then an automobile blocked his view. Ben and Sol and their families got out of the car and greeted Abraham and me. When we went inside my father made me take off my overcoat and jacket right away and said, "You can't be all sweated, or you'll catch cold." We all had breakfast together, and I kept repeating to myself parts of the service I was to sing. I wanted to be the best.

My cousins David and Jack arrived at the synagogue late. The two sons of Jacob Kagan had been drunk the night before, and though rare for Jack, the condition of intoxication was common to, almost expected of, David. Ben walked over to them and sat next to David, intending to discover his nephew's present sobriety: he leaned across him, reaching for a prayer book. He smelled whiskey but he did not say anything; the ark was about to be opened and I was singing, "Hear O Israel . . ."

ONE

MORNING

I

My great-grandfather on my mother's side was known as Yitzhoc the peddler, and he was a wanderer living in a world of poverty and ritual. Every spring, he walked from his village of Swislow, in White Russia, to a region hundreds of miles away, near the Caspian Sea, where he bought fur skins; then he returned north, peddling the skins to village tailors. His profits were very small and his family rarely had enough to eat. From the time they were boys, his three sons travelled with him; they were uneducated, illiterate except for a slight reading knowledge of Hebrew. The father and sons wore the long black coats of the orthodox Jew; they never shaved or cut their hair. Because they were Jews they had entrance only into certain small towns, for, even to enter a city, a Jew needed a permit, and to do business in a city, he required a license. One summer, while Yitzhoc and his sons were travelling, his wife and two daughters died in an epidemic. Yitzhoc heard the news a fortnight later, and he and his sons rent their clothing and made the prayers, but they did not return to Swislow until they had sold all their furs.

In 1877 there was a drought through the entire Ukraine. That year, Yitzhoc and his sons returned to Swislow with no money and only their unsold furs to barter for food. The eldest son, Abraham, worried as was his father that even if they could survive the winter they would have no money with which to buy furs the following year, decided to take the unsold skins to a big city. Unlike his father, who dismissed the idea, and believed, with the other Jews of Swislow, that prayers alone could alleviate their distress, Abraham found the means to exist in such times in his own strength—he was six feet tall and broad of back. Yitzhoc refused to allow his younger sons to accompany Abraham and he left Swislow alone. He had no idea which city he was going to; he barely knew the directions of the big cities, and certainly did not know their distances. He carried one hundred skins on his back. When it grew dark and he was nowhere near a village, he laid down his pack and slept in the open, using the tightly packed furs as a pillow. When his clothes began to tear and fall apart, he exchanged a fur skin for a blouse and pants, and when it grew cold, he obtained a heavy jacket in the same way. Nights, during the winter, he would knock at the door of any house he might chance upon. Often he was allowed to stay under the roof and given straw to sleep upon; and in the morning he might be given directions. "Riga? Of course, it is over that way," his host of the night before might say, pointing north. "But Krivichi is nearer, and I know exactly how to go there."

Sometimes Abraham walked with peasants going fifty miles to visit relatives, and sometimes with pilgrims or beggars. When he arrived in Riga, three months after he had left Swislow, he spoke the crude and vulgar Russian of these people. He had no difficulty in gaining entry into the city—he not only spoke like a peasant, but he looked like one. Walking in the streets of Riga, wandering through residential and business areas, pausing to stare at buildings, carriages and monuments erected to honor generals, poets and nobility, he was dumfounded by the grandeur of the city and the thousands upon thousands of people he encountered. He stopped once to watch a plump lady alight from a carriage. The coachman opened the door for her; she was wearing a foot-high fur hat and she had to bend her short neck to an almost horizontal position to be able to angle out of the carriage. She leaned on her coachman's arm and as she stepped down, the skirt of her fur-lined coat swept the snow. Once she was sure of her balance, she put her gloved hands inside a muff and walked within three feet of Abraham, her nostrils twitching in obvious distaste as she passed him. "That is a real lady," Abraham thought without malice. Just before sunset, reflecting that in all of Riga there must be at least one synagogue where he might say his prayers and perhaps meet someone who might help him, he stopped a man and asked in Russian, "Could you possibly direct me to the house of a *zhid?*" knowing only one way to refer to a Jew, the word actually meaning *dirty* Jew.

"Bum!" the man exclaimed in Yiddish, not breaking his pace and glancing angrily at Abraham. Abraham took three strides and was abreast the short and heavy man whose feet moved so rapidly and mincingly.

"You are Jewish?" Abraham asked in Yiddish.

"Get away from me, you bum!" the man exclaimed.

Abraham watched him cross the street and walk up the steps of a large building. There was a Star of David over the doorway—it was a synagogue! But how large it was! In Swislow there was a cabin; this was a stone building. Abraham entered and sat down on a cushioned bench in the rear. There were over a hundred people praying and there was room for more. The voice of the cantor, singing prayers Abraham had heard spoken but never sung so beautifully, the exquisite lush carpets and the stained glass windows distilling light into brilliant red and blue were all too rich for Abraham; he could not concentrate enough to say his prayers. He looked all around the large room and saw the small man praying, rocking back and forth on his heels. Abraham stared at the man's back and when his eyes blurred, he began rhythmically to incline his neck and shoulders forwards and backwards and to utter the prayers the way he had intoned them three times a day as far back as he could remember. When he finished his prayers and opened his eyes, the services were already over and the people had left the synagogue. He walked up to the podium at the front of the building and stared at the mahogany-panelled ark where the *Torah* was kept. The floor and the railing around the podium were covered by a thick, dark red velvet. The *Shamus* of the synagogue, arranging prayer books, noticed Abraham and silently approached him. He stared at him for a moment and when Abraham finally turned, seeing him, the *Shamus* asked, "What are you doing here?"

"I'm just looking," Abraham said.

"Who are you?"

"My name is Abraham *ben* Yitzhoc Kagan. I sell furs," he added, tapping the pack that lay on the floor next to him.

"Are you alone in the city?" the *Shamus* asked, and, looking quizzically at Abraham's baggy, home-made pants, and his brightly colored woolen shirt showing at the neck beneath his jacket, he said, "Come, my wife will give you a special price for dinner and a bed." Abraham ate and slept in the boarding house of the *Shamus'* wife and in the morning he was told to see *Reb* Meir, a furrier. Abraham took his furs, leaving one skin in lieu of money with the *Shamus'* wife, to the address that was given him.

"You sell furs, eh?" *Reb* Meir asked. "They must be good, not damaged, you understand? What kind of furs?"

"Caracul, broadtail, Persian. I buy them in Lerki."

"The price must be right. I buy from a Gentile and he overcharges me."

Abraham showed him his goods and *Reb* Meir agreed to buy seventy-eight of the eighty-one skins Abraham had left. With approximately eight hundred rubles stuffed into his purse, Abraham departed the following day, joyful that he would return a Joseph from Egypt. He travelled by train to a town about fifty miles from Swislow, then bought a horse and continued on. When he was still several miles from home, he saw large smoke clouds and, as he approached the town, he smelled the stale odor of charred wood still burning. There was not a house left standing; small fires glowed under debris. Abraham's horse reared back. A woman was lying in the middle of the burnt wreckage of a house, her clothes torn and caked brown with dried blood. Her face was contorted even into eternity by pain. Abraham ran. There were ashes and debris where his father's cabin had been. He ran to the synagogue. Burned down! There was the rotten smell of burnt flesh. Abraham sank to the earth, and his hands dug into the soil.

After a while he thought he heard someone repeat, "Abraham? Abraham?" He turned his head in the direction the voice seemed to be coming from. His youngest brother, Leazar, his face and clothes covered with soot and dirt, stood several yards from him, holding a shovel in his bleeding hands. Abraham rose slowly, disbelieving, and then ran to his brother and embraced him. Stepping back, he asked, "Is everyone dead?"

"Abraham, I need help. Will you help me?"

Abraham gripped his brother by the shoulders and shook him. "Is everyone dead?"

"I've been alone two days." Leazar looked at the wreckage of the synagogue and said, "I saved some from burning, but they are dead. I've dug twelve graves."

The two brothers worked until early the following morning. When it was still dark, they mounted Abraham's horse and rode several miles from town, to a peasant's hut. "I want drink," Abraham said in Russian to the peasant.

"Go way, *zhid.*"

Without an answering word Abraham walked up to the glaring peasant and, as he drew back, suddenly afraid, Abraham's arm shot out above the peasant's head and swung down hammer-like in a short arc, smashing him on the side of the neck. Abraham found vodka, and then he and Leazar walked through the fields, leading Abraham's horse. They sat down, chilled by the early morning freshness, and drank.

In the darkness Leazar's eyes shone brightly and he said slowly, the vodka thickening his voice, "Just before noon, Schmulka told us. Papa hid the flour and linens and we went to the synagogue. No one was left home; everyone was there, and we waited. Suddenly papa stood up and he began to beat his breast, and then everyone was praying, all of them, and they cried like little babies and then I heard the horses—a thousand horses. It sounded like thunder, and they shouted we had caused the hunger, that they were being punished because of us, and we were all quiet and began to crowd together. Then they began to shoot." Leazar's voice rose. "Papa was shot right away. They never took aim, but they shot like we were cattle. A bullet grazed me. Then I began to bury them." He drank again and said, "Tomorrow I am going to America." Later he was sick, and then they slept.

When Abraham awoke, his brother was nowhere to be seen. Abraham called out his name several times but received no answer. For a moment he stood still. The horse was gone. Suddenly he slapped his right trouser pocket. His purse, with the money he had gotten for the fur skins, was not there. His fists clenched, and he looked around once more. "Leazar's on his way to America," he thought, and then he said aloud, "The *goniff's* already halfway there!" and his muscles relaxed and he laughed.

For several weeks, Abraham walked from village to village, working at odd jobs to pay for food and shelter. He knew of no relatives, nor would he resume the way of life of his father and his father's fathers. His faith was rooted in his own strength. One night he slept outdoors in a field; he made a mattress of wheat and, when he lay down, the stars were brilliant and the sky was open above him. A breeze blew across the fields, and he stood up and let it touch his face. He watched the wheat sway in wave-like undulations, and he felt, at that moment, that his body was God's temple.

In the autumn, he worked in the forests of Lazar Starobinetz, not far from the river Berezina, relying now on his arms and his body and not on good fortune. He knew exactly what he was doing each time he unconsciously cut at a tree and, knowing his strength, he took pleasure in living. Often it was the silent physical pleasure of work, being in the sun, breathing cold air, swimming, eating; and sometimes he found pleasure in the sober knowledge of his independence from the worries and the responsibilities his father had been able to face only with fear and faith. In his woolen shirt, stuck by sweat to his back, his trousers pulled in under muddy, leather boots, he hacked and sawed at trees three and five feet in diameter, and when the men stepped back to watch a tree topple and yelled, "Timber!" he yelled with them and enjoyed the feeling of the earth shaking for that instant beneath his feet.

He learned the ways of the lumbermen quickly and more than held his own working with the Ukrainian peasants. Every autumn, these peasants, their harvests in, their fields about to freeze, travelled several hundred miles north to work in the forests of Prince Alexi Alexanderovitch, brother to the Tsar, the forests of Graf Potofsky, and the forests of the Jew, Lazar Starobinetz. Prince Alexi allowed only certain of his trees to be cut, protecting always the immense, virgin forest that surrounded his isolated villa. He had uniformed, armed guards patrolling his grounds; trusting no one, least of all his brother, he kept to himself and was rumored to be a drunkard. Graf Potofsky was a man of the world; educated in Switzerland, Germany and France, he travelled abroad six months every year. He was handsome, an excellent horseman, and a businessman who, up to a few years before, had rarely interfered in his business. A bachelor with one nephew—the prodigal, Prince Sligorin—Graf Potofsky, perhaps the wealthiest man in all of White Russia, had unwittingly helped the Jew, Lazar Starobinetz, start a competing business. He had given to Lazar, the director of his company, a personal loan of fifty thousand rubles. The Jew had used the loan and all his savings to buy for himself forests he was supposed to have bought for Graf Potofsky. Several years later, when Lazar Starobinetz had expanded his business until, like Graf Potofsky, he owned mills, barges, and some of the finest forests in Russia, the two men met in St. Petersburg. "Starobinetz," Graf Potofsky had said, "I still have affection for you, *malgré tout*, but in the future I shall know how to deal with your kind." Lazar replied, "It's good you have learned something from our acquaintanceship. But you know, that was only the first step in your education."

Abraham worked four years in Lazar's forest and was made foreman over thirty Ukrainians. In the spring, when the melting snows made the forests swamp-like, the felled trees were dragged by horses to the river Berezina to be sent to a town in the Ukraine. Many logs were tied together to make a huge raft that Abraham was appointed captain of. It was a trip of several hundred miles down the meandering Berezina and there was much work to do; the size of the raft and the width of the line of logs trailing behind the raft often had to be changed. There was a giant ton-weight block of iron that was used as an anchor for steering, and in the evening for halting the raft. Sometimes, at night, the Ukrainians, returning home, sang of their girls. One of them sang in a high tenor voice and repeated a melody over and over, a refrain from a love song. The river was gentle, and the evenings were warm. When the raft was safely secured, Abraham would sit alone and listen to the songs and watch the path of the moon across the surface of the river.

When he returned from the Ukraine, Abraham went to the city of Minsk, to the house of Lazar Starobinetz. He was let into the house by Lazar's niece, Heika, who, orphaned as a child, lived with her bachelor uncle. She was short and inclined to stoutness; her hair was black as night. Abraham reported to Lazar and was invited to remain in his house several days.

"Where do you live?" Heika asked that evening during dinner.

"Nowhere," he answered. "I have no home. My father and brother were murdered," he explained. "Sometimes I stay with a friend in Nishkovitz, a small village near the Berezina."

"Ah!" Heika sighed sympathetically.

Lazar had invited Abraham to stay a few days, and Abraham stayed a month. He spent much time with Heika; one evening they listened to her cousin, Chaim Eliah Starobinetz, play melodies on his violin. Another day they went skating on a pond, and when Abraham caught her around the waist to keep her from falling, she told him that he had the strength and gentleness of an angel. One year later, in 1883, they were married; they settled in Nishkovitz. "Think of it," Chaim Eliah, putting aside his violin, said at the wedding, "You are stealing away the best woman in Minsk, and you are taking her to a dull village. There is no culture, no music, no one to carry on an intelligent conversation; you will die of boredom."

With a gift from Lazar, they built a house in Nishkovitz directly over a well. There were two stories and an attic; there were ten rooms, a bathroom and a kitchen with running water. The kitchen was the largest room in the house. Abraham and Heika owned poultry, cows and horses, and raised on their three or so acres of land all the vegetables they ate. Every year, Abraham was away from Nishkovitz for six months, working in Lazar's forests, but Heika, though she certainly missed him, was never bored or inactive. Over a period of twenty years, they had twelve children, eleven sons and one daughter. Heika nursed her children and raised them. The children played outdoors even in the cold; they dared each other to climb the tallest trees they could find. In the winter, they improvised wooden ice skates and sped and tumbled on the thick layer of ice that topped the river. During the warm months they swam in the Berezina and watched the lumber barges that came from the north, and sometimes yelled questions to the men on the barges: "Hey, where are you taking all that wood?"

"To the Ukraine. Where we come from there are trees that touch the sky."

2

The eleven sons of Abraham and Heika Kagan were named: Jacob, Mendel, Samuel, Laban, David, Mordecai, Joshua, Elihu, Reuben, Solomon and Benjamin. The daughter, my mother, was born a year after Solomon and three years before Benjamin and was named Esther and called Eshka. Of all her brothers, Jacob, the first-born, was the most extraordinary. When he died and the migration began, only the stories of the old country, of Jacob Kagan, could recapture for the uprooted brothers, the five who came to America, the sense of size and power, the urgency and excitement of life they had experienced in Russia.

At the age of sixteen, Jacob was the best wrestler in Nishkovitz. He stood six feet four and weighed two hundred and thirty pounds. The peasants told stories of Jacob Kagan, who could lift a man over his head and throw him twenty feet. They told the story of how, one day, he was walking in a forest with his brother David, when he saw a bear not more than fifteen yards away. The bear was standing by a tree, calm as you please, looking right at them. Jacob told David to remain still, then he walked towards the bear. "Eh, my black brother," Jacob said, "have you lost your master, are you all alone in the cold? Come, dance for us," he said smiling broadly. The bear did not move. When Jacob was only about a yard away from him, he arched his back and yelled in his magnificent basso profundo voice, "Dance!" and though the bear did not actually dance, in no more than half a second, he had dropped to all fours and had scampered off.

Jacob, Mendel and David were the closest of the brothers and the closest to their father. A year older than Mendel and five years older than David, Jacob found in the first a quiet and ready strength, a wrestler almost as large and as powerful as himself, and in the second—a boy—a restlessness and intelligence. "You're a poet," Jacob once said to David. "By your burning eyes and your pale face, I can tell. One day all women will love you. Look, Mendel, how the color comes into his beardless face."

"And one day," David answered, "I'll be big enough to beat you."

"One day . . ." Jacob repeated, and suddenly embracing David, lifting him off the ground and glancing then at Mendel, he said, "we will be richer than Starobinetz."

After Jacob and Mendel each reached his thirteenth birthday, their schooling was discontinued, and they went to work with their father in the forests. They had each attended, in turn, the Jewish Basic School in Nishkovitz, had been Bar-mitzvahed, and, not having shown any inclination towards learning, had been put to work. Their teacher, Ziptchik, the single instructor and chairman of the Basic School, as well as the Rabbi and *Mohel*—performer of circumcisions—of Nishkovitz, had said disparagingly of Jacob, "He is already taller than I. No, his future is not in the world of scholarship." During the four to six months they were home each year, their education was continued by their mother, whose physical methods of instruction, pulling by the ears two sons who were from the time that they were adolescents nearly twice as big as she, slapping them on the hands, or kicking them in the shins when they did not pay attention to her lessons, resulted in their learning to read and write Russian. But their education really took place in the forests, where they worked with the Ukrainians, listened to their stories, and invented their own. And, where they came to love the rivers and the tall trees.

By the time he was eighteen, Jacob had worked five years in the forests of Lazar Starobinetz, and he could walk with Mendel and predict with great accuracy the quality and quantity of the lumber of an uncut tree. When their father did any job for Lazar, his two oldest sons were his first and sometimes indispensable assistants. One autumn, Abraham was sent to a Ukrainian village to contract for extra workers; Jacob and Mendel accompanied him. But Abraham could in no way persuade any of the peasants to leave their straw covered huts for the six months he wanted them to work in the forests. "No use," he finally said to his sons. "Starobinetz will have to do without them."

Jacob nodded his head in apparent agreement and then, smiling, whispered something to Mendel. "Papa," Jacob said, "you wait for us right here."

"And what should I wait for?"

The two sons had already mounted their horses and Jacob answered, "Papa, it's just to see if I can win a bet," and then, at a motion from Jacob, they raced off. They rode through a field to the only wooden house in the village. The owner of the house, a general store as well as a home, met them outside and looked admiringly at Mendel's proud horse. "A beautiful animal," Jacob said dismounting and drawing his hand along its flank. "He's fast as the wind, smart as a bear, loyal as a hound." He paused and said, "My brother, who is quite a horseman, got him as a gift from Prince Alexi Alexanderovitch. His father was the favorite stallion of the Tsar himself. As a riding horse," Jacob concluded, "there is none to match him." Then Jacob looked at the Ukrainian and said as if the thought had just occurred to him, "Do you want him? A one-in-a-million horse? No! No, don't say a word! He's yours!" The storekeeper fed them, insisted that they sleep in his house as his guests, and the following morning assured Abraham, whom Jacob had introduced as Lazar Starobinetz himself, that the peasants would go to the forests. "In this village where there is no mayor and no Jew, I am both mayor and Jew. They shall go when you want them."

On the first day of the two-week-ride back to Nishkovitz, Abraham was very thoughtful. He shook his head from side to side and finally said aloud, but not addressing either of his sons, "Whose blood is it? Surely it's not from me. Mendel is not so smart, but *he,* he's already like a millionaire. When we work, the peasants no longer fear me, but my son. I may not be as big as he, but I am big. You know," he said, now looking at Jacob, "I think I could beat you wrestling."

Jacob laughed.

"At your father you laugh," Abraham said and reined his horse to a stop. "I'm not that old. Come on," he said and dismounted.

"Mendel," Jacob said, "to fight such an old man is a disgrace, I think."

"Come on," Abraham said impatiently.

"Papa, you insist?"

"Come on," Abraham said, beckoning and then squashing his fist in his other hand.

"Mendel?" Jacob said.

"You must wrestle," Mendel said. "If not, then I'll tell everyone Jacob Kagan is afraid of an old man."

"You come next," Abraham said to Mendel.

Jacob dismounted. The father and son, hands on partially bent knees, circled each other. Jacob's hand darted towards his father's neck, but Abraham sliced it with the edge of his own hand, knocking Jacob off balance and, with a grunt, Abraham was sprawling across his son and exclaiming ironically, "Eh, Jacob? Eh, Jacob?"

"Papa, don't push your luck," Mendel warned. Then Jacob suddenly threw his body up, thrusting his father's body off his own and, turning in air without touching ground, he landed on his father's back.

"Eh, papa?" Jacob said when he had gotten Abraham's arms bent behind his back in an unbreakable hold.

Abraham later took great delight in relating this story to Lazar, who, a short and stout man, respected Jacob chiefly for his strength. "Jacob," Abraham said to Lazar, "is a real giant. I am little more than a baby to him."

Of all the sons, Ziptchik regarded only Samuel and David as potential scholars, and he advised that they be sent to continue their education in Minsk. Samuel, hardly more than a capable student—never industrious but always pleasing (he knew a hundred ways to get around Ziptchik and used them all)—was sent to Minsk, where he lived in Lazar Starobinetz's house and attended a formal Hebrew School. And two years after Samuel, David was sent to Minsk. Brilliant and curious, he had early become too much for the plodding Ziptchik. Mathematics fascinated him; on his own, he solved equations that Ziptchik could hardly understand. "An engineer," Ziptchik had pronounced proudly to Abraham. "The boy is a born engineer, or an architect at least." After several months of preparation, David passed with high honors an entrance examination to the regular Minsk *Gymnasium* and, one of ten Jews in a class of two hundred, was admitted as a student. He too lived with Lazar, and whenever Lazar asked him about Nishkovitz, or about his brothers, none of whom Lazar had ever met, David responded by telling a story of Jacob. Some evenings they ate in the house of Lazar's nephew, Chaim Eliah Starobinetz. Chaim Eliah had been set up in business by Lazar, and now owned the largest general store in Minsk. He was recognized in the town as an intellectual, and could, with equal facility, refer to the Bible, the Talmud, or Russian literature. A lover of poetry, he often read Pushkin to his five children. His wife, Bassya, ran the store and was, both by virtue of her being married to Chaim Eliah and the sharp aspect of her face, also considered an intellectual, though her mental activity was generally confined to the computation of customers' bills. The conversation about the dinner table would start in fine generalities, but would ultimately descend to an interesting and gentle kind of gossip. And nearly always, David, who otherwise hardly ever spoke, turned the conversation to his brother Jacob: "There is no one in the entire world who can possibly beat my brother."

"His strength is in truth the strength of ten," Sam, who was learning the scholarly nod, said in the Hebraic sing-song of his teachers.

"Say," Chaim Eliah's oldest son, Isaac, said, imitating the sing-song and the nod, "his strength is the strength of thirty."

"He is very big," Chaim Eliah agreed. "Heika has written."

"What of it?" Bassya asked. "He was not smart enough

even to come to Minsk to study," she said, looking proudly at Isaac, who was to leave shortly to study medicine at Yourieff University in Riga.

"Not everyone can be smart," Chaim Eliah said.

"He is very smart," David said. "He is the smartest; he is so smart that none of you is as smart as he is."

"Well, he may not be that smart," Chaim Eliah said, "but I'm sure he's very clever."

"He is a real genius," Sam said.

"We'll all soon see what kind of genius he is," Lazar stated. "I've invited him to Minsk."

And when Lazar met him, he was not disappointed. Taller than his father, Jacob smiled more naturally, spoke with confidence, and his deep laugh easily filled Lazar's large sitting room. "Boy," Lazar began, "your father's worked for me many years, and you know I've great affection for him—he's always made a comfortable living. But if what I hear of you is true, then you've the qualities of your father and more. Sharp! Listen, in two days you'll journey to Riga with my nephew Isaac. I want you to have a good time, but I want you to learn. You'll go to the auctions in Riga and observe! One day you may have to know all things, you will have to be very sharp."

That evening Lazar and Jacob ate in Chaim Eliah's house. Jacob's two brothers were not invited, and, as a matter of fact, they saw very little of Jacob. During the day they had to be in school, and in the evening they ate alone in Lazar's kitchen as punishment, for the last time they had eaten dinner at Chaim Eliah's, David had kicked Isaac so hard that Isaac had not been able to walk for three days. Chaim Eliah gave the place at the head of the table to Lazar and sat down next to him. Bassya sat at the other end of the table. Jacob sat in the center, across from Tania, the sixteen-year-old daughter of Chaim Eliah and Bassya. Tania's hair and eyes were brown, and her lips, which she hardly opened even for food during the meal, were pale and thin. She would look at Jacob for a few seconds at a time and, when Jacob caught her looking at him, she threw her gaze to some object in a proud and disinterested, but nevertheless blushing, manner. After a while, Jacob found himself staring at her and smiling foolishly each time her gaze inevitably fell on him. The sons, Isaac, seventeen, and Grisha, a boy of eight, sat on either side of Tania. Grisha wanted to test Jacob's strength, and the two younger sisters, Sonia and Rachel, seated on either side of Jacob, insisted that he flex his muscles.

"Don't pester Jacob," their mother said. "I'm sure he's very strong."

"He's a powerhouse," Chaim Eliah said, "and that is as it should be. His father is a strong man and his mother is a *balabusta.* When I first saw Abraham I said to myself, here is a soldier of Israel, and when I look at you, I see a young lion." Chaim Eliah caressed his full beard thoughtfully, and then, smiling, asked, "Your mother's to have another baby, eh?"

"In a few weeks," Jacob answered, forcing himself to look away from Tania.

"Such a small town," Bassya asked. "Isn't she afraid?"

"She's no time to be afraid," Chaim Eliah answered his wife. "She has eleven children."

"Ach!" Lazar exclaimed, looking up from his plate for the first time. "I shall never forgive her leaving my house to marry your father. No one in the world makes potatoes so well. Even these, delicious as they are, somehow just miss that extra spice."

Chaim Eliah explained to Jacob, "My wife may not cook, but she shows the girl how it's done."

"How can I cook when I work in the store?" Bassya asked. "And raise my children?"

"Mama," Isaac interrupted, "I know why I'm so short and Jacob so tall—you haven't been able to raise your children."

"As a comic you'll make a fine doctor," Chaim Eliah said and then, rubbing his stomach, said, "Gentlemen, now some brandy."

In the afternoon of the second day that Jacob was in Minsk, there was a farewell picnic for Isaac. The Starobinetzes drove out of town in Lazar's carriage; Bassya's maid set a tablecloth on the ground, in the shade of a tree, and Chaim Eliah placed cushions around it. They ate cold chicken and drank imported white wine. When they had finished their meal, Chaim Eliah took his violin from the carriage and asked Jacob what he would like to hear. "Tschaikovsky?" Chaim Eliah asked rhapsodically. "Do you know the *Swan Lake?*"

Jacob shook his head and Tania said, "Play that, papa."

Chaim Eliah tuned his instrument, nodded his head once, and was about to begin, when he looked up and said, "You must excuse my arrangement. The music, you know, wasn't written for violin alone." He raised his bow like a baton for silence and commenced playing. His arrangement of the theme of the swans, so soft and melodious, and his playing, were exquisite. Jacob watched Tania, who rocked, her eyes closed, almost in a trance. When he looked away, he retained an impression of loveliness and beauty that was interrupted only when Chaim Eliah finished playing. Then, while everyone else relaxed, Sonia, Rachel and Grisha stood about Jacob, silent for a moment, till Grisha asked, "Do you cut down trees?"

"Yes," Jacob answered.

"All alone?" Sonia asked.

"Usually someone helps me."

"I want to be an engineer," Grisha said and paused. "Sonia wants to be a journalist, and Rachel, a dentist."

"You want to pull teeth?" Jacob asked incredulously, and then smiling as if at a joke, said, "You have to be very strong."

"Oh, I'm strong enough. Look, I've already pulled one."

Jacob looked into Grisha's agreeably open mouth. "She's very strong," Grisha said, keeping his mouth wide open to show a gap in his teeth. Jacob, shaking his head, left the three children and walked to where Tania was sitting. He leaned over her and asked impatiently, "And what will you do when you grow up?"

Tania stared at the ground and answered, "I don't know. I suppose I'll marry."

"You don't want to be a dentist?"

"Oh, no!" she exclaimed, and, looking up at Jacob, they both began to laugh.

Suddenly Jacob felt a small fist strike him on his thigh. "A fly," he said, grabbing the hand that had hit him.

"Show us how strong you are," Grisha said. He was standing with his smiling brother, Isaac, who said, "Show us, strong man."

Jacob looked at Tania, then at Isaac, and said, "Come here, little man." Isaac approached Jacob hesitatingly. Jacob suddenly grasped him, his two hands nearly spanning Isaac's waist, and, lifting him, held him up in the air at arms' length. "Now," Jacob said, "how far shall I throw you?"

"As far as you can," Grisha called.

"Shush," Tania said. "Put him down, you brute."

"So I am a brute?" Jacob said, and then laughing so hard that he nearly dropped Isaac, he said, "Here, here, my sweet, is your brother," and Jacob set Isaac down with great care.

The following morning, Isaac and Jacob left for Riga. During the long and tedious train ride, neither of them slept and they sat up, talking for hours. Jacob told Isaac that he thought Tania was very attractive.

"Attractive? She's all right," Isaac said and shrugged his shoulders. Then he looked at Jacob in a conspiratorial way and whispered, "She can be very mean, you know?"

"Mean?"

Isaac nodded his head seriously and grunted his affirmation.

"When is she mean?" Jacob asked.

"You have to get to know her," Isaac said, and, shaking his head sadly, said, "Grisha's only a small boy and he's very sensitive. Perhaps he's too sensitive," he continued, as if he were having an abstract conversation with himself, "but still, that would not excuse her."

"What are you talking about?"

"Grisha had a dog and she hated it. Oh, how she hates animals! It was only a small thing, but how many times have I seen her kick that dog so it went flying."

"I don't believe that," Jacob said.

"Believe what you want. I tell only the truth. When Grisha saw her kick his dog, he cried for three days. He didn't eat and he hardly slept."

"You're a liar," Jacob said.

"But what's the difference?" Isaac asked. "You don't really like her?"

"No," Jacob answered, and, smiling, continued, "even if I did, I could never see her too often. What with a dentist sister and her sharp-nosed mother. One of my friends says, and he speaks with great wisdom, that before you marry, be sure to look at the girl's mother, for one day you may be cursed with a wife who is a mother-in-law. And her brothers!" Jacob exclaimed. "I think, Assoc," he said, calling him for the first time by his nickname, "as a doctor, you'll make a good prankster. I would not trust you to heal a cut on my littlest finger."

"A cut on your smallest finger is like a gash on my thigh."

"Little man," Jacob said, "you are so ugly, you'll frighten your patients to death."

"If I'm so ugly, how is it that you think my sister so beautiful that every time you look at her your face becomes the face of a homeless dog?"

"Did I ever say she was a beauty? She takes after your mother—she's a scarecrow."

"You may not be a scarecrow," Isaac said, "but you show great resemblance to a circus bear."

"A circus bear?" Jacob repeated and smiled. "Tell me, Assoc, have you heard about me and the bear? No? Well, when I was sixteen . . ."

When they arrived in Riga, they rented rooms in the same boarding house, and in the evening they walked about the city, forming, this small man with an intellectual background and professional future, and the large man who was in Riga to learn about the methods of business, a friendship that lasted all their lives. The following day, while Isaac registered for his courses at the University, Jacob sat with Lazar's broker at the auctions. The broker explained to him that several weeks before each large auction, announcements were made as to what forests were to be sold. Agents of each lumber company were immediately dispatched to the forests to investigate them and determine their worth (Jacob, with his father and Mendel, had several times acted in that capacity). Their evaluation was communicated in code to the director of the company who then, in turn, told his broker—at the auctions in Riga and St. Petersburg only licensed brokers were allowed to enter bids—whether or not to buy, and what the approximate figure they could offer was. Jacob watched the brokers give their bids, written on small scraps of paper, to attendants, and then wait several hours till the winning bid was announced.

The brokers were cautious men, suspicious of one another, professional gamblers knowing the limits of each competitor, knowing and afraid of the brokers who represented Prince Alexi, Graf Potofsky and Lazar Starobinetz. When these men made bids, one of them got what he wanted and no other broker even had a chance. They bid only on the huge forests and, never speaking, not able to make a second bid, knew with gamblers' instincts who had won. It was rumored among the other brokers that the night before each aution, Graf Potofsky's broker dreamed the exact figure he would bid. Lazar's broker, not a mystic, was a careful analyst who did not make his bid until the last moment, hoping to hear a passing remark, to catch a careless expression on a competitor's face. He was given great leeway in determining his bid and, more often than not, when Lazar Starobinetz wanted a forest badly, he, and not Prince Alexi or Graf Potofsky, got it. During the two weeks that Jacob was in Riga, Lazar's broker, out of the ten times he made bids, won seven times. Nor did he ever show elation when he won. "Never let them know what you're thinking," he advised Jacob. "If you yourself know, that is enough."

Jacob arrived back in Nishkovitz a fortnight after his youngest brother, Benjamin, was born, on the day the circumcision was to be performed and celebrated. The large house was a mass of steam, boiling water, linens, men, women, boys, girls, infants. Ziptchik, who was to perform the circumcision in the sitting room, washed his hands and wiped them on his trousers, rubbing them dry on his black jacket. His knife was brought to him in a pot of just-boiled water. He fished it out with his hand and dropped it on a clean white towel. He wiped it dry, picked it up, and approached the baby, held on a table by Abraham and Mendel. The baby screamed once, and the circumcision was accomplished; the baby cried, and the men smiled. Then everyone went into the dining room, where Abraham toasted Ziptchik. But it was Jacob whom all the children clustered about; he had been to Riga! Ziptchik soon joined the group about Jacob and, panting from shortness of breath and the constriction of a tight vest, said as an experienced man says, "So, Jacob, what happened to you in Riga?"

"In Riga? What happened to me?"

"It is a big city," Ziptchik said, spreading his arms and nodding his head. "Beautiful, but it's really too large. I hear that people who have lived there all their lives often get lost. Just imagine!"

"Listen," Jacob said, "I shall tell you about Riga! My first day, I am walking on the widest street you have ever seen, when a big black coach made of black ebony wood, pulled by six horses, each of them the purest of stallions, passes me. I am that impressed by the city that I do not even notice the coach. To that city Nishkovitz is a twig, Minsk only a branch, but Riga, Riga is the tallest tree I have ever seen! To think of it, but you will not believe me, you will not believe what happened to me on this my first day; you will say that Jacob Kagan is a liar, yet it is true, it is as true as I am standing here on this very spot."

"You met the Chief Rabbi?" Ziptchik suggested. "He is truly the greatest scholar in the world."

"Who was in the coach, Jacob?" a neighbor's son asked.

Jacob looked from Ziptchik to the boy and closing his eyes for a moment, he continued. "Suddenly I heard a voice call out, 'Mister Kagan! Mister Kagan, come here!' I turned around wondering—(who in Riga should know my name)—

and let God strike me dead if it wasn't—what a fine picture in his tunic covered by medals—the Tsar!" Jacob paused now and, nodding his head, looked at the rapt faces of his listeners. Then he continued, "Shocked, but still in possession of my wits, I approached him and knelt before him. With his own two hands he raised me from the ground and kissed me on both cheeks."

The children remained with their mouths agape, and Ziptchik had not breathed for a full minute, when three-year-old Esther Kagan asked, "Is the Tsar as big as you, Jacob?"

Starobinetz put Jacob to work now in different and important capacities. He bought equipment, estimated the value of forests up for sale and directed operations in various forests; he, not yet twenty years old, in charge of five hundred men. Sometimes he shared responsibility with his father, but more and more he was given jobs where he alone was in charge. Lazar was preparing Jacob in order that he should one day be director of all his enterprises. For Jacob, the next five years were years of work and travel; he saw St. Petersburg, Moscow, Warsaw, and Odessa. And, he had great expectations. The world, closed to his grandfather, whom he had never known, partially open to his father, was unfolding before him like the panorama of a still distant city.

When he needed advice, Jacob spoke to his father, and when he needed assistants, he hired his brothers. Mendel was always with him, a partner in all his endeavors, and Laban, the fourth brother, was for a short while a third partner. He, who later emigrated to America and changed his name, my uncle Larry, was the handsomest of the brothers. Tall and lean, muscular from years of work in the forests, an expert horseman, he was stubborn and inconsistent, dogmatic and ambitious. Once he assisted Jacob when Jacob was in charge of the operations in the Criasti forests. Laban was foreman over fifty men and, for a week, his crew accomplished more than any other. The trees of that dense forest, the most valued single holding of Starobinetz, were enormous; any one of them could bring more money than passed through a peasant's hands in years. Only certain trees were supposed to be cut; they had been clearly marked even before the workers had come to the forests. On an inspection tour, one day, Jacob discovered that his brother's crew had been cutting trees down indiscriminately. Jacob spoke in anger to his brother, and Laban exclaimed, "To hell with all of it! I should like to burn it! What right has Starobinetz to all this?"

"It's his," Jacob declared. "These are his trees."

"And you're his lackey."

Laban left the forests and went to Minsk.

In Nishkovitz, Heika received a letter from her uncle Lazar. He suspected that David belonged to a clandestine Political organization. And, by the time Jacob next went home, his brother David had been both expelled from school and put out of Lazar's home. The Russo-Japanese War had begun; unverified reports of victories became actual reports of defeats. Laban and David Kagan slept in their parents' home, but were otherwise rarely there. Laban rode from village to village, wearing a bright red blouse and a revolver strapped about his waist, organizing meetings at which David, a short and stout adolescent, made fiery speeches revealing the plot behind the war, speaking about injustices, and speaking against the Tsar.

In that year, 1904, Jacob, Mendel, and Samuel were called to serve in the army. To avoid the draft, Mendel had his trigger finger sewn to his middle finger, and Samuel had an ear punctured. Jacob was advised to do any one of a number of things: he could have his big toe amputated, could find a way to raise his pulse to some impossible rate, or, by eating sugars, could appear to be diabetic. Jacob refused to have anything done to himself. Laban scorned Jacob for being a fool, and Mendel and Samuel for being cowards.

"Let them take me," Laban declared, "but first they'll have to find me!"

"To die fighting for the Tsar," David said, "that is insane.

If you are first a Jew, then this is not your war. If you are first a Russian, then there is a real war right here."

"Shall I cut off my arm and my pride both at the same time? My arm I need to work, and my pride I need to live."

"No one said you should cut off your arm!" Abraham exclaimed.

"Even a finger," Jacob said slowly and with finality.

Jacob received two months of training in a camp not far from Nishkovitz, and was then transported across Siberia. The trip took twelve days; once a day the train stopped to allow the soldiers to be fed thin, tepid soup. There was hardly any room to lie down on the straw-covered floor of the bare cars the soldiers were shipped in, and by the time they reached the front, they were exhausted and sick. On the first day in the trenches, Jacob was smoking a cigarette, looking at the enemy lines, when someone prodded him in the back. *"Zhid!"* his company officer exclaimed. "Put out that cigarette! You're not home, this is the front."

"Relax," Jacob said calmly, "or I shall throw you to the Japanese."

The officer drew his revolver and shot Jacob in the leg. Several minutes later, the enemy attacked unsuccessfully, and the company officer was killed leading a counter-charge. Jacob's wound was treated, he was given a medal and hospitalized for several months, then discharged and sent home. He returned to Nishkovitz; only his mother Heika, and the children Esther, Sol and Ben were home. He embraced his mother, and she cried and gave thanksgiving that her eldest son was safe. At dinner, the evening of his return, all but two of the family were present.

"David and Laban still speak against the Tsar?" Jacob asked.

"They're known by the police; one day they'll be arrested," Abraham answered.

"They speak against the Tsar while I'm wounded protecting his honor?"

"Laban rides from town to town; he looks fine on a horse,"

Abraham said sarcastically. "David reads books and sees things no one else can see."

"The poverty of the peasants," Sol said excitedly, "you can see that."

"You too?" Jacob asked.

"To hell with their poverty!" Abraham exclaimed angrily. "I don't give a damn about them. Do you know why I've no father and no mother, only one brother, and that one an American crook?"

"Give the people education and there will be no pogroms," David said, entering the room with Laban. "The only education the peasants receive is in the army, and what can you expect of that?"

"Well said, brother," Jacob said smiling, and he rose to embrace his brothers. When everyone else had gone to bed, Jacob, Mendel, and David went outside. There was a chill in the air and a wind brushed the trees about the house. Jacob looked up, past the trees, at the clear sky. They walked, and Mendel asked, "How was it, Jacob?"

"So, so," he answered and then told the story of how he was wounded. The physical appearance he ascribed to his officer was distorted, and even before Jacob reached the part where he told of his being awarded a medal, his brothers could hardly contain themselves.

"Did you really say that?" David asked.

"He was a bastard."

"That I understand, but to say such a thing to an officer?"

"To speak against the Tsar?" Mendel remarked and poked David in the shoulder with his two, sewn-together fingers.

"That is a belief," David answered quietly.

"And the Tsar is not four feet away from you," Jacob said and smiled.

Jacob stayed with his family two weeks. Once, he went to hear David make an outdoor speech in a neighboring village. He stood with Laban at the rear of a crowd made up mainly of workers from a lumber mill owned by Graf Potofsky. Laban enthusiastically counted the number of people and said,

"We're growing stronger every day. You'll see, there'll be a time when you'll thank your brothers because your name will be our name."

David stood at the center of a makeshift platform and, looking at the audience, he began his speech. He spoke of the mistake of the war. Siberia, he said, was far away. He described the land, the frozen wastes, the few cities and the monstrous cold. Then he said that he knew the names of men who had died in prisons there and, truly, they were greater patriots than any dead soldier. These men were fighters against the greatest enemy of all, tyranny, the tyranny of the Tsar! He spoke of war and hunger and those who dared expose the truth. He read from no manuscript, and though at the beginning of his speech he looked at the faces of his listeners, later, he lifted his gaze, and it seemed as if he were looking at the whole Russian horizon.

He had spoken eloquently and passionately and, afterwards, riding back to Nishkovitz, Jacob said to David as if he were making a final distinction, a cleavage between them, "You're an idealist."

"A man may be an idealist," David replied, tired.

"That is a dreamer," Jacob said.

"And you want money," Laban said.

"Yes. That's one thing I want."

Jacob occupied himself playing with his one sister and his infant brother. He gained weight and decided it was time to see Starobinetz. Jacob rode to Minsk and was received warmly; the two men talked for several hours, sitting in Lazar's study, smoking long, thin cigars. After Lazar had asked Jacob about his service, and Jacob had told of having been wounded, though he did not tell how, Lazar, smiling, asked, "You know, Tania was almost married?"

"What do you mean, almost married?"

"Every day for several months she was with this writer fellow, Shmyola Bernstein. She gets older every day, just like the rest of us. But what a character that Bernstein was! I think he's in St. Petersburg . . . his nose always itched and he would either be wrinkling it, rubbing it, or scratching it."

"Does he make money?" Jacob asked.

"A little now, just a living. You know how it is in the arts—you can be going along, very nearly starving, when boom! you can make a hundred rubles," Lazar said, and smiling, continued. "Tania loved his being a writer; she reads books . . ."

"So?" Jacob interrupted impatiently.

"I thought you might be interested."

"I came from Nishkovitz to talk about my job, my future."

"Your future is good," Lazar said seriously and went on to discuss just what his plans for Jacob were. Jacob left Minsk the same day. He travelled through the night and arrived in Nishkovitz in the morning, before Abraham had left the house. "Today you do not go anywhere," Jacob said to his father, "nor Mendel. The others can go about their business. We shall talk and make plans."

"Plans for what?" Abraham asked.

"Plans to make money," Jacob said abruptly. They went into the kitchen and sat around the wooden table. Jacob felt the thickness of the table as if for support and then said, "Starobinetz is old. He wants me to travel for him, to be sometimes in St. Petersburg for him, or Riga. He wants me to be able to take over his business."

Mendel moved forward on his chair, and Abraham, sensing that the news he had so hoped for was not satisfactory to his son, clasped his hands and asked, "You accepted, eh?"

Jacob ignored his father's question and continued, looking now at his brother Mendel. "When Starobinetz dies, what will he leave me? Nothing. The training to be director of a lumber company. His nephews and cousins will get what he has always owned, and the company will fall apart."

"It's existed since before you were born," Abraham said. "Why, smart one, should it fall apart?"

"Because today, everything's in the palm of his hand. Tomorrow his relatives will want money, not lumber and not forests."

"Stupid ambition!" Abraham exclaimed. "You won't be satisfied until you're as rich as Starobinetz. Accept his offer."

Jacob stood up and leaned over the table towards his father. "I'll tell you about Tsar Alexander III. Dying of consumption, he called in a famous doctor from Germany, a Jew. The doctor said that the Tsar could live only five months and the Tsar screamed, *'Zhid!'* and reared back and spat like a snake in the Jew's face. The doctor returned to Germany and the Tsar died in five months." Jacob paused and said, "On the front I was wounded, not by the Japanese, but by my own officer. He had the authority to do with me as he liked because I was a plain soldier and because I was a Jew. I saw him die, but I am not satisfied to be spat at and then to watch, as though God takes a late vengeance. To me that's no vengeance. Not even the Tsar will spit at a millionaire."

After a moment, Mendel said, "You are the leader. Where are we to follow?"

"To the auctions in Omsk. Lazar asked me to go there and bid for him. One of the largest Siberian forests will be suddenly put up for sale. Lazar had information that a certain Count Igor has arranged, by the suddenness of the sale, to obtain the forests at a fraction of what they're worth."

"I don't understand," Mendel said.

"We have no money to bid for even a small forest," Abraham added. "Will you bid for Starobinetz?"

"Count Igor will think so," Jacob replied, smiling.

Jacob and Mendel travelled by train more than one thousand miles. Tired and unkempt, wearing peasant blouses and cheap mackinaws, they arrived in the city of Omsk. The day after their arrival, they rented two horses and rode to the forests. They returned after dark and were met at the door of their hotel room by a servant in a dark green uniform, who saluted them and said, "Sirs, his excellency, Count Igor, awaits you in his rooms. He will see you immediately."

Count Igor, a handsome young man smoking a long cigarette in a holder, tilted his head, not looking at either Jacob or Mendel, but peering around the smoke at a spot on the wall, and said, "I have been informed you are in Omsk for the auctions. Your names, I know . . ."

"Kagan, your excellency," Jacob said. "Jacob and Mendel Kagan."

"Yes. I have never before heard that name, but then, gentlemen, I do not know everyone." And now he turned his head and looked directly at Jacob. "I shall be brief. I am here for the auctions, and I do not want to be outbid. Have I made myself clear?"

"Perfectly, but the man we represent is a very particular man who always gets what he wants," Jacob said in apologetic but firm tones.

The count looked back at the spot on the wall and, exhaling smoke in a thin stream, asked, "Who is he?"

"I can't tell you his name, your excellency, but it's true that he's interested in buying the forests up for sale," and Jacob winked, just the slightest twitching of his eyelid, at Mendel. The count caught the wink and smiled cynically. "It is my brother's and my job to evaluate the forests, and today, even though we only saw a little, we've decided that these forests are much richer than our employer ever imagined." Jacob paused and said, "Now sir, if you'll excuse us. We've had a very hard day and want to be rested for the auctions in the morning."

"Eccentrics!" the young count exclaimed after Jacob and Mendel had left his rooms. "A great pity that the aristocracy must protect such people. They are obviously themselves the buyers, the invisible partners . . . representatives of the Jew Starobinetz, or the financiers of a prince, perhaps even Alexi."

Just before dawn, someone knocked at the door of Jacob and Mendel's room. Jacob opened it and the uniformed servant said, "Sir," addressing himself only to Jacob, "Count Igor will see you now." Jacob dressed and followed the servant. The count was in the same chair and the room was smoke-filled. The count spoke calmly at first. "Kagan, I know whom you represent. You people are never content, you connive . . ." The count stopped himself and, controlling his anger, continued slowly and threateningly, "I give you warning, if you bid against me, you and your protector will be revealed."

A look of amazement flashed across Jacob's face.

"Yes. I know who he is."

"Sir," Jacob said, finally understanding the count's assumption, "as you might guess, the gentleman we represent is willing to bid far more than . . ."

The count nodded his head and indicated that it was not necessary for Jacob to go on. Then he took an envelope from his inside tunic pocket. He held it out to Jacob and said, "There's a hundred thousand there. It's too much; I do not want to bargain. You will not have to share this with your prince and you can buy elsewhere."

Jacob took the envelope and bowed to the count; then, straightening, he turned and left the room. Like fabulous Marco Polo returning wealthy from the East, Jacob and Mendel returned to Nishkovitz resplendent in fur-lined coats, derbies, five button suits, and silver-knobbed walking sticks. In Moscow, on the way back from Omsk, they had bought presents for the entire family, and when Jacob told the story of Count Igor, smoking through the night, wondering who those two Jews really were, and deciding finally that they must be financiers, Rothschilds, the pleasure of the Kagan family was complete.

3

"Eshka! Eshka! Oh, the water's cold!"

"Baby Ben," Esther said. Then her whole body shivered as she lowered her bare feet deeper into the freezing water of the Berezina. Later, Esther and Ben sat on loosely stacked grain not far from the river, and while Ben looked back towards their home, worried that they would be late for dinner, Esther watched a number of ice slabs float past her. "Today's a holiday," Esther said. "We've a letter from Laban, from New York City. Of course, you're too young to remember . . ."

"I remember like it was yesterday," Ben protested.

"We'd sometimes sit here or walk," she said. "How handsome he was!" She nodded her head, smiling. Across the river she saw a solitary rider racing across the fields. How slowly he seemed to be moving! He disappeared into a forest; Esther glimpsed him once more and then he was lost.

"Eshka, we'll be late."

Ben followed several paces behind Esther. She walked quickly, agilely, knowing the fields between the river and her home perfectly, where each path was and just where it led. Her heavy torso swayed slightly to each side as she walked and her arms swung out like a soldier's. Once, her long, full skirt caught on a dry twig and with only a sweeping backward motion of her arm, not even losing her stride, she freed herself. Ben, trying to keep up with her, thought that the fields opened up only for her, that if he fell too far behind, they would close in on him.

When they got home, Abraham, seven of his sons and a visitor were eating. The visitor was a short, stout man in his fifties, whose yellowed gray beard was more round than long though it hung several inches from his face. "Eshka and Ben," Abraham said to the visitor. "My two late arrivals."

The visitor looked up from his soup, glanced at them, nodded his head, and then continued eating.

"Who is he, mama?" Esther asked when she went into the kitchen to help her mother.

"Chaim Eliah Starobinetz. Jacob wants to marry his daughter, Tania."

"He's fat," Esther said.

"He plays the violin."

After dinner, Abraham, Chaim Eliah and Mendel sat in soft chairs and discussed the match. Chaim Eliah leisurely stretched his legs, sipped brandy from a gold-rimmed narrow glass and said, "Jacob spends much time in St. Petersburg, also Riga. I've heard stories from tradespeople in Minsk. It's said that he's often in the company of the Princess Helene."

Mendel brought his right hand to his face; smiling, he stroked his black mustache with his two sewn-together fingers, and replied, "She entertains for him."

"I know he's a big businessman," Chaim Eliah interrupted. "We hear stories of him," he said, and his tone indicated the unsavoriness of the stories.

"Listen," Abraham said, "Jacob and Tania wish to be married. Let us talk about the marriage."

"Ah, it's not so simple," Chaim Eliah said.

"He is Jacob Kagan!" Mendel exclaimed and, pointing his two fingers at Chaim Eliah, leaning over and poking him in the shoulder, he said, "A catch!"

Jacob married Tania in 1910. The wedding took place in Minsk, and never had that city seen anything like it. The name of Jacob Kagan was famous beyond the name of any Jew in Russia. Certainly Lazar Starobinetz was wealthy, perhaps even richer than Kagan, but about Kagan there were stories. He was a giant, as strong as a bear, as cunning as a fox. Wasn't it Jacob Kagan who sued the Tsar and won? In the summer of 1908, when Nicholas II blocked off a fifty mile stretch of the river Berezina because he was to cross the river in a month and was afraid that preparations to assassinate him might be made, Kagan circumvented the river blockade, transporting his logs overland till they could again be set in the river; but, incensed and amused by the action of the Tsar, Kagan hired a lawyer, a member of the first *Duma,* and sued the Tsar, declaring he had been unable to fulfill contractual obligations because of the blockade. The case received a great deal of publicity, became a political issue, and, as an indication of the Tsar's liberality, was decided in favor of the plaintiff. The stories of Kagan, clouded by exaggeration, by hero-worship, or by hate, were often the inventions of men who had never met him. It was told that he had swindled Lazar Starobinetz, who had the reputation of a miser, to make his first start; that once, attacked by six robbers, he alone had smashed in their skulls with only his fists. But though many of these stories were untrue, they were believed; Kagan was capable of anything, be it only great!

Jacob and his family left Nishkovitz in three closed sleds; they wore their wedding clothes beneath heavy flannel shirts and fur-lined coats. It was snowing and so cold that Mendel and Esther, driving the first carriage, had to change off holding the reins every quarter of an hour. When Esther was not driving she stamped her feet and beat her arms across her chest. Only their eyes were exposed to the blizzard and they could hardly see twenty feet ahead. Esther urged the horses as well as a man and when she thought that her fingers, covered as they were by heavy gloves, were going to snap off if she held the reins another minute, she would still hold on till Mendel forcibly took the reins from her. They rode for many hours and arrived in Minsk on the eve of the wedding.

There were crowds of people outside Chaim Eliah's house, curious, waiting to see Kagan. Esther jumped to the ground from the driver's bench and opened the door of the sled. Abraham came first and helped Heika out. Then, as Abraham walked with Heika towards the house, Jacob appeared, stooped, in the entrance to the sled. He looked up for an instant and then stepped to the ground, took Esther's arm and walked with her: she, no taller than five feet; he, several inches above six feet and wearing a tall Caracul hat. Then, as in a procession, came the brothers.

From all of Russia there were guests—the aged *bon-vivant,* Graf Potofsky, his nephew Count Sligorin, the Princess Helene, the international financier Meyer Rabin, the Chief Rabbi of Riga, Lazar Starobinetz, and the famous author Shmyola Bernstein. The author, anxious to meet Jacob, was introduced to him by Tania. Bernstein was of average height and physique, but his face was strange, even more, bizarre, composed of single ridiculous features. If, for instance, a man asking God for a face received but one feature at a time, he might look at his ears and say, "They are queer, but perhaps the mouth will be better." Then, when the mouth is as bad as the ears, he might say, "Perhaps the nose will be noble, or the hair blond and the eyes blue." Bernstein's short, dull red hair stood straight up, and his nose was broken right in the middle, so that from that middle break his nose did not extend even a millimeter further out from his face, but dropped abruptly, a sheer precipice.

"Jacob Kagan," Shmyola Bernstein repeated. "Kay-gan! It is a beautiful name. Yacobe Kaghane, there is a melody to the name, an exquisite tune. But who is this charming girl? What sparkle in those eyes . . . my dear child."

"Hold," Jacob said as Shmyola reached out to pinch Esther's cheek. "My sister Eshka," he said smiling, "may be quiet now, but she uses her teeth and feet. Once she whipped a regiment of Cossacks."

"Ah, that's a story I might have written. But you know, Kagan, I'm working for the St. Petersburg *Verloffen* and want to do an article about you."

"Jacob," Tania interrupted, "isn't that the Graf Potofsky?"

"Excuse us," Jacob said to Bernstein.

"I shall see you in St. Petersburg, eh?"

"Of course," Jacob said and taking Tania's arm walked away from Bernstein.

"Do you like your brother?" Bernstein asked Esther.

"Where did you get such a funny nose?" she responded.

Bernstein was hardly taken aback and said, "It's a long story . . ."

"You almost married him?" Jacob asked Tania incredulously.

"Oh," Tania said, "he is charming, but imagine, Madame Shmyola Bernstein!"

Graf Potofsky, Princess Helene and Count Sligorin were standing together and Potofsky was saying, "That one, over there; you've never met Starobinetz, have you?"

"He is the man who once worked for you?" the princess asked, smiling.

"The man who swindled you," the Count remarked under his breath.

"Exactly! Lazar," he called, seeing that Lazar was looking at him. "Starobinetz, come say hello."

Lazar turned around and, smiling, approached the three. "Starobinetz, this is the Princess Helene, and this my nephew, Count Sligorin."

Lazar nodded his head twice and asked, "So how do you like my niece's choice? He's maybe a little too smart, but . . ."

"An excellent choice!" the Graf exclaimed. "Absolutely excellent!"

"It does look like a fine match," the Princess said and Sligorin smiled.

"And just imagine," Lazar said, "what will happen when I give my holdings to Jacob. Why, he'll force everyone else out of business."

"Ah?" Potofsky exclaimed, and then smiled as Lazar, laughing, nodded again and left them.

"Pig!" Count Sligorin exclaimed, and then said to the Princess, "To know such people, it is an embarrassment."

"Graf Potofsky, Princess Helene and Count Sligorin—my wife to be," Jacob said, introducing Tania to them.

"She is a beauty," Potofsky whispered into Jacob's ear, but loud enough for the others to hear.

"You're not the first to think so," Jacob said. "That man over there, the author, also . . ."

"You don't mean Shmyola Bernstein?" Potofsky interrupted. "Is he here?"

"You know him?" Jacob asked.

"*Bien sur*. He is a wonderful companion. I must say hello to him."

The writer was standing alone in the corner of the room, sipping from a brandy glass. "Bernstein," Graf Potofsky said, "it's good to see your Jewish face."

"Your excellency."

"You know, Bernstein, you astonish me. I've heard you referred to as the Yiddish Dickens, but I have never seen you any place but in the drawing rooms of the best homes in St. Petersburg and, now, here in Minsk. Where do you get your experience?"

"I listen, your excellency. When I was younger, I travelled third class and listened to the poor. You know," he said, pausing reflectively, "I have not talked with a scholar in years, and yet yesterday I finished a tale of one." Bernstein took off his spectacles and scratched his left nostril. "It is a tale of all of Judaism."

"You must tell it to me," the Graf said. "Here, wait one minute and I shall bring back the princess, I'm sure she loves Jewish stories."

SHMYOLA BERNSTEIN'S TALE OF YEHUDA THE ASCETIC AND MOTTEL THE BALAGOLA

Yehuda the ascetic and Mottel the *balagola* lived together in a cabin close to the Berezina. These two bachelors lived apart from the Jewish community of Thokva. Yehuda, a scholar, measured his years by the number of years he had studied the Talmud. His beard extended like a starched white collar beneath his chin. His tall, thin body was stooped as though the strict discipline necessary for the reading and contemplation of the Talmud had bent and bent him until it was impossible for him to look at the face of another person. And when he did look at the face of anyone, the terrible effort it required gave a sharp, bulging effect to his eyes and creased his forehead with hundreds of tiny, condemning folds of empty skin. In his cabin, when contemplating, he reclined deeply in a soft, cushioned chair, so that the nearly impossible feat of his staring straight out was achieved. Seated like this, facing the door, his hands on the arms of the chair, his black, crown-like skull cap placed squarely on his head, his lips pursed, he would nod to Mottel, and in a slow, heavy Yiddish would ask, "So, Mottel, tell me, what's new?"

Mottel would hang up his cap and coat, wash his hands in a basin placed on the top of the stove, vigorously rub his completely bewhiskered face, seat himself on a stool near the stove, roll a cigarette and say, "Surely." Mottel, not as tall as Yehuda, but heavy and strong, his hands calloused from lifting crates on and off his cart, stiff from holding the reins of his horse, might laugh and say, "Today I rode all the way to Strovnitz and for only one ruble, but when I got there, I heard a story . . ." Yehuda would place his hands together beneath his chin, nod his head and say, "So?"

Sometimes this rough *balagola* and the frail ascetic would discuss Spinoza. Yehuda might murmur, "He would have been a genius, had he only understood."

"Who?" Mottel would ask.

"Spinoza," Yehuda would say as if he were talking to himself.

"Surely, he was a real genius."

Yehuda might talk about an interpretation of the Talmud but he would invariably lapse into a puzzling question that abstracted his eyes. All the while Mottel sat on his stool, occasionally standing up to warm his hands over the stove. Once, every day, Yehuda left the cabin and walked to the house of one of the Jewish families. For two hours he would sit in the warm living room and listen, his eyes closed, to a boy read Hebrew; he would correct the boy's pronunciation and stop him when he skipped. Then he would return to the cabin. Mottel left at dawn and rarely returned before late evening. On some days he would travel many miles to a neighboring village, but on days when he had no deliveries he would sit on the bench of his cart and slowly ride up and down the single street of Thokva, often loudly hailed by peasants he knew. Sometimes he would be approached by the daughter of a Jew, and he would bring his right hand to his cap in a salute. The girl would tell him that her mother said he should come to her house and pick up some meat and soup for Yehuda. Late at night, Mottel would play his flute, and Yehuda would close his eyes, relaxed in the peace of that which should be.

In this way the two lived together, but one year life became unbearable to Yehuda. Mottel's presence in the cabin made contemplation impossible; some days, Yehuda never even left the cabin.

"Yehuda, are you hungry?" Mottel asked him one evening.

"Hungry I am, but it is not for the food you eat."

Mottel suffered Yehuda's silence and curtness but finally said, "Yehuda, we have lived together many years. You are a scholar and a philosopher, I am only a *balagola,* but until now we have never had trouble. What has happened?"

"I have wasted my life. Now I discover I must have someone to talk with, someone who will understand me, and I am too old."

"Other days you have talked to me and I have listened."

"You never understood what I said, Mottel. What can you know of Spinoza?"

The next time Yehuda the ascetic left the cabin, he encountered Mottel, who was driving his cart on the main street. Mottel turned his cart around and brought it close to the raised wooden walk where Yehuda was standing. "So what do you think of Spinoza?" Mottel asked. "Do you think he believed in a God of the mind, eh Yehuda?"

Yehuda remained silent, and Mottel nodded his head and continued. "Is that your thought? Well, you may be right, my learned friend, but my theory is that he believed in a God of the sky. The trouble with you philosophers is you don't know where to place God. For example," and while Mottel gesticulated and talked several Jewish townspeople stared at and followed them, "you read books and find God in them. I have thought a little bit, and God is not in you; you are in God." But then Mottel paused and, looking at Yehuda's face, exclaimed, "Yehuda, my friend, come get beside me, and I will take you home."

Yehuda did not say a word but continued walking. Mottel stopped at the end of the street. Near evening a Jewish girl came up to the cart and said to Mottel, "My mother wants you to come to our house to take some chicken for Yehuda the ascetic."

"Surely," Mottel said.

Shmyola Bernstein paused a moment and then said, as though he had just finished reciting a tale by an author he did not know, but agreed with thoroughly, "It is so."

"Charming," the Princess Helene said.

"It's very nice," the Graf Potofsky added, "but why does Mottel go back to that fool?"

"Ah!" Bernstein exclaimed, "that is the whole story."

It was far past midnight when Chaim Eliah announced, "A toast! I wish to offer a toast!" He waited for silence and continued, "To the Kagans—a great family. Many years ago I knew Abraham when he was working for my uncle. Who would ever know? He is the father of a dynasty. Not just the business, though that is part of it, but the family. It will have many, many generations, and its greatness will multiply with each generation. To the Kagans!"

The services were over. I had stood facing the Torah, the Word of God, on the platform at the front of the synagogue, and had sung not merely the Bar-mitzvah portion, but the entire three-hour Sabbath service. Abraham had stood at my right, turning pages, careful to see that I did not miss anything. And, at about the middle of the service, when I had sung full-throated, "Hear O Israel, the Lord is God, the Lord is One," Abraham had looked at me, then had closed his eyes and had himself begun to pray as if at that moment he thought that he was no longer my teacher. In the afternoon we held open house at the apartment. I stood with my parents in the small hallway and was kissed and congratulated.

"So how does it feel to be a man?" Jack asked me as he pressed a bill into my hand. Fifty dollars. Add that to three hundred-dollar bonds, seven fifty-dollar bonds, sixteen twenty-five-dollar bonds, two hundred ninety dollars in cash, five albums of phonograph records—the complete *La Bohème*—a Parker 51, and uncle Larry and Ben haven't given me yet. "I don't know," I answered.

David, the eldest son of Jacob Kagan, stood beside the marble-topped bureau and mixed himself a double Scotch with water. He noticed his uncle Sam watching him. Sam looked like a wax dummy; his smile was frozen onto pasty white cheeks, and he could move only with the greatest difficulty. Then David saw Sam's hands. They were vibrating like the strings on a violin, moving only fractions of an inch each way, but shaking uncontrollably. Sam tried to hide his hands; David felt his own body begin to tremble. He looked away and, seeing me, he raised his glass, smiled, and drank. Then he said, "This is what you sounded like," and he sang a line from the service in high falsetto.

"Never mind," my aunt Gertie said to David, "he has a *goldene* voice. You wish you had such a voice. Yoselle Rosenblatt," she said turning to me, "you'll be another Yoselle Rosenblatt. You made me cry."

"Where is Ivan?" David thought. "Where is he?"

"What time are we going?" I asked David, anticipating the opera he was taking me to that evening.

David looked at his wristwatch and said, "Not till seven-thirty or eight." His father's watch. A timepiece outside of time.

His brother Jack stood with Abraham, Larry, Ben and my mother. "Give me five years," he declared, "and I'll be the biggest Jewish shipper in the U.S."

"I'd tell your fortune," my mother said, "but I need cards."

"I don't need any fortunes," the younger son of Jacob Kagan said, "just a break."

"Ah, there's Ivan," Abraham said.

Ivan was standing with David and they were speaking in Russian. I heard David give him an address and the name of a bar, The Merchants' Café. Then Doctor Deutschman called me.

"Sam," he said, "it was wonderful. I see where you already take the responsibilities of a man. To sing the entire service, that was a real feat."

"Abraham taught him for five years," my father informed his colleague.

"Five years? You know, you could be a doctor by now," Deutschman said.

"He wants to be a singer," my father said, and laughed.

"A singer like Frank Sinatra?"

"He'll be a businessman," my father said. "He has too much of his mother's blood."

"No. Like Caruso," I said.

TWO

AFTERNOON

I

Just three months after Jacob's marriage, David was arrested by the Tsar's secret police and sent to Siberia. In 1911, two years later, he escaped and returned to Nishkovitz. He had lost a great deal of weight and he looked consumptive. Jacob was in St. Petersburg and did not see his brother or even learn of his escape until days later. David spoke with his father.

"Switzerland," Abraham suggested. "You can rest, and then maybe Jacob can work something out."

"I want to study," David said and Abraham nodded his head. "I want another chance. If I can get my health back, I'll return."

Heika sat with them, and Mendel, who was in charge of Jacob's first lumber mill, located not far from Nishkovitz, was called from work. David went to sleep in his old bed, and his father and brother considered how they could get him to the border and then across it. They decided to dress him as a Rabbi and to have Ben, not yet seven years old, accompany him in a cart. When David awoke, he was disguised and given money, and then he departed with Ben. He was captured not more than a few miles outside of Nishkovitz. The police had known of his return and had waited to arrest him until he was alone and outside of town. They let Ben go, but took

David to a cabin where they held him for a short while. Then they took him outside and summarily shot him. Ben came back to the house and only Esther and Heika were there. Esther sent Ben to her father, and then she rode bareback, retracing Ben's steps, and finally coming upon the cabin. The police were gone. She saw David's body lying in the snow. When it got very cold, she pulled her brother's body into the cabin and waited there until Mendel found her several hours later.

They brought back David's body still clothed in the black silk coat of the orthodox Jew. When Heika saw the horse carrying her son, she ran out of the house and, stopping several feet away, threw her head back and clapped her hands to her ears, pressing them against her head until her eyes were slits. "Oh, my God, oh, my God! You were too good to me!" she wailed, and did not speak again for longer than a year.

The sudden death of David, the emigration of Laban, and the marriages of seven of the brothers—only Sol, Ben and Esther remained single in 1911—left the large house in Nishkovitz empty and vast. Heika wandered through the house, conscious of her family as little more than shadows. Abraham tried to comfort her, to share the sorrow that she had made her own, but she never heard him. She shaved her hair and wore a coarse brown wig. Once she tried to speak to Esther, but her lips only trembled. When, like a dream-walker suddenly wakened, she was able to talk again, it was easy to see that she was mad. Detached, she never made judgments of people, but trusting all people equally and implicitly, she accumulated random facts; sometimes she knew a hundred facts about a person: his occupation, avocation, his wife's name, how many children he had, if he could read, how often meat was served in his house. "Starobinetz has a bad temper," Sam was saying to his father one day, when Heika entered the room and said, "He eats four times a week in Chaim Eliah's house."

"He's lonely and he visits his nephew," Sam explained to Heika, who was leaving the room and who did not require any explanation at all. She spent many hours every day sitting alone in the kitchen, reading prayers aloud. On the Day of Atonement she read prayers meant for the Passover, as if the Day of Atonement should have been a feast day. She gave up all household activities, and though she had formerly always cooked—(from the time of her marriage she had had a hired Gentile girl for cleaning)—and taken pleasure in cooking, her menus now became so strange—she might have a meal of asparagus one night, or of sliced raw potatoes another—that the job of cooking for Abraham, Ben and Sol fell to Esther.

The married sons rarely visited Heika; she was an embarrassment to their wives. Their name, the wealth of their brother, had made them sought-after young men but, once married, it developed with four of the brothers that their wives were jealous not only of Jacob's success, but also jealous of each success and each purchase of any of the brothers. Jacob's business enterprises, continually expanding, employed all the Kagans in responsible positions: Sam and Mordecai were the directors of two new lumber mills, Joshua was Jacob's broker, Elihu and Reuben were agents, and Sol and Ben worked in various capacities in the forests. If Jacob acted as general, then his father was counsellor, Mendel his special envoy, and his other brothers his captains and lieutenants. The brothers were absorbed into a network of acquisition and control that often carried them to the big cities and the isolated forests; by a message from Jacob in St. Petersburg, any one of them might be dispatched to the Ukraine, Siberia, or Poland.

The largest of the lumber mills that Jacob owned had been erected on the Berezina, several miles from Nishkovitz. Virtually the entire peasant population of Nishkovitz and the two small neighboring villages was employed there. Sam was director of the mill. His Talmudic education had made him argumentative but also a disciplined worker. He received his orders from Jacob but introduced his own techniques to accomplish the job with a minimum of expense and effort. Though Sam lived with his wife in Nishkovitz, and though the mill was only a few miles from his home, Sam was often in Riga for weeks at a time. His wife Berryle, it was universally agreed, was a witch! She was not a witch in the sense of a conjuror, or a hag with long black hair covering a pock-marked face, but she was just not of the family, never could be part of a family that had a central figure, whose women, no matter how jealous or foolish they were, were either *balabustas,* such as Heika had been and Esther was, or beauties like Jacob's wife, Tania. By no stretch of the imagination could Berryle have been called a beauty, and she could hardly prepare borsht and blinis. She was disliked even while Sam courted her. He was warned, called "idiot," by Jacob, "fool," by Mendel, and "stupid," by Abraham. But Sam, wanting a wife as one might want a pet, not from love but from a vague desire to have a completed household, thinking her ambition might be a driving force in his own life, thinking her unique (which she most certainly was), stubbornly concluded that he loved her, married her, and, after six months of growing doubt, decided that he had been dreadfully wrong.

He visited Jacob in St. Petersburg and spoke as a man tormented and hounded by evil spirits. "Jacob, you knew; you told me, but I was blind! In my eyes, she was beautiful. I could see no wrong. Oh! if you could understand how miserly she is! I'm served meat only twice a week. What can she do with all the money I give her?"

"Perhaps she saves it for a dowry?" Jacob suggested sarcastically.

"Listen, my brother, I can't endure it! See how I cry! I'm in everlasting hell! Every time I look at her, she says, 'See, see what you did.' 'What did I do?' I ask. 'I'm fat with child.' For six months she says that, and she still looks like a broomstick, she isn't getting fat at all. Jacob! Don't smile! It's eating my heart out."

Jacob waited while Sam blew his nose and then exclaimed, "Every night! Every night, Sam, you should beat her with a cane. And then, when you finish beating her, you should stand in front of a mirror and beat yourself for having been such a fool as to have married her."

"Jacob!"

"Shall I really tell you what you'll do? You'll find a *shiksa* and this time you won't sign any contracts."

Berryle was immediately suspicious when her husband began to take extended trips. Before, when one of the Kagans visited her, she might offer tea and a stale cookie; now she did not even open the door to them. Once, when Esther had left her mother alone for a moment, Berryle stormed into the house. She ran through the rooms and, when she saw Heika sitting on a wooden stool in the kitchen, reading a prayer book, she screamed, "Where's your son, where does he keep his whore?"

Heika closed her book and, screwing up her eyes, said, "I've heard that the Tsar is only five feet four inches tall, just an inch taller than you."

"You crazy old woman, your son lived with a whore, and you pray to God and talk about the Tsar! When I see him again . . ."

"How can the Tsar be only five feet four inches tall?"

"How should I know? What do I want to know about the Tsar? I want to know whom your son is sleeping with tonight."

"He's in Riga," Esther said entering the room. "Jacob sent him there to buy barges," Esther lied.

"Your mother's crazy and you're a liar! What a family!"

"God must be taller even than Jacob," Heika said and nodded her head.

"He'll be back in one or two weeks," Esther said.

"Better for him if he never comes back," Berryle declared and turned and left.

Sam returned to Nishkovitz at the end of a month and found his house closed to him. He knocked on the door for several minutes, then tapped on a window. There was no answer, and it was only when he picked up his suitcase and turned to go, that a second floor bedroom window was flung open and Berryle, screaming "Scoundrel! Whoring son of a crazy mother!" capsized on him a soup tureen full of just-melted snow. Soaked and shivering, Sam took asylum in his parents' home. Jacob and Abraham in St. Petersburg were informed of what had happened, and Abraham returned to Nishkovitz. When he saw his son, so very pale and nervous, Abraham could only shake his head from side to side.

"Can't you even look at me?" Sam exclaimed. "You must do something—people laugh at me when I walk on the street. I'll die if I stay here another day. I feel her on my shoulders so I can hardly stand straight. What a witch! What a horrible woman!"

"Patience," Abraham counselled. "I'll talk to her and we'll see."

"I can't wait. Don't you see how I die a thousand times with each breath?"

"You know," Abraham said gently, "everything happens for the best. There is always compensation," he philosophized.

"What kind of compensation? Where compensation? Papa, I want to be rid of her . . ."

Abraham and Esther went as a delegation to Sam's house. Berryle let them in and then suddenly burst into tears. "My family wasn't rich," she said. "My father was just a shopkeeper, but they were good. What did they ever do that I should deserve this? Tell me, Abraham, and you, my sister Eshka, tell me they were devils and then I'll understand."

"It makes no difference whose fault it is," Abraham said. "You're married to my son, and we must find a solution. He cannot go on living in my house forever."

"A solution? An answer to the devil? You answer the devil only one way," Berryle exclaimed and spat on the unswept floor.

"If you don't want to live as husband and wife, you must separate for good," Esther declared angrily.

"I will not," Berryle screamed. "How dare you say such a thing! I can never marry again! He's ruined me, taken everything from me, and now you want I should free him to live with a whore!"

"You must live as husband and wife," Abraham said rising from his chair.

"Oh, my God!" Berryle sobbed, hiding her face in her hands. "Why can't I hurt him like he's hurt me?"

For just four days there was peace in Sam's house, and then he was thrown out. He went to his brother's house in St. Petersburg, and Jacob, the news having already been telegraphed to him, asked, "You infected her?"

"I never touched her," Sam answered.

"But you have syphilis?"

"Syphilis? There! There, see how she lies and distorts! I've a small gonorrhea and she calls it syphilis."

Jacob gave Sam the equivalent of ten thousand dollars, and Sam, diseased, went to the United States, where he joined the revolutionary, Laban, and his uncle Eleazar who, as a young boy, had robbed Abraham of all his money.

2

The St. Petersburg society that Jacob was a member of was cultured and moneyed. His acquaintances were the sons and daughters of wealthy Jews. They had been educated in Germany; they never spoke Yiddish, but spoke German and French as fluently as Russian. These were the merchants and their wives, the directors of the large organizations. They were sharp, invested only in sure things, added to their wealth gradually, and lived leisurely, taking vacations each year in Switzerland, France or Italy. Licensed as merchants of the first guild, they earned more than fifty thousand rubles a year. Jacob was a giant among them; his untutored speech, his fantastic wealth, made him envied and admired, and often an object of ridicule. Shmyola Bernstein, working for the St. Petersburg Jewish language newspaper, the *Verloffen,* contributed to Jacob's fame by writing articles about him and everything he did. In 1909, when Jacob's first son had been born, Bernstein had written a series of sketches about the family Kagan. In it he had written about Jacob's brother David, at that time in Siberia, and had likened Jacob's son, named David after the same grand-uncle, to the David in Siberia and then to King David: "These are the blessed, the children of truth, the singers to God." In the same series, he had traced the name Kagan back to a Mongol tribe that in the sixteenth century had converted to Judaism. He had compared the gigantic size and power of Jacob to that of the warlike Mongols and had concluded, "With the name Kagan, he could have been only a king, which indeed he is." In the course of some of the more accurate research for this series, he had become an intimate of Jacob, and over the years was a frequent guest at his St. Petersburg mansion. Often Jacob, Tania and Bernstein went to the opera or theatre together. They were an extraordinary trio: Jacob in his sable lined and collared brown overcoat, so big, looking from a distance like a bear; his wife, her features so soft, she—so beautiful, so small standing beside her husband; and Bernstein with his red hair and broken nose. Bernstein always wore some article of clothing that would be stared at. "If I had been born a Gentile," he once explained, "I would have worn crosses or medallions, but as I am a Jew, I wear a violet cravat and even a fur skin round my neck." Bernstein contributed to Jacob's fame, not only by his articles and the glamour of his own company, but also by his remarkable ability to concoct stories about Jacob on the spur of the moment. Once, at a theatre, he stood with two acquaintances, and during an intermission one said, "Last night I saw 'the bear' at the opera. He sat through *Faust* for three hours, and when the performance was over, he announced his displeasure. It seems he had come to hear Chaliapin sing *The Flea.*"

"The Flea?"

"Yes. He wanted to see Chaliapin scratch himself."

"Ah, that would make him feel at home."

"Gentlemen, you are unjust," Bernstein said. "I'm sure he wanted only to relive his youth, when he worked in the forests. You know, he educated several fleas, he kept them as pets, and when he became wealthy, he sold them to a circus."

"Not really?"

"He actually sold them?"

"He made an enormous amount on the sale," Bernstein said.

And Bernstein did more for Jacob than help to make his name famous. It was Bernstein who first suggested that Jacob visit Paris.

In 1913, Bernstein was assigned by his newspaper to be their first foreign correspondent in Paris. He had been to Paris, once, when, before he had published any of his books, he had travelled there third class and had earned whatever money he had made by translating Russian stories into Yiddish for a Jewish publishing house. Now, on a salary, with a small expense account and a growing reputation, he made ready to return, and spoke to Jacob about Paris. "I shall show you a city," Bernstein said, spreading his arms wide. "The city of lights." Jacob was unimpressed and Bernstein said, "Listen, you have more than enough. Take a vacation! Broaden yourself! Your father and Mendel can handle your affairs. After all, why should you be the only Jew who has not been to Paris?"

Tania took to the suggestion enthusiastically—it was her desire, she explained to Jacob. Paris was a magnet whose irresistible pull she had always felt. Jacob agreed to the trip, and in two days' time she had prepared an itinerary that included not only Paris, but Warsaw, Berlin, Vienna, Berne, and Florence and Venice, if the weather permitted. Jacob changed the itinerary to include Minsk and Nishkovitz and wondered if he would be able to go through with that kind of adventure. When they visited Tania's family in Minsk, he spoke with his brother-in-law, Isaac. "You know," he said, "I'm very rich, but I think I'm different. Shmyola wants to educate me, and Tania wants to dress me up like a fancy cake, but I suppose I'll always be the same."

Isaac suggested that he give some of his money to the Jewish Hospital of Minsk, where Isaac was Chief Resident. Jacob laughed and said that he would when he returned to St. Petersburg.

"Frankly," Jacob said, "I am very nearly frightened. I have no manners," he finally stated.

"But that is your charm," Isaac said.

Before they left Minsk, Isaac warned Jacob not to take David with them. "The change of climate," he said, "it would be stupid. A child can't adapt that easily. Leave him in Nishkovitz. The country air will do him good. Just look at yourself."

Jacob stayed in his parents' home in Nishkovitz, and his son was adored. Heika sat with him for hours, reciting prayers that he soon learned. Esther walked with him miles around, to show him to all her neighbors. But in this large, carelessly furnished and carelessly run house, Tania was uncomfortable. Esther ran the house her own way, preparing large meals of her own choosing. She made a cabbage soup with tomatoes and *flanken* that Tania could hardly look at, and which lasted two days. The visitors who came to see Jacob and his son were strangers to her; their clothes were coarse, their beards untrimmed, and many of them smelled as if they had not bathed in months. Her mother-in-law and all her ways upset her, and Esther's incredibly arbitrary running of the house confused her. The once shy Tania had, as the wife of one of the wealthiest men in Russia, blossomed into a fashionable and discriminating woman.

"You should wash your hair more often," Tania said one day to Esther.

"Would I be beautiful then?"

Tania blushed, and Esther, laughing, said, "If I washed my hair so much that it was as pretty as yours, still no one would take me to Paris."

"But if you really wanted to go . . ."

"Why then I still wouldn't go."

"I don't understand you at all," Tania said. "You can be beautiful. Jacob and your brothers certainly have enough money; you can do anything you want."

"Taniashka, I've told my fortune a thousand times, and it's never said I'll go to Paris. Maybe if I become a great actress . . ."

"Is that what you'd like?" Tania asked and continued quickly, "Then you have to study; you should go to the Institute at St. Petersburg and live with us."

"No," Esther said, "the cards also say I'll never be a great actress."

"But what *do* you want to do?"

Esther put her hand on her chin, caressed her mouth with her thumb, and said seriously, "Ice-skate in the summertime."

"Oh, you're joking," Tania said.

David and his nurse remained in Nishkovitz. Jacob, Tania and their maid travelled to Warsaw, from where they had reservations on the Berlin-Paris Express. They met Shmyola Bernstein and departed in the late afternoon. Dinner was brought to their suite of five compartments, and afterwards, Tania took out her Russian-French dictionary and made Jacob pronounce certain French expressions: *bon jour, comment allez-vous, je vais bien, je suis Russe, j'ai mal à la tête.*

"Bon soir, mon mari," Tania said, and explained, "That means husband. And you say, *bon soir, ma femme.*"

"Ah," Bernstein said smiling, pointing his index finger straight up, "but *bon soir ma faim* means goodnight my hunger."

Jacob woke before dawn; Tania was sleeping. Perhaps it had been the scraping of a branch against the moving train that only he had heard. Her breathing was regular; Jacob, careful not to disturb her, got out of the bed noiselessly and opened the door to the sitting room. He picked up a volume of poetry Tania had taken with her; he started to read a poem and then put the book down. He placed his chair near the window and, resting his elbow on the sill, cupping his chin, he stared soberly into the darkness. He tried to distinguish features of the land they were passing through, but could see only his own reflection. He stood up to turn off the light and then nearly stumbled finding his chair. It was much better; he could distinguish a little now. Looking up, he saw thousands of stars, and he drew strength from his present solitude. For months he had felt himself growing weak, had wanted to break away from his home and business and work as he had once worked. Oh, what a beauty there was in the raw cold of a forest in winter! He saw a hill, so black against the black of the sky, and then, after a few moments, the sky grew lighter and was gray. All quiet, with only the dulling noise of the train's strong and steady rhythm. An hour after dawn, the train stopped at the German border. Jacob threw his overcoat over his shoulders like a cape and left the train. He walked on the deserted platform and felt the chill of the spring morning. He clasped his hands behind his back and breathed deeply.

"You can't sleep, eh?" Bernstein said, approaching Jacob from behind.

Jacob turned about. Shmyola's eyes were red, and he appeared very tired. "My bed is too small," Jacob explained. "Unless I bend myself double, some part of me is always uncovered. But why are you up so early?"

Bernstein took off his spectacles and, rubbing the bridge of his nose, replied, "I've been writing a story."

"Ah."

"It's about my own trouble. A very short story; perhaps you'd care to hear it?"

"By all means."

Bernstein scratched his ear and began: "The very famous *Gayon* of Vilna, at the age of sixty-three, having spent his entire life studying and teaching, decided to travel through Russia, to stop at small villages as well as cities, to explicate the Torah and the Talmud. Surely he could have travelled in high style, but he chose rather to ride in a cart, with an ordinary *balagola* as his only companion. They drove through thirty villages and the *Gayon* was feted in each of them. One day, on the road, the *Gayon* overheard the *balagola* talking to himself. 'Ah! If only I was the *Gayon* of Vilna, then I too would be given dinners fit for a Grand-Duke. How lucky one is to have an education.'

"The *Gayon* smiled behind his thick, gray beard, he scratched his ear and said, 'Yoselle,' for that was the *balagola's* name, 'I've come to an important decision. I want to see whether the scholars really understand and appreciate my explications, so, in the next town we come to, you will be the *Gayon* of Vilna and I will be Yoselle.' The *Gayon* was very amused by his idea for he knew that Yoselle had no understanding of the Torah or Talmud, that he could not even read, and that he would be discovered the first time he was asked even the simplest question.

"They arrived at a village, the *Gayon* holding the reins of the horse and Yoselle, anticipating a feast, sitting in the rear as if for all the world he were the *Gayon*. Yoselle was greeted by a delegation from the local synagogue and was taken to the home of the wealthiest Jew in the town. He was fed as if he were a Grand-Duke, and, later, he was taken to the synagogue. In the dim lights, he was brought to the ark and shown a section of the Torah. 'Venerable *Gayon*,' the rabbi of the village said, 'for fifteen years I have bent my back and studied this one section, but I have never understood. See? Tell me, venerable *Gayon*, how can . . .' and at this point Yoselle stepped back and exclaimed, 'You mean that I've come all the way from Vilna to be insulted? Why, even my *balagola* knows what that means. Yoselle,' he called, 'show them how simple it is.' "

"That's a very funny story," Jacob said.

"You see my problem?"

"What problem?"

Bernstein explained: "I am at the same time both the *Gayon* and the *balagola*. Sometimes I'm very clever, sophisticated even, and other times I'm ignorant, but maybe wise. But always I'm not sure what and whom I'm supposed to be. You know, Jacob," he continued reflectively, "one comes to understanding in peculiar ways. A job you feel you're not right for, a woman who you realize doesn't love you. Why? Why, indeed! You are a man with aims, with desires you yourself don't understand, and for a woman to love, she must give herself completely. How, Jacob, could any woman do that for me, when I understand so little of myself?"

"You're too much of a thinker—a philosopher and dreamer," Jacob said smiling.

"Ah, no. I do not dream. I see clearly; sometimes my vision blinds me, and I want to die."

"You're a dreamer because you want too much. You want only the beautiful when there's very little that's beautiful, and, in fact, Shmyola, you know, you're not the handsomest of men."

"Of course," Bernstein agreed, blushing. "To be a writer, one must be ugly."

They arrived in Paris, at the *Gare de L'Est,* the following day. Jacob sent his maid with their luggage to their hotel, and then they left the station and hailed a cab. Bernstein said to the driver in French, "To the Eiffel Tower." They drove along the Seine and stared out of the open windows while Bernstein gave a running commentary on everything they passed.

"How exquisite," Tania said when they crossed the bridge dedicated to Alexander the Third.

"Voilà!" Bernstein interrupted. "All of Paris in that one edifice! It rises and rises and for no reason at all."

They got out of the cab and walked around and under the tower. "But enough," Bernstein said, taking Tania's arm. "Now to Montmartre."

They drove all afternoon, and finally, at about six, Jacob dropped Bernstein off at his pension and then continued with Tania to the Ritz in the Place Vendome. The Russian bear had arrived in Paris!

At nine that evening, Bernstein burst into Jacob and Tania's suite exclaiming, "Any adjective, any other word destroys it!

It's only," and Bernstein drew in his breath and then exclaimed, "Paris!"

"You're taken in," Jacob said, smiling at Bernstein's enthusiasm and the fur skin he wore about his neck.

"No!" Bernstein said, "it's more; it's the air here."

"Perfume," Jacob said and looking at himself in a full length mirror, adjusted his white silk cravat.

"Shmyola understands," said Tania. "It's clear and beautiful. It's absolutely elegant. St. Petersburg's nice, yes, I do like it very much, but how can it be compared? We're at our source. Whatever culture we have all comes from Paris. *Notre culture est une culture française.*"

Bernstein's face became very thoughtful.

"What did you say?" Jacob asked Tania.

"I said our culture is French."

"Oh," Jacob said.

"That's not true," Bernstein said, enunciating each word slowly and deliberately. "Our culture is . . . *our* culture. And it's not French, though we try to make it that." Bernstein shook his head from side to side and said, smiling pensively, "Ah, my dear friends, just look; one minute ago, I could think only of Paris, religiously I thought of it, as a scholar would wonder in amazement over the wisdom of an ancient. There was no geometry, no logic. I was, like Tania—my sweet flower, I was like you—in love, but love blinded me. Do you understand? I thought only of the beauty . . ."

"Not a word," Jacob said.

"It's a serious matter, a question," Bernstein stopped himself and exclaimed, "You see, I'm Jewish and I'm Russian."

"That I understand," Jacob said still smiling. "So am I."

"But one can learn," Tania said, "one can watch, can enjoy the beauty of the language, the parks, yes, and even the churches."

"That's escape," Bernstein said. "Yes, it's escape from the realities of heritage. I am a Jew and my heritage is—Moses. I'm a wanderer."

"And mine, Jacob—a wrestler with God."

"You're Jacob Kagan," Bernstein said shrugging his shoulders.

"And you're a fool! And look, it's after nine o'clock. Come on, let's go. I'll eat in spite of everything, even our culture."

On Bernstein's suggestion, they went to the Restaurant Armenonville in the Bois de Boulogne, and were seated at the far rim of the circular terrace. It was past dinner time, and most of the other patrons were finishing their meals, having coffee or smoking. A small orchestra had just begun to play dance music. A waiter put menus in front of Jacob, Tania, and Shmyola and then stood behind and slightly to the right of Jacob's chair. Tania and Shmyola studied the menus, but Jacob, never even opening his, turned to the waiter and said in Russian, "Cabbage soup and boiled beef."

Tania looked up from her menu and whispered, "Jacob!" and the waiter said, *"Pardon m'sieu?"*

"I said," Jacob repeated slowly, "cabbage soup and boiled beef."

"Je ne comprends pas," the waiter said and shrugged his shoulders.

"He does not speak Russian," Jacob said to Bernstein, "perhaps . . ." and Jacob repeated his order in Yiddish.

"Jacob!" Tania exclaimed.

"M'sieu!" the waiter said.

"He speaks neither Russian or Yiddish. Let's go to another restaurant. This one is too French for me," Jacob declared.

Bernstein laughed and explained to the waiter in halting French that Jacob wanted cabbage soup and boiled beef.

"Mais," the waiter said, *"quelle sorte de boeuf bouilli?"*

"What kind of boiled beef do you want?" Bernstein asked.

"What kind?" Jacob repeated and his face became dark and ominous. "Boiled beef is boiled beef. In St. Petersburg and Nishkovitz, in Moscow and Odessa, there is one kind of boiled beef."

"People are looking at you," Tania said.

"Let them look," Jacob said, and then nodding his head thoughtfully, he looked at the people at every one of the tables around him. He looked from the irritated but still attendant waiter to Bernstein, who, beginning to feel self-conscious, adjusted his fur scarf, and then to his wife, who stared at him reprovingly. He gave a last definite nod and pronounced, "What must be, must be. There's no other way. Tell the waiter to bring three of each dish on the menu."

"I will not," Tania said.

"I'll yell at you if you don't," Jacob said smiling.

"I'll do it," Bernstein said and laughed.

It was done, and what a stir! An army of suspicious waiters trooped out fifteen different appetizers, twelve different soups, forty-five bottles of wine, and twenty-four different main courses. The orchestra conductor's baton remained motionless in his hand as he watched the proceedings, and the music stopped. When the waiters saw that Jacob was laughing, not especially at them, but good-naturedly at himself, at his wife who remained blushing, and at his fur-scarfed companion, they gave up their suspicions and executed their movements with flourishes and turns worthy of ballet dancers. After Jacob had selected, of all the appetizers, the one he wanted, Tania and Shmyola ordering the same, the waiters walked in single file back to the kitchen. Several minutes later, when they came out with the soups, the orchestra conductor raised his baton, and the orchestra played *In A Persian Market*.

All the eyes in the restaurant were on Jacob when he began to select his main course. He did not say a word while eight plates were brought before him, but on the ninth plate, his face broke into a smile and he exclaimed, "Boiled beef, *oui*."

Suddenly a voice boomed from across the terrace, "Kagan!" and all the people who had been staring at Jacob's table now turned towards the tall, stooped, bare-headed and gray-haired man who had called out Jacob's name and was now approaching him.

"Potofsky, you rascal!" Jacob exclaimed, and leaving his boiled beef, he rose and embraced the Graf.

"Ah, *mon ami*," the Graf said, "how good to see you and here in Paris! There I was, sitting on the other side of the restaurant, my dinner not agreeing with me at all. You know, I was very uncomfortable, I desperately wanted to, well, you can imagine how grateful I was, but you know, Jacob, my eyesight's no good, I can hardly see ten feet, every day I see less and less . . . well, one of my dinner companions, what boring chaps, told me a man who looked like a bear was cursing a waiter in Russian, and then, when he told me you ordered every dish on the menu, I knew it could be only one person, of course; Kagan had come to Paris!" The Graf laughed and then saw Bernstein. *"Mon Dieu!"* he exclaimed. "Bernstein, I had no idea you were here! How are you; you have a cold, eh?"

"I'm fine, your excellency."

"Bernstein, you look as though you have all the aches a man my age should have."

"How are you, your excellency?"

"Bad, very sick. Always you Jews are healthy, even when you look sick, that's why you survive. You see, I shall die soon. No, Bernstein, don't shake your head; it's true. I can hardly stand straight any more."

"But do sit down," Jacob said.

"It will make no difference, but here now, see how I sadden you, your first time in Paris," the Graf said and then looked at Tania. He scrutinized her for a moment, not recognizing her, and then winking lecherously at Jacob, said, "My dear mademoiselle, your gown is *charmante*. Did you get it at Paul Poiret?"

"My wife," Jacob said, "bought it in St. Petersburg."

"Stolen from a Poiret style, I'm sure," the Graf said.

"You see, we just arrived this afternoon," Tania explained.

"Ah, of course, of course . . . but is this then your first evening. Oh, I'll make it memorable! No! No protests! I say I'll give you an evening you'll never forget." The Graf motioned a waiter to bring a chair and then, sitting down, leaning over the table, he said in low and confidential tones as Jacob indicated to the waiter that his boiled beef was too cold, "Listen, there's a tango ball tonight. The Countess Sonia. I'll tell you this, she's the wife of the Norwegian match king, but," and placing a finger over his lips, he whispered, "she's a Hungarian Jewess."

"Really?" Tania asked.

"I know from reliable sources, it's a fact all right. Tonight she's giving a party; many, many people—the aristocracy, the wealthiest, the most cultured, diplomats—everyone will be there."

"Wonderful!" Bernstein exclaimed.

"But," the Graf said, "she never invites Jews to her parties."

"Oh," Tania said, disappointed.

"Jews are themselves the worst anti-Semites," Bernstein said.

"Nevertheless," the Graf continued, "we shall all attend. You," the Graf said to Bernstein, "you will be my nephew, the scoundrel Prince Sligorin."

"With his nose," Jacob said, "he passes for nothing but Jew."

"And you, Kagan, I'm sure people will have heard of you, will also change your name. It will be *un vrai coup*."

The Countess's palatial home was in Neuilly, not far from the Bois. She kept it open only in the spring, at the height of the Paris season, and spent the rest of the year at her residences in Oslo, Venice, and Biarritz. There was a tall, iron fence surrounding her home in Neuilly, and within the gates there was a cobbled driveway that led up twenty yards to the main entrance of the house. The house itself was massive—three stories high, covered by layers of creeping vines; it seemed to be an impenetrable square. Thirty carriages were standing outside the gates, and there were several inside, waiting in line to get up to the main entrance.

"It's larger than your house," Bernstein said to Jacob. "I think perhaps I should remove my scarf."

"You cannot!" the Graf exclaimed, and then, smiling, said, "It'll be a sensation." They entered the house and were ushered by a servant in brilliant green livery down a wide and dark mahogany-panelled hallway to the glass doors of the ballroom. The elaborately jointed, waxed wooden floor glittered under the lights of enormous crystal chandeliers; windows on two sides of the room looked out on a terrace. The ballroom was painted light blue, and red velvet draperies that seemed so rich you could bury your hand in them hung partially over each window. The room was filled; there were at least a hundred and fifty people present. To the left of the door, there was a small orchestra, and at the extreme right of the room, there was a fifty-foot table, covered by a single white heavy cloth on which were placed flowers, cakes, and ice buckets with champagne.

"There," the Graf motioned with a shake of his head, "the Crown Prince of Serbia."

"Is it really?" Tania asked.

"A rake," the Graf said. "I met him when he was *incognito* at *Le Théâtre des Capucines*." Then, allowing the servant to open the doors, he said, *"Eh bien!* Follow close, *l'action commence*."

He led them directly to the Countess Sonia, who exclaimed in French, "Ah, my dear fellow, so good to see you. Germaine," she said to the young woman, her ward, who stood with her, "this is the man I've told you so much about, the wildest man in all of Russia, Graf Potofsky."

"My dear Sonia," the Graf said, "I bring you one wilder than any man, by all means the wildest: Boris Sloboda, and his wife Tania."

"Oh," the Countess said, feigning fright, "you will not bite?"

"What does she ask?" Jacob asked the Graf.

"She asks you not to bite her."

"I'd die of indigestion," Jacob said smiling.

"He says," the Graf translated, "that with one bite, he could eat you whole, but that as he is a guest, he shall refrain." Then the Graf, turning to the grinning Bernstein, scowled at him, and pulling him by the arm until he was almost against the Countess, said, "And this is my worthless nephew, Prince Sligorin."

"What a charming scarf," the Countess said. "Do all Russians wear them? Is it a custom in St. Petersburg, like in the orient—you know, cutting legs off so women are never taller than men?"

"It's a good-for-nothing custom for good-for-nothings. He's a writer," the Graf said scornfully.

"Ah, an artist," the Countess said. "It's wonderful! Every spring Paris is filled with artists; it seems everyone is creative but me. Germaine is a singer, very, very good too. Prince Sligorin, you will feel quite at home here, all of you shall, but tell me," the Countess said, noticing Tania's full skirt, "How long have you been in Paris?"

"We just arrived," Tania replied.

"Ah, that explains it. We are wearing narrow skirts this year, for the tango, you know."

"That is a dance of America of the South, isn't it?" Bernstein asked.

"It was," the Countess said, "but I have it now. How long shall you stay?" she asked Tania.

"Perhaps a month."

"Perfect," the Countess said. "Germaine will help you shop, and you, Prince Sligorin," she said to Bernstein, "I shall introduce you—you are not married, eh?—to the most beautiful girls, the most exquisite Parisiennes."

"What did she say?" Jacob asked Bernstein.

"She told me she'll introduce me to beautiful girls," Bernstein (who was beginning to think that he actually was Prince Sligorin) impatiently translated, and then said in a slow French, dropping his arm from across his chest in a clumsy flourish, "If sometimes I can be in your presence, I could ask for no other thing."

"Ah, you have your uncle's blood! Both scoundrels!" the Countess said. "But I do not want to hold you; there are so many interesting people here and I am such a bore. I shall see you all later; you must come one night to the opera with me. *Manon* is simply wonderful."

It took longer than an hour for the Graf to exhaust the number of acquaintances he wanted to introduce Jacob, Tania and Bernstein to. Tania, awkward and unsure of herself at first, after a while gained assurance, smiled more regally, as though Jacob's ease, in spite of the fact that he could not speak French, was transmitted to her. She was beautiful when, like the consort of a reigning monarch, she walked at his side. They were stared at and wondered about. "Who are they?" a small royal Italian guest asked the Countess. "And who is that ridiculous fellow with the pelt around his neck?"

"My dear Carlo," the Countess said, "that fellow is Graf Potofsky's nephew and the others are his friends."

"But you don't believe that?" the Italian asked incredulously. "He is no more his nephew than I. Why, just look at the nose, Countess! Just look at the nose!"

"I've seen his nose. It is very unfortunate."

"It's not Roman," the Italian said, "nor Greek, though it is the size of two Greek noses. Countess, it is beyond a doubt, that man, he is a fraud. The Graf Potofsky is having a joke at your expense. His nephew indeed! That man is a Jew!"

The Countess glanced quickly at Bernstein, and then, reassured, snapping her head back, looking right through the Italian, she said indignantly, "Impossible!"

The Italian left the Countess and joined the group of guests he had been with a moment before. "She will not believe me," he said.

"Then there will not be a scene? Pity," someone said.

"Not that kind," the Italian remarked, "but truly we do have a show. That Jew with the fur scarf, his giant of a bodyguard. What a crew! And who is that man over there—there," he pointed with his chin, "the man who almost fell over himself dancing the tango, that one with the fantastic cigar holder?"

He was a heavy man of average height and he smoked a long brown cigar in an ornate gold holder shaped like a flower vase. He held an empty champagne glass in one hand and every once in a while made a show of sipping from it. He seemed to be bored except when he spoke to his elegantly dressed male companion, and then he seemed annoyed. Jacob had noticed him and, his eyes roaming a second more, he had brought his gaze back to him and now stared at him intently.

"That man," Jacob said distractedly, "what a remarkable similarity."

"What is?" Tania asked.

"Do you see him?" Jacob asked the Graf.

The Graf glanced at him and said, "I don't know him."

"He's very familiar," Jacob said.

"He's an American," the Graf said, imitating the expression on the man's face when he clenched his cigar holder between his teeth.

"He has my father's expression!" Jacob exclaimed. "We must find out who he is. Potofsky," he said, taking his arm, "introduce us."

Jacob and the Graf approached the man and the Graf said in French, "My friend, M. Sloboda, is sure he has seen you before . . ."

The man's companion interrupted the Graf and said, "His name is Jean Smeeth."

"What did he say?" the man asked in English.

"The tall one thinks you are very familiar and wants to know who you are," his companion answered.

"Well, tell him my name and it's not Jean Smeeth. My name's Louis Cohen," he said in English to Jacob, "That's my name and I'm not ashamed of it."

"What's he saying?" Jacob asked the Graf in Russian.

"I think he's speaking English," the Graf answered.

"You speak Russian?" Louis Cohen asked. "I was born . . ."

"*M'sieu* Cohen," the elegantly dressed companion remonstrated in English, "you will be discovered."

"Look," Louis Cohen said, "I paid you to show me the

sights, not to be bored stiff. You said this was gonna be exciting . . ."

"Extraordinary, *M'sieu* Cohen. I did not say exciting."

"I don't give a damn what you said," and then he turned to Jacob and said impatiently in imperfect Russian, "And what's your name?"

"Kagan," Jacob said smiling. "Jacob Kagan."

"My God," Louis Cohen exclaimed, "you're my nephew!"

The royal Italian guest, observing Louis Cohen and Jacob Kagan embrace, declared, "They're invading from all sides. They meet in our ballrooms. The Countess is a Jew and the Divine Presence will have it known by the company she keeps."

Jacob, Tania, Bernstein, and Louis Cohen left the Countess Sonia's ball after midnight and went to Jacob's suite at the Ritz. Jacob ordered two bottles of champagne, and when they were brought up, Bernstein took great pleasure in popping them open. Then he raised his glass and said in Yiddish, "Drunk I am not so much with spirits, no, not even with the Countess! I am drunk from seeing beautiful feelings. When you embraced, an uncle never met, lost for so many years, I wanted to cry. Oh, Jacob, in your business, all of Russia is your province, but in my business, all of humanity is mine."

"Noble," Jacob said.

"Beautiful," Bernstein said and, draining his glass and then adjusting his loosened scarf, he bowed and left.

"A funny man," Louis Cohen said. "Does he make a living?"

"He lives," Jacob said.

"He writes beautifully," Tania added, "he is very famous in St. Petersburg."

"That's a long way from New York," Louis said, clipping the end off a cigar with a gold cutter, and, not using his ornate holder, putting the cigar between his teeth.

"St. Petersburg?" Jacob asked.

"Is a long way from New York," Louis repeated, nodding his head.

"I think it is," Jacob agreed.

"What I'm saying is that it's New York that's the center of the world. Not St. Petersburg or Paris—they're out. The money's in the U.S.A., and if you're smart, you'll follow your nose."

"My nose?"

"And come to New York."

"I'm too tired to go to New York, though I'd like to very much," Tania said, rising unsteadily, and then excusing herself, she left the room.

"So tell me about Laban," Jacob said.

"We call him Larry. A smart one he is. He put an advertisement in the papers when he came over, if anyone knew an Eleazar Kagan. I read it and gave him a job. You know what that son-of-a-bitch did when he first came to work?" Louis asked, smiling. "He started organizing a union right in my factory. Me, his own uncle."

Jacob laughed and asked, "And Sam?"

Louis shook his head and answered, "Not so smart. No sense. Comes to America, thinks he's dressed like a diplomat, striped black pants, homburg, silk cravat. He looks like a—in English there's a word—yokel. You know, like a foreigner. I invite him to sit down, give him a cigar, and he says, 'Eleazar, my proposition is you invest fifteen thousand dollars in my company!' 'What company?' I ask. 'The company I formed.' " Louis drew on his cigar and smiled indulgently. "Coming over on the ship, he and another yokel formed a company to sell lumber. The other guy never saw a tree in his life. Well, I told Sam I had a job for him but no money. He got mad and left. Six months later he comes back, broke, so I put him to work sweeping floors."

"He makes enough money?" Jacob asked.

"Now he does," Louis said expansively. "He doesn't make

as much as me, but he makes plenty. Listen, Jacob, in America everyone makes a living, and if you got just a little more up here," he said tapping his nearly bald skull, "why, no one can stop you. I came to America, a kid; I went to work, small time stuff, carting things around, and I got to know a lot of people, and they liked me. I worked hard, and when one of them made some money, why I just tagged along. I was a partner in a dress business; now I own one of the largest factories in the city. I started real estate. Some nights, I play poker and lose as much money as I used to earn in five years."

"It's a wonderful country," Jacob said.

"It sure is," Louis insisted and flicked some ashes off his white shirt front.

After that evening, Jacob tried to avoid his uncle, but what with Louis staying in the same hotel, there were several inevitable meetings. Whenever they went out, Louis picked up the check, as if to prove his wealth. Perhaps they did not become friends because Jacob was so much wealthier than his millionaire uncle, or, because they had no common language. Jacob did not understand English, and Louis spoke Russian crudely and only with much difficulty. They did both speak Yiddish, but two varieties of it. In Russia, Yiddish was a language in which an author like Bernstein could write classic stories, but in America, in the New York garment district, Yiddish had already become an imprecise language of businessmen who defined the state of the world, their businesses, and their health with single words and much facial anguish, as if there could be no real communication except through physical expression and consummated business transactions. When Louis Cohen finished selecting and buying the dress fashions he had come to Paris for, he returned to New York. He was the first of my family to have settled in the United States and though I never knew him (he died, committed suicide in 1931 by dunking his head into an already filled gas oven, kneeling to get his head inside, his knees on a cushion), I draw my American pioneer heritage from him.

3

After Jacob had settled in St. Petersburg, the stories of his great size, his strength, his wonderful laugh, though not forgotten, were rarely retold by the people of Nishkovitz. He was their employer: Kagan—the first person in St. Petersburg to own two automobiles. But if Jacob had lost his place in the imagination of the people of Nishkovitz, his sister Esther had captured it. She was called *schwartze* because of the dark coloring of her hair and skin, and *zigeunerin* because she had learned to read palms and tell fortunes, and because of her restless and daring nature; on a bet she would run barefoot in the snow and, more often than not, it was the person who had made the bet, who had stood in his overcoat and heavy boots and had just watched her, who caught cold. She acted in plays that the young people of the town presented, and though she was not an actress and not a raving beauty, whenever she was on the stage, every eye was on her. Perhaps it was the way she walked, never afraid to take a step, always moving with an easy grace and confidence no other girl in Nishkovitz had. Sometimes she frankly searched out friends in the small audience and winked at them; if the play were a comedy and an actor told a joke she had heard five times before but still enjoyed, she might forget her lines for a moment and laugh. When Shmyola Bernstein had gone to Nishkovitz to get background material for a sketch he was doing about Jacob, she had filled his notebook with untrue, fantastical stories that Shmyola had believed and later published. She gave him a photograph of herself as a baby that she said was Jacob as a baby, and that, too, was published. But of all the things she ever did, the most wonderful was her falling in love with and marrying my father.

In the summer of 1913, when Jacob was in Paris, the directors of the Minsk Jewish General Hospital received reports of a typhoid epidemic in Nishkovitz. Isaac Starobinetz and one nurse were given several crates of medical supplies and sent to Nishkovitz.

When Isaac arrived, he found only four incidents of the disease. After a week, each day saw one or two more people fall sick. Isaac immediately imposed sanitary and other measures to prevent the further communication and spread of the disease. No one was allowed to leave Nishkovitz, and the houses of the sick were closed to all except Isaac and his nurse. The epidemic had broken out while Jacob and Tania were in Paris, and their son David was living in the Kagan house with his governess, his grandparents, Abraham and Heika, and his aunt Esther. Isaac stayed with them, using the large sitting room as his office and storeroom. At the end of two weeks, the number of sick had jumped to nearly fifty, and Isaac's nurse was one of that number. He could give the sick only the most basic of treatments, keeping the temperature down, watching out for complications and, most often, just comforting them. And when there was no sign that the epidemic was letting up, when the first sick began to die and he could do nothing, he felt suddenly impotent, but continued his work. Every day, hours after dark, Isaac returned to Abraham's house and, in the carriage shed, he stripped, sponged himself with alcohol, and changed his clothes. Abraham and Heika rarely left the house, and David and his governess never came down from the second floor, the governess thinking that the higher altitude might deter the transmission of the disease.

Esther was unable to remain inactive during this time. She first volunteered to assist Isaac, who told her it was not her job, that it was too dangerous and arduous, and then she went herself, disobeying all of Isaac's strictures, to the homes of diseased neighbors. Isaac discovered her at the bedside of one of the sick, and his face blanched. But afterwards, once she had already been exposed, he allowed her to assist him. She cooked for the sick, washed and cared for them, and worked through the same long hours as Isaac. Every morning, just before dawn, she woke Isaac, and they had breakfast together. She was seventeen years old, twelve years younger than he, but she fed him as a mother feels a child, insisting always that he eat the food she put before him. She drank her coffee from a glass, or a saucer if the glass was too hot, keeping part of a lump of sugar in her mouth, and she ate only a thick, buttered slice of corn bread. So early in the morning, having slept only a few hours, he talked as if he were thinking aloud, of the disease, of the sick. He himself supervised the cremation of the dead, stood by to make sure that only crumbling bones were left. All during the epidemic, Esther watched him weaken, his fleshless body no more than covered by skin, and when he said, "It's all will, that's all. There alone is resistance," she understood that he was not referring only to the recovery of the sick. After breakfast, they left the house together, he telling her to remain with a patient who had no one to care for him, and then making his own rounds.

One afternoon, during the third week of the epidemic, while Abraham was on the staircase passing food up to David's governess, who still refused to come down from the second floor, and now also refused to allow anyone all the way up, Heika left the house unobserved. It was cool outside; the fields on both sides of the Berezina were swept by a steady westerly breeze. Heika was short and very stocky, and when she reached the river, she sat down on damp ground to catch her breath. The sky was broken by clouds, and she watched the sun disappear and then suddenly reappear from behind them; she watched the river sparkle when the sun played on it, and then become cold and of infinite depth when the sun was hidden. She folded her hands and smiled, her face creased by hundreds of small wrinkles. Walking back from the river, she entered without knocking the house of a woman whom she had not visited since before her son David's death. It was very familiar, as if she had been in it only the day before, and she sat down in the living room. She fingered the lace on the arm of her soft chair. The house was dark and stuffy. Her hands froze on the lace as she heard the sound of someone crying. After a moment, she rose and walked to the kitchen. There was a basket of food on the floor and she selected ingredients from it and prepared a thick soup. When it was steaming, she brought it to the room from which the sound of crying had been coming. A man and his son stood on either side of a bed, afraid even to touch the woman who lay there, covered by several blankets. The woman's skin hung loose and dry; she perspired freely. Heika fed her, and then, stripping the blankets from her, washed her and changed her sheets.

When she returned home, Abraham asked her where she had been and she answered, "I walked by the river." Six days later, she had great fever, and upon examination by Isaac, showed the telltale rose marks of typhoid.

Heika lay in bed fifteen days, and in her suffering almost never said a word. Outside was a world of sounds—people whispering, footsteps, liquids being poured—she had no desire to penetrate; she surrendered to the heat and darkness of her fever.

Esther nursed her night and day. Abraham prayed at the foot of her bed; he let his beard grow and fasted on crackers and tea. He was cursed by his grandson's governess each time he brought her food, as though he were responsible for the sickness, for the epidemic. In his despair, he became suddenly religious, and he seemed to the governess to be related to God by blood or guilt. His wife dying, Abraham resigned himself in prayer, just as Isaac was resigned in knowledge. He watched Isaac feel Heika's forehead, and then mechanically look for blood under the blankets, and he cried.

"She won't fight," Isaac said.

It was raining the day she died. At odd intervals, she repeated in Yiddish, as if she were interjecting an exclamation into a tedious monologue, "Oh, my God, You were too good to me." Just before she died, she called for her sons, and there were none.

And there was no funeral. Her body was burned. Abraham just watched as her body was carried out of the house.

Two days later, Jacob arrived in Nishkovitz with a team of four St. Petersburg doctors. He arrived none too soon; Isaac, a week after Heika's death, fainted in a patient's home.

When Isaac regained consciousness, he saw only Esther. She fed him, and when the fever seared his skin, she washed him.

Delirious, he felt her hand on his head, felt her hand gripping his; her very touch brought relief. She nursed him through his crisis, and through his convalescence she was his bedside companion, telling his fortune with cards, joking with him, or just listening to him. When he felt well enough to walk outside, the epidemic was over.

He did not leave Nishkovitz until several weeks after he had completely recovered, and had built up enough courage to ask Esther to marry him. A second after he asked, she accepted, and they planned to marry in the spring of 1914.

The sun disappeared at about three in the afternoon, and it began to snow. After supper, there were only a handful of guests in the apartment; Abraham had gone to his own small apartment around the corner on Manida Street to rest. My mother, Anna, and Lily were washing dishes in the kitchen, and my father, Larry, and Doctor Deutschman were playing pinochle. My uncle Ben and my cousin David were the only others there. Ben suggested that they end the game so that he could drive Doctor Deutschman home and go home himself. "It's really coming down. We should go before it freezes over," he said to no one in particular.

My father glanced through the open Venetian blind and then looked back at his cards. "Three fifty," he bid. "This is too good a hand to stop now," he lied, leading Larry to believe that he held a good hand.

"Sixty," Larry raised.

Deutschman passed and my father said, "It's yours."

"How are you going to take Sam downtown?" Ben asked David. "By subway?"

"On his Bar-mitzvah day, by subway? By cab!" David answered and poured himself another drink.

"Faker," Larry exclaimed angrily at my father, who smiled. Larry threw down his cards and said, "Enough!"

David and I drove across the Triborough Bridge and down the East River Drive. The falling snow disappeared, melting into the East River; the heavily trafficked streets were already dirty and slushy. We passed the terraced apartment buildings facing the river and, in the seventies, I saw Christmas trees all lit up, illuminating some of the apartments. David cleared his voice and said, "He's not Caruso, Gigli, or even Martinelli, nothing extra special, but you should see it. Do you know the story?"

"It's about artists," I answered.

"It's about love, Sam," David corrected. "All opera's about love. Here's a poet, very poor and very talented; every day he writes a masterpiece, but he never has any money. He meets a girl, very beautiful and very tubercular; she always coughs. They fall in love; she dies," David said and then, in a tenor voice that did not dare reach too high, he sang the aria, *Che Gelida Manina.*

"Bravo!" the cab driver exclaimed when David had concluded. "You sing at the opera?"

"No," David answered, "I sell whiskey."

"Sometimes you drink it too." The driver laughed and looked into his rear-view mirror. David nodded his head and lit a cigarette. "The whiskey business's a good business?" the driver asked.

"I hope so," David replied.

We had orchestra seats at the Metropolitan Opera House. David checked my coat, hat, and rubbers, and we went in. It was warm, almost overheated, inside. The seats were soft, covered with wine-colored velvet, and when I looked up at the gold of the stage curtain and the ceiling, I thought I had never seen anything so rich. During the first act, so soft and lovely, I saw and heard nothing but the singers. At the intermission, David asked me how I liked it, and I said it was terrific. "The tenor's not so bad tonight," David said.

The fast pace of the next two acts excited me, and I began to wish for a happy ending. Then suddenly, in the third act, when Mimi, hiding behind a tree, coughed, I knew that she was going to die. I cried during the last act and when Rudolpho screamed, "Mimi! Mimi!" I said to myself that I would sing at the Metropolitan, that I would sing so beautifully when my love died.

THREE

EVENING

I

According to orthodox Jewish law, a child cannot be named after a living person; children are never given the same first name as their parents. But they are named after relatives who are dead, and sometimes several children are named after the same grandfather, grandmother, great-grandfather or granduncle. In a family as large as my own, first cousins were often given the same first name. There are three Davids, all first cousins, and two Samuels, my uncle and myself. In conversation, the cousins would be distinguished one from the other by affixing their father's name to their own. So that David, Jacob's son, would be called David son of Jacob, *Dovid ben Jacob.* In this country, one would say, according to the comparative ages of the cousins, David senior or junior. The marriages in the old country between near or distant relations, the number of cousins with the same name, or in the United States with slight variations on the same Hebrew name—(someone named after Jacob might be called Jacob, but more often would be called Jack, as Jacob's youngest son, Yitzhoc, renamed himself upon arrival in America)—all are particularly revealing of the tight circle that is my family.

And just as the name Jacob became Jack, the name Kagan became Cohen. When Eleazar Kagan, not yet thirteen, was on a ship going to America, he was told by a Jew who had already established himself in New York and was returning from Europe with a bride, that his name was very "un-American," that, with a name like Kagan, he would always be marked as a foreigner. The Jew suggested he change his name to something more suitable, something like Louis Cohen,—"A name like that," he said, "would not be strange in New York City." When the ship docked, Eleazar told the immigration officials that his name was Louis Cohen, and afterwards, when one by one the Kagans came to America, their names were Americanized—they all became Cohens.

The older members of my family have always been conscious of the origins of their own names, and the names they gave to their children. By naming a child after someone dead, they perpetuated the life of someone they had known or had heard stories of. Thus a child named after Chaim Eliah (he would be called Charles Edward) would naturally be given music lessons early. I believe that they were also conscious of the Biblical significances of Old Testament names, so that to them Davids were always, in some way, misguided, and Samuels were always wise, sometimes too wise.

In the spring of 1914, Jacob's second son was born. He was named Yitzhoc after Jacob's grandfather, the peddler. Tania objected to naming him Yitzhoc. "Why, it's so Jewish! Everyone will joke at his name."

"Let them," Jacob said. "That'll help a boy with as much money as he'll have."

"Do you want him to be like Shmyola Bernstein? What a name!"

"I want him to be a little like Bernstein, a little like my grandfather and my father and my brothers, and a lot like my sister, and maybe a little like you."

"I refuse to give him a name like that," Tania declared.

"Refuse or not, Yitzhoc will be his name."

Tania did not speak to Jacob for a week and then announced that he could call him what he wanted but she would call him Joseph because of his beauty.

The month that Yitzhoc was born was also the month of Esther and Isaac's wedding. It was soon to take place in Jacob's house in St. Petersburg; the Starobinetzes were to come from Minsk, and the Kagans from all of Russia for a week-long celebration. Shmyola Bernstein, returned from Paris, was already staying in Jacob's house, but Shmyola hardly had one opportunity to talk with his host. Jacob was immersed in a frenzy of business activity sweeping St. Petersburg, that culminated for him with an enormous sale to a German firm. Because of his sale, lumber prices fell off considerably, and Jacob closed his offices, not expecting prices to rise again before the end of a month. The day after he closed his offices, Jacob and Shmyola went for a walk, the former carrying David on his shoulders, and the latter wheeling Yitzhoc's carriage.

"So now that you're up so high, what do you see?" Jacob asked David.

"Flowers."

"Only flowers?"

"I see the sky."

"Which sky?" Bernstein asked.

"That sky," David answered, pointing, after a moment's hesitation.

"That's the Russian sky," Shmyola said. "My child, there's no other sky in the world like it."

When they returned to the house, Jacob and Shmyola waited outside the music room where David studied voice with Signor Montinelli.

"You have a favorite already," Bernstein said.

"No," Jacob protested. "It's just that he's older."

"You don't deceive me," Bernstein said. "But listen," he added, smiling, "you must leave something to both."

The Italian came out of the music room after an hour and Jacob asked, "Tell me, Montinelli, does he sing well?"

"Your son has possibilities," the Italian said impressively. "Signor, do you know the difference between a Russian and an Italian tenor? One sings high like a woman or a boy, but the Italian, he sings strong, from the lungs and heart and stomach. Your son may sing like an Italian. It is too soon to tell, but he may sing, with training and much study, like an Italian."

"And if he becomes a basso?" Bernstein asked.

"You think him to be another Chaliapin?" the Italian said. "But no, he is not that strong."

"I think him to be another Kagan," Jacob said, smiling.

"But I have nothing to do with that," the Italian said.

During the week, Jacob's and Tania's families arrived in St. Petersburg. Every day there was another party: one for Esther, one for Isaac, and even a birthday party for David, though his real birthday was months away. He received many toys: a woolly dog that barked when pinched on the nose, a model house, a three-foot-high soldier who marched and played a drum with martial precision.

Before the birthday cake was served, Esther dressed David in his new black seal hat and white ermine knee-length coat, and took him for a walk. The coat was elegant, with three large black seal buttons and a high, tight collar of the same fur. Esther wore a black broadtail coat Jacob had given her, and kept her hands warm in a sable muff. They walked to a park and Esther began to laugh.

"What's funny, aunt Eshka?"

"Oh, it's your coat. You're the most beautiful clown I've ever seen."

David looked down at his bell-shaped coat.

"Haven't you ever seen a circus?" Esther asked. "Not even once? Then you haven't seen clowns or bears that walk like people and sometimes even dance."

"Bears don't dance," David declared angrily.

"Not all of them, but lots of them do. They're dressed up just like princes going to dinner, and they bow and stand straight and dance better than most people."

"How can a bear dance?" David asked.

"It's simple," Esther said. "Just watch me," and she lifted one foot and brought it down slowly and heavily, and then lifted her other foot. "See?" she asked.

"But that's not dancing."

"No," Esther said, looking beyond him. A gray bearded beggar was standing to one side of a clump of dry, bare bushes, with his hand outstretched. His clothes were dirty and torn. There was a large blister on the palm of his hand. Esther gave the beggar a coin. She watched his fingers close so tightly that she thought his blister must burst. Abruptly, she turned around and walked off with David.

When they returned home and entered the dining room, the drapes were drawn and the electric lights were off, but on the table, around which everyone was standing, there was an enormous chocolate cake with seven flickering candles. "You have to blow them all out," Grisha Starobinetz said anxiously. "And you can't even let one remain, 'cause that's for good luck."

David approached the cake, inhaled deeply, and then blew with all his might. The electric lights were switched on just as the smoke began to rise from the extinguished candles. "Hurrah, hurrah!" Lazar Starobinetz exclaimed and everyone clapped.

"It's a beautiful cake," Grisha said to Ben and Ben nodded.

"David must sing for his cake," Chaim Eliah said. "Before he eats, he must sing a song. Tania, perhaps you have a violin here?"

"What will you sing, maestro?" Jacob asked his son.

"The song you taught me," David answered.

He closed his eyes and sang in a clear, high alto, a Ukrainian song about lovers separated by hundreds of miles.

"But that's my song," Abraham said when David had finished. "How many times did I hear that song! Oh, so long ago, so many years." He smiled at his grandson and said, "Before your father was even born, when I was as old as Ben, I sailed for weeks and weeks on the Berezina, the Dnieper—some nights I heard that song for hours . . . oh, it was different then. Lazar, do you remember how we took our lumber to the Ukraine, no steamboats and barges, just rafts? But they were the largest rafts you've ever seen."

"Cut the cake already," Ben interrupted. "David's starving."

The cake was cut and the portions served. Ben and Grisha each had three pieces and then, with Sol and Isaac, they went into the library to play cards. Tania, her mother Bassya, her two unmarried sisters, Sonia and Rachel, and Esther went to the music room, and while Tania played Chopin nocturnes, Esther told Sonia and Rachel's fortunes.

"But what about you?" Rachel asked after Esther had told her fortune.

"Well, I'll tell my own," she said and spread out the deck of cards. She opened one card; it was a dark jack. "Someone short and dark will become part of my life," she interpreted.

"What else?" Sonia asked, smiling.

Esther picked up a light three and said, "Marriage."

"How can you tell?" Rachel asked.

Esther looked seriously at the card she held in her hand and said, "One is Isaac, I'm the other and the third is the rabbi."

In the dining room, young David sat at the head of the table, his chin barely three inches higher than the tabletop. His father, his two grandfathers, Lazar Starobinetz and Shmyola Bernstein, sat about the table. "He'll be a singer," Chaim Eliah said proudly. "All my children are musical. That's Tania playing now," he said, nodding his head.

The conversation passed from David's future to the impending marriage of Esther and Isaac and then to business. David understood very little, and he began to watch his grandfather Abraham with his full round beard, and his large black eyes. David remembered his grandmother's funeral. After the epidemic in Nishkovitz was over, they had held a funeral service for Heika and had buried her ashes. When they had returned to his grandfather's house, Abraham, who had not cried during the service, who had stood stiff and pale even when the soil had been thrown and sounded hollow on his wife's virtually empty casket, had, upon sight of David, suddenly begun to cry, as though he had precipitated a rain of memories. Abraham now sat at the table, and every once in a while, he ran a finger across his lips and entered the conversation. More often, he was silent; he could hardly keep up with Bernstein, Jacob, Chaim Eliah, or even Lazar. Once he pulled his three-stoned diamond stickpin out of his cravat and carefully reinserted it about an eighth of an inch to the left of where it had been.

"There have been wars before," David heard Abraham say.

"This will be like no other war," Bernstein said.

"The Tsar's friendly with the Kaiser," Chaim Eliah remarked.

"And the Tsarina's German herself; she'll never let Russia fight Germany," Lazar added.

"They're children; you can twist them like that," Bernstein said, intertwining the fingers of his hands and then, jerking his hands apart, breaking the knuckles of his fingers.

"So what?" Lazar asked.

Bernstein slammed his hand on the table and the empty china clattered as he exclaimed, "Rasputin!"

"The monk?" Lazar asked.

"Yes, the monk!" Bernstein exclaimed, and then said slowly and more emphatically, "The hypocrite, the horse-thief, the murderer, the anti-Semite friend of the usurer Simonovitch. I see in him the end of our society, of St. Petersburg, Riga, and Moscow."

"No," Lazar said, shaking his head and smiling, "you mean the drunkard and the seducer . . . I saw him drunk in a nightclub once."

"Did you look into his eyes?" Bernstein asked. "Did you see . . ."

"He has eyes like the rest of us," Jacob interrupted. "Shmyola, if there's going to be war, there'll be war, but not because of Rasputin. The Tsar has alliances with England and France."

"You don't understand," Bernstein said. "You don't understand how different all this is. Nationalities mean nothing to them; alliances are scraps of paper. The Tsar and his advisors are supranational; they are not worried about Russia. Yes, Graf Potofsky and perhaps even the Grand-Duke Alexi have some connection to the land, to our own Russia, but the Tsar is more German than Russian, more English than German and more stupid than smart."

"You speak like a bolshevik," Lazar said.

"And you are a fool!" Bernstein responded.

"Enough!" Jacob exclaimed. "No more talk of war! If it comes, I stand to make a profit; if it doesn't come, I won't be sorry."

"You stand to make a profit?" Bernstein repeated angrily. "Are you crazy? Do you know what will happen? Are you a prophet that you see so clearly?"

"I see that the price of lumber will rise," Jacob said curtly.

"Is that all? Do you see anything about St. Petersburg? About Russia?" Jacob did not answer him, and Shmyola went on more calmly, in a softer voice. "Listen to me, Jacob. I tell you it's coming, not just a war, but a collapse."

"There's no war yet," Chaim Eliah said. "Anyhow, what could we do even if we were sure of everything you said?"

Bernstein looked intently at Chaim Eliah and then at Jacob. When he saw Jacob's stony face, he shrugged his shoulders and said, "At least we would understand."

"Understanding's all right," Lazar said smiling, "but profit's much better," he said looking at Jacob.

Abraham stood up and said, "A walk will do us good."

"I agree," Chaim Eliah said. "A walk in the spring is like a broom that sweeps out all dust and debris from the mind. I know a first-class bassoonist, now at the Imperial Opera House in Moscow, who said that he could never play so well as after a walk; it does something for his wind. Indeed, I myself never feel so healthy as when I feel the still cold ground hard under my shoes. Fresh air is a fine tonic, a brisk refreshener . . ."

"I'll join you," Lazar said.

"You, Jacob?" Chaim Eliah asked.

"I'll just sit here."

"Bernstein?"

"My father died of pneumonia," he said.

"You can't frighten us," Chaim Eliah replied. "We're three gentlemen of the old school." When Chaim Eliah, Lazar, and Abraham left the dining room, Jacob sent David upstairs to bed. Then he turned to Bernstein and said abruptly, "Excuse my anger."

"No, my friend, it was my fault. I should never have talked of war to begin with."

They remained silent, each waiting for the other to say something further. Finally Jacob said, "Shmyola, I have lost touch."

"What do you mean?" Bernstein asked.

"I am afraid. I have too much—you know, my arms are not strong enough to hold on to all that I have."

2

In the first days of August 1914, Tsar Nicholas mobilized an army and then, almost immediately, sent his poorly trained and badly equipped troops into battle. Everywhere in St. Petersburg there was excitement; society rode about in automobiles and entertained more frequently than ever, unassigned army officers wore their handsomely tailored uniforms to parties, and old warriors of the Russo-Japanese War were admired for their medals. The newspapers were filled with exaggerated, second-hand accounts of the war; Shmyola Bernstein, working now for both Yiddish and Russian-language newspapers, wrote of the courageous French army, of the only strategy that the Allies could use, that of encirclement. "We must advance, advance, advance," Bernstein wrote one day, "until we enter the homes of the Germans, and we must not stop until, coming from opposite sides, we embrace with our allies." It was more than a year later, as rumors of losses began to filter into and then race through the cities, as the defeated and deserting soldiers returned, that the reality of the war was made clear.

Isaac Starobinetz was called to serve in the army in the latter part of August 1914, three months after he married Esther. Unlike the Kagans, of whom only Jacob had served, Isaac felt his call to duty to be a responsibility he could not, with conscience, evade. So he was given a uniform and a parchment that declared he was a captain in the medical corps, was presented with an orderly and a horse, the horse immediately presenting the element of danger necessary in war, and the orderly, a soldier six feet three, exactly twelve inches taller than Isaac, adding a touch of glamour to what might otherwise have been a most ignoble and even fatal army career.

Isaac's orderly was a Ukrainian, Ivan Ragushenko; he performed his duties, his every motion, with a singularly proud and military bearing. On receipt of his orders, Isaac with Ragushenko, travelled east by train to Nidzica. They remained there five days, until reports of an impending German offensive reached the regimental commanding officer. He was Prince Sligorin, the disinherited nephew of Graf Potofsky; now a colonel in the army of the Tsar, he had been formerly an infrequent and generally unwelcome guest at Jacob Kagan's St. Petersburg home. The Prince equipped Isaac with one of his own revolvers, and then ordered him to the front. Isaac returned to his quarters and was packing a suitcase when Ragushenko knocked and, entering, said, "Sir, the horses are ready.

"Well, take my suitcases and let's go," Isaac commanded briskly.

"Your suitcases, sir?"

"That's right."

"Sir, we're travelling horseback," Ragushenko said, betraying just a trace of a smile. Isaac's face reddened and, unpacking his suitcase, he took out twelve pairs of heavy socks and four suits of long underwear, which Ragushenko then tied together in a neat bundle.

Never an equestrian or an outdoorsman of any sort, Isaac mounted his horse with some difficulty and, after sitting motionless for a moment, he turned to Ragushenko and asked, "Now which way?"

"Over there, sir," Ragushenko pointed.

They had ridden for nearly a half hour when they began to hear the sounds of explosions. As the sounds grew louder, as if with each foot of their progress mobile artillery were also advancing towards them, so that there would soon be an inevitable and horrible meeting, Isaac began to perspire. His body felt as heavy as lead as he thumped hard in the saddle; his stomach knotted spasmodically, and he began to feel queasy. Suddenly, Isaac drew rein and dismounted. Looking first at the flat, vast, empty horizon, and listening to the sharp reports of the artillery, he relieved himself while Ragushenko held his horse and discreetly looked elsewhere. Then, trembling from chills, fever and fear, he remounted and proceeded to the front.

For six weeks, Isaac lived in the trenches. German artillery shelled the Russian lines every day, but there was no offensive. Casualties from the shellings, from snipers, and patrol losses were numerous, and Isaac, one of two doctors, was busy twenty hours a day. Hitherto fastidious in his personal habits, he was now oblivious of the dirt, lice, and rats that infested the trenches. He had to operate on a makeshift wooden table in a dugout adjoining a trench. Amputation was the common operation; most of the wounded died. Once, a Cossack was brought in. Left for dead by his comrades, he was found three days later with two bullets in his stomach. Isaac just glanced at his wound and then turned to leave, for he could not be saved, when the Cossack grabbed his arm and gripped it with enormous pressure. "Listen," he said, and before he died, he confessed to the murder of his best friend. With one blow he had killed his friend, holding him on the floor, sitting on his back, his hand tensing more and more, never sure that he wanted to kill him, that perhaps it had been his girl who had really been the unfaithful one, until, with a final explosion of energy, he had brought his fist down on the back of his friend's neck and had killed him. Several times Isaac heard the confessions of dying men; he listened to them and knew that he was not afraid of death—his fear was of violence. He had heard the Cossack's story; more than the bullet-ridden bodies of machine-gunned soldiers did that bloody fist frighten him.

One week, it snowed for two days, and at the end of the storm, in the late afternoon, the Germans recommenced shelling, but now with a fury the Russians had not before felt. It seemed to Isaac that there were ten thousand artillery pieces firing all at the same time, firing every second like clockwork. "Now," Ragushenko said to Isaac, "they'll attack in a minute."

"How can you tell?"

"I can tell," Ragushenko replied. "There's not much time, my captain. Put on your coat."

"Where do you want us to go?"

"There," Ragushenko said, pointing to the rear.

"And those men?" Isaac said looking at the dugout where the wounded were.

Ragushenko shrugged his shoulders and said, "They're goners, anyhow."

The artillery firing had ceased.

"No. If you wish, go ahead," Isaac said and turned his back on the orderly. Ragushenko, astonished at the little man's declaration, picked up a rifle and placing it over the parapet to give himself a view of the whole plain before him, began to laugh.

"A soldier!" he exclaimed. "A god damned soldier!"

And then the Germans came. Sweeping forward towards the center of the weakened Russian line, they suddenly divided and attacked the flanks. The right flank held; the left flank collapsed and was overrun. When the remainder of the troops saw the Germans coming at them from two sides, when a German machine gun opened fire at them from behind their own lines, the Russians clambered out of their trenches and ran.

"Enough," Ragushenko said, taking Isaac by the arm.

"Oh my God!" Isaac exclaimed. Running, he heard the

loud staccato of the German machine gun and saw soldiers folding up and falling as if cut by a gigantic, invisible saw that sliced horizontally several feet above the ground.

"Follow me," Ragushenko said. They ran inside the trench until Isaac could hardly catch his breath. "In here," Ragushenko directed, and pulled Isaac into a dugout. "Quiet." After a short while, the firing ceased, and then they heard the Germans talking softly among themselves. For five hours, until long after dark, Isaac and Ragushenko remained in their cramped positions; finally, Ragushenko stepped back into the trench. "Let's go," he whispered, and he lifted Isaac onto the parapet. Their muscles stiff, they moved slowly and cautiously, stopping behind large rocks, dropping into shell holes. They reached the new Russian lines just before dawn.

Prince Sligorin had moved his headquarters up to the line. Upon seeing Isaac, he threw aside a map he had been studying and exclaimed, "You got through! I'll give you a medal! My revolver, I bet it helped you out, eh? Did you kill any Germans? Heroic! The Jews of St. Petersburg and Minsk will be proud of you! Now listen; the wounded have been evacuated to town. You report there. Bravo, Starobinetz!" Worn out, wanting only to sleep, to sink into some place of warmth, Isaac immediately set out for Nidzica with Ragushenko.

For two years, Isaac and his orderly retreated with their army. In 1916, when there was virtually no food and no ammunition, when officers and soldiers were fighting without will, generals openly accusing the Tsarina of Germanophilism, the soldiers began to desert *en masse,* and the Russian lines absolutely collapsed. Isaac and Ragushenko walked and rode freight cars, and, just twenty miles from St. Petersburg, they were stopped on a road by a six-man Russian patrol. "And where do you think you're going?"

"To report to our new headquarters," Ragushenko replied. "My captain is to report to St. Petersburg."

"A lie," the sergeant in charge of the patrol said. "Where are your orders?"

"They're lost," Ragushenko said.

"Have you lost your voice, *my* Captain?" the sergeant asked.

"We have no orders," Isaac replied.

The sergeant told two of his patrol to take Isaac and Ragushenko to regimental headquarters. After they had walked several minutes, Ragushenko asked, "How far is it?"

"Far enough," one of the guards answered curtly and pushed the barrel of his rifle hard into Ragushenko's back. Ragushenko glanced over his shoulder and then suddenly snapped his right arm behind him and, with one sweep, pulling the rifle out of the astounded guard's hands, he swung the rifle at the other soldier, just missing him. "Ivan!" Isaac shouted in warning, and the soldier shot Ragushenko in the thigh. The rifle still in his hands, Ragushenko dropped to the ground and shot in the stomach the soldier who had just wounded him. Isaac hesitated only a second, and then rushed the disarmed soldier who was reaching for his comrade's rifle. Clasping both hands together and swinging them like an axe, Isaac smashed the soldier across the face. The soldier collapsed, unconscious. Isaac stood by him. The soldier's nose was broken, the flesh was torn open over his mouth, and his whole face was bloody. Isaac's hands were cut, his left wrist felt sprained. He wanted to run.

"Captain," Ragushenko called.

Isaac bandaged Ragushenko's wound and then, Ivan using the rifle as a cane, they walked to a clump of trees a hundred yards away. Isaac sterilized his knife over a small flame and extracted the bullet from Ragushenko's thigh. They moved on immediately, and a half hour later found an empty hut where they stayed the night. In the morning, when Isaac awoke, Ragushenko was gone. There was a note scrawled on a piece of crumpled paper: "Sometime we'll meet again. Ivan."

Isaac smuggled himself into St. Petersburg in the back of a horse-drawn cart. Once within the city gates, he jumped out of the cart and into a taxi. He went directly to Jacob's house. Only Jacob's two sons and the servants were home. Esther and Tania were out shopping.

"Uncle Assoc, Uncle Assoc," David cried on seeing him.

"Ah, David," Isaac said and smiled.

"Look, look at Yitzhoc. Isn't he big?"

"Captain Starobinetz," one of the servants said, "it's an honor to see you again. Can I do anything for you? A bath?" the servant suggested.

"Yes," Isaac answered, "please."

He had just finished bathing when Esther and Tania arrived. He stood several feet from Esther, and she began to cry. Nearly a skeleton, he went to her, and they embraced.

Later that evening, Jacob came home.

"See how changed he is," Tania said.

"I'm all right. My wrist is sprained, that's all."

"Two years, and your wrist is sprained," Jacob said, smiling. "A long two years, eh? And you haven't forgotten your Eshka?" he asked, smiling again.

"Sometimes I thought I was in Nishkovitz," Isaac replied, "that all I had to do was see one more patient and then return to Abraham's house. But I'd realize where I was and then I don't think I thought at all."

He spoke softly. They retired shortly, and Esther smiled at Isaac and said, "I won't cry again. I promise I won't cry."

The following evening, Shmyola Bernstein came to dinner. He arrived late and Jacob, Tania, Isaac, and Esther had already begun to eat. Upon entering the dining room, he rushed over to Isaac and clasped his hand. "What a tragedy," he finally said.

"Sit down," Jacob suggested.

"That we should have to run before the German. How was it, Assoc? I know. No. I don't want to hear. Every day I get reports—the Germans have taken this town and that town. You are well, though? You've lost weight. Ah, the lines on your face!"

"They show suffering," Tania said.

"This afternoon I told Assoc's fortune," Esther said, "and it's a little trouble, but all happiness."

"Ah," Bernstein said, raising his eyebrows and nodding his head, "life should be so simple."

"You won't be served standing up," Jacob said.

"Yes, my great financier," Bernstein said. "Where are the children?"

"In bed," Tania replied. "You're quite late."

"Too bad, too bad. I had a story for David."

"And I have a story for Assoc," Jacob said as if Shmyola had just reminded him. "About Alexi Alexanderovitch."

"The Tsar's uncle?" Isaac asked.

"The Tsar's uncle or not the Tsar's uncle," Jacob said smiling, "let me tell you how a Jew outfoxed him, and, understand, I did this strictly for pleasure though the profit was considerable. There comes to town a colonel of engineers. He is supposed to build fortifications along the Berezina and his commission, signed by the Tsar, allows him to requisition all the lumber he needs, to be paid for, of course, but not at the best prices. Alexi, he thinks to be very smart, he tells the officer who goes first to him for advice, not that Alexi is even as important as your uncle Lazar, to see me. 'I'll fix that Jew,' he must have thought. 'They'll requisition his lumber and Kagan will not be able to compete on the open market.' The colonel is a fine man, an aristocrat, very smart," Jacob said smiling, "and he asks me. 'Lumber for fortifications!' I exclaim, 'But there's only one tree strong enough, enduring enough, big enough, only one tree, colonel.' 'Where?' he asks. 'Alexanderovitch's forest, the forest about his palace—if you use anything else you'll do a disservice to the Tsar.' 'But why,' the gentleman colonel asks me, 'didn't he tell me?' 'Why?' I repeat. 'Haven't you heard? He hates his nephew!' The colonel believes me; after all, I did tell the truth, and Alexi's private forest is without a doubt the finest in Russia. Then he asks me to suggest a construction company to put up the fortifications. 'Why colonel,' I say, 'it'll be a slight inconvenience, but I'll give you my men. If you go to Nishkovitz, my brothers will assist you without charge.' The colonel protested that I was too good." Jacob paused and lit a cigarette. "It was a very profitable venture. We stripped Alexi's forest, but still hadn't enough lumber, so we had to buy from another concern at extraordinary rates."

"You've made money," Isaac said.

"Hand over fist," Jacob said emphatically.

"My friend," Bernstein said cynically, looking at Isaac, "wars are made for people to make money."

"You," Jacob said to Bernstein, "write of people in another world—you write of defeat, but not of death. Your army will always be the brave Russian army that's losing because of reasons. I give no reasons. We're losing; what'll happen only God knows. The truth is defeat, and the truth of life is power. The beautiful," he said, "cluster about the strong."

"Because I have not become a millionaire," Bernstein said, "I cannot see the truth. That is a philosophy I do not understand."

"You speak," Isaac said to Jacob, "as if one lives for and by himself. That is false."

"Ah," Jacob said smiling.

"Wait," Isaac interrupted. "You told a story, now let me tell one. It is not about profits and it is not amusing—it is about war."

Bernstein shook his head sadly. "War is never amusing."

"Nor is there profit for the dead," Isaac added. "How many were killed, I don't know. Only this—for two years I operated, I amputated limbs, knowing first that this man and that man would have to learn to live without an arm or a leg, without arms or legs, and then I no longer thought in terms of after the war. I was helpless in the face of all that suffering, and nobility and courage became meaningless words; fear and death were the inescapable presences. But two years of war made me one with the Russian soldier, and rats, lice, dirt, sweat and trembling were our common lot. This is not philosophy, but fact."

"And are you still one with the Russian soldier?" Jacob asked.

Isaac hesitated. "That's beside the point."

"To argue with him on his second day home!" Tania exclaimed to her husband. "And besides, I'm sure you're wrong."

"And I, positive," Esther said.

"No," Isaac said, "we did not each live for himself. Soldiers were killed saving their comrades."

"Ah!" Jacob exclaimed. "But I suppose," he added, smiling, "there are some things I would die for."

3

The October revolution bankrupted my family. The Bolsheviks took control of Petrograd, exiled or shot the leaders of the Provisional Government and, throughout Russia, hundreds of years of mounting fury exploded in a tide of revolt. The Tsar and Tsarina—the incredible "Alix"—and their family were murdered with the kind of carelessness with which the Tsarina had often recommended that the Tsar have someone shot. Fantastic wealth was buried in gardens and cellars, the owners expecting to be able to retrieve their fortunes in just a few months. Speculation in rubles became a flourishing lottery in all of the world's exchanges.

The Bolsheviks confiscated the house and possessions of Jacob Kagan. Jacob left Petrograd and journeyed to Nishkovitz with Tania, their two sons, David and Yitzhoc, and Isaac and Esther. And he took with him one wooden box containing a fortune in jewelry. Tania, always a frail woman, distraught by the experience of the last two months, caught pneumonia on the trip and died shortly after they reached their destinarion. She was buried next to the ashes of Heika and the body of David. Her funeral was attended by her husband and sons, and Abraham, Mendel, Benjamin, Sol, Isaac and Esther. Afterwards, Esther again took over the management of the house; she cared for her nephews while their father wandered about the village, looking in on the telegraph office every day to find out the state of the revolution. For several months, there was peace in Nishkovitz, and then one of the small wars that were ravaging Russia passed across Nishkovitz.

Prince Sligorin, ex-colonel in the army of the Tsar, entered Nishkovitz commanding a cavalry troop that was being pursued by a Red army. Sligorin took control of the town in a matter of minutes after his arrival. He established headquarters in Abraham's house, and when he met Jacob he asked, "So, Kagan, where are your sympathies?"

Jacob shrugged his shoulders.

"*Zhid!*" Sligorin screamed. "You may once have been something. Now you're nothing. Do you understand?"

Before Sligorin left, he confiscated food and livestock, whatever could be carried or led away. And he drafted Isaac into his army, giving him the rank of colonel. Isaac deserted from his undisciplined, irregular army only three miles outside of Nishkovitz.

The Reds arrived several hours after Sligorin had left. They ascertained that there was no food, and they drafted Isaac into their army, not apologizing, but stating the fact that they had no doctors, that wounded soldiers were being left to die. The Reds left the town, and for two months their only contact with the Whites was in patrol action. Then there was a sudden attack by Sligorin, and the Reds retreated through Nishkovitz, where Isaac again found it easy to desert. When the Whites reached Nishkovitz, Sligorin went out with a patrol to find the fugitive Starobinetz. They rode first to the house of an informant and then to Abraham's house. Isaac had just enough time to clamber upstairs and hide in the attic before they entered the house.

"Starobinetz," Sligorin intoned when Abraham, Esther, Jacob, David and Yitzhoc, Mendel, Benjamin and Sol were lined up in front of him. "Starobinetz the deserter, where is he?"

"The Reds took him with them. He had no choice," Esther said.

"Would he hide here?" Jacob asked. "He'd have to be a much greater fool than he is."

"Enough shit!" Sligorin exclaimed. "I know he's in Nishkovitz! Search the house," he ordered his men. He stared at Abraham and said, "Seventeen wounded. I left them in the snow to die because the warmth of this house . . ." Sligorin turned around and hit his hand hard on the mantle above the fireplace. "I'll kill him."

"He's only one Jew," Jacob said, and Sligorin turned back to face Jacob.

"Everyone!" he screamed. "Deserters of Christ, murderers of God. Where's your gold, Kagan? Where do you hide it?"

"In the pockets of the Bolsheviks," Jacob replied. "They got to me first."

Esther nudged Jacob and Sligorin said, "I'll shoot you."

"Go ahead," Jacob said.

His revolver trembled in his hand and Mendel said, "Shoot him and you'll have to shoot me," and he walked towards Sligorin.

"And me," Abraham said.

"And me," Esther said and all of them stepped forward.

"All of you," Sligorin said, "one day you'll all be dead."

The soldiers examined each room downstairs and went up to the second floor. Isaac heard the stamp of their boots and heard one soldier say, "He could hide behind a chair, or under a bed like a mouse." Isaac crept on his hands and knees to the window and climbed out onto the roof. It was far below freezing, and Isaac, without an overcoat, lay flat on the roof for several hours until Sligorin, having searched every house in the village with no success, rejoined his troops outside of town and proceeded after the Reds. Isaac was unconscious when he was discovered on the roof by Jacob, who climbed out and carried him back inside.

"As a deserter, you make fine fly-paper," Jacob said to a warmly covered and sneezing Isaac the following morning.

"As a man of importance, you're like a tree without branches," Isaac answered.

For several months, the Reds and the Whites fought east and then south of Nishkovitz. And one day, a detachment of twenty Reds arrived in Nishkovitz to gather food. One of them, a tall, limping man went to the house of the Kagans. He wore two belts of cartridges crossed on his chest, and he carried a rifle. "Ragushenko," he said to Esther when she opened the door. "Tell your husband that Ivan Ragushenko is here."

The two men greeted each other warmly.

"And you remembered my talking of Nishkovitz?" Isaac asked. "Ah, what a fine fellow you are!" They sat down and Isaac asked, "But how is it you are fighting for the Reds?"

"One army," Ragushenko answered, "is as good as the other. The Reds have some idealists, volunteers," he said, "and I have always liked idealists."

"You will die a soldier," Isaac said. "No. I have a much better idea. You'll remain in Nishkovitz in this house. Jacob expects the English to send their fleet to take Petersburg, and then everything will be better."

"And what will my idealists do without me?" Ivan asked.

"They'll be disillusioned. Or, perhaps not, but that's not my concern."

Ivan did not return with his detachment. He deserted and remained in the Kagan house.

When the White armies became little more than roving troops of gangsters, the Reds began to establish themselves, and they attempted to restore the economy of the country. A team of Bolsheviks was sent to Nishkovitz. Jacob was visited by one of them, who asked him to get his lumber mill back into operation. "The equipment," the Bolshevik said, "is rusty and damaged. But if anyone can do it, it's you. What will you need to begin?"

"A miracle," Jacob replied. "Nothing less."

But two days later, Jacob went to the Bolshevik and said that he would attempt it. "You must send me to Petrograd; that's the only place that has the equipment I need. Without the equipment, we'll never accomplish anything."

Jacob left the following morning, having told only Abraham of his real intention. He was escorted by a troop of Red soldiers thirty miles through White infested territory to the nearest railroad station. He carried onto the train just one suitcase, containing three shirts, several pairs of heavy socks, warm underwear, and a wooden box in which was all of his wife's jewelry. When he reached Petrograd, he immediately phoned a German business acquaintance and then went to various government offices to order equipment for the mill. He left for Nishkovitz at the end of a week.

PART TWO

COHEN

The sun. Jacob watched the flat, desolate land. Half an hour more, then a three hour ride. How long would it take? The jewelry would be sold in Germany. A carriage would be waiting at the Polish border. Maybe two months. Paris. He would wait in Paris, then return in a private car and reclaim what was his!

"Comrade Kagan, this is your stop." They were approaching a station. "The White bastards still run loose here," the railroad attendant said.

Jacob brushed off his clothes and picked up his suitcase.

A man standing by a horse and cart tipped his cap and asked Jacob where he wanted to go. "Nishkovitz."

"Ah, no," the driver said. "It is a dangerous ride."

Jacob gave the man a gold ring and told him that he would have the horse and cart returned.

"It's dangerous," the driver called out as Jacob left him and the small town behind.

He drove slowly. It was a cool autumn day. There had been no snow yet. After an hour, he reined the horse and tied up the cart. He took off his jacket and loosened his pants.

He was squatting beside the cart when two armed Whites came from behind a thicket of trees. One of them pointed his rifle at Jacob and said, "I am going to shoot you."

"Wait until I finish, will you?" Jacob replied.

"He is Kagan," the other said. "We'll get a reward for bringing him in alive."

FOUR

MORNING

I

It had stopped snowing when David and I left the Opera House. I looked up Broadway, past Times Square. News bulletins ran on panels of electric light bulbs around the Times building. Theatre marquees blinked. Not a single sign was off that would not switch back on in an instant. Brilliant neon advertisements sent reddish glows even over the skyscrapers of the city. David and I were pressed into a crowd surging uptown to the subways and restaurants. David took my arm and pulled me through the crowd, until, south of the Opera House, we could walk at our own pace. When we turned a corner and walked east, all the sounds and lights of the city were suddenly very distant, as though a glass door had silently slid shut behind us. Huge buildings with offices and factories on every one of twenty stories, empty of people on this day and this hour, protected by solitary watchmen, lined the narrow streets we walked on. The snow on the sidewalks was still white. So very still. The buildings, like trees in a primeval forest, or like high Gothic arches in a cathedral, leaned over us and the sky was a sliver of dark black.

"There it is," David said.

A glass window, a glass door, and on the door a stenciled cardboard sign: DAVID COHEN AND ESTHER STAR, WINES AND LIQUORS. OPENING JANUARY 13.

"We can't go in," David said, "the burglar alarm would go off."

I could not see into the store at all. I looked at the display of bottles in the window.

"The best Scotch. Your mother'll wait on customers and I'll drink up the stock. How's that?"

"Maybe you'll let her take some home?" I suggested.

David put his hand on my shoulder and said, "Sam, she won't take anything home but money. Nothing but profits. This is the perfect business, not just to make a living, but to really live—a fortune if we're lucky. Jack's the president of the shipping corporation, he wants to be a big man, but all we want is to have some money, to live like men out of that stinking dress business. *Comprennez?"*

"Do you think it'll really be good?" I asked.

"I not only think it, I guarantee it, and you'll have a car of your own in a couple of years." David smiled at me. "Come on, I'll buy you a coke."

We walked down the street and turned onto Sixth Avenue. There was a bar right around the corner, The Merchants' Café.

The doors swung shut behind us. The large, long room was nearly empty; there were three men sitting at different sections of the bar. The bartender said, "Hello, Mr. Cohen," and we sat down in a booth.

"The cornbeef's the best," David said to me when the waitress came over. "Do you want cornbeef?"

"Sure," I answered.

"A cornbeef sandwich and a Coca Cola for the gentleman, and a double Scotch on the rocks for me."

"Yes, Mr. Cohen," the waitress said and left us.

"Everybody comes here for lunch, the great dress manufacturers. Jack'll be here later; maybe he'll be with his girl, a blond like in the movies, like Betty Grable," David said, and smiled.

"Are they gonna be married?"

He laughed. "She thinks so, and a *shiksa* has a right to an opinion."

The waitress brought a tray with our orders, and I ate my sandwich while David drank.

"So Sam, you wanta be a singer?"

"Uh," I answered.

"Why? Because you'll be famous?" he asked, smiling.

He was not a singer. He had tried and had failed, but I would not fail. "To make a million dollars," I answered and laughed apprehensively. Would he laugh?

"A million dollars, if you're lucky and smart, you might make in business, you might be another Jack Cohen, but in singing—you'll be lucky to get a chance to sing."

"Why I can sing right now . . ."

"But with dignity," David interrupted. "With dignity. To sing in a bar is not to sing."

I put my half-eaten sandwich down and asked, "What difference where you sing?"

"You're too young to understand," he said, and he saw my lips press together in anger. "Listen, Sam," he said after a moment, "our whole lives aim for one thing, and that's death. There's nothing anywhere, and everywhere you look there's only that last breath, and life's agony, agony of knowledge, agony of dream and reality, of beauty and filth. Every once in a while I wake up in the morning, and I spit blood, spit right out of my throat—I know how human I am. And tonight they were human, they sang fair and fair's never good enough, only *it* is good enough. When you have that voice on loan that's given, never to be owned but to sing with, to protect and to use, and only Caruso and Chaliapin had it, and one didn't know when to stop and the other was a clown; but they had *it* like no one else, and do you think you'll have *it?* Hello, Yankel," he greeted a tall, red-faced man, and then turned back to me without waiting for an answer.

"A *shmuck.* The whole world, from Vladivostok back to Vladivostok, the whole world is *shmucks.* Do you know what life's all about?" he asked. "It's breathing and eating and make-a-living, and there's only Caruso who wasn't a clown but who choked on his own voice. Annie!" he called to the waitress. "So you sang in the synagogue today, and so you went to the opera, and you want to be a singer . . . Annie! God damn it! When I was your age, I'd studied ten years already, and when I was twenty and said to hell with it, I'd studied seventeen years. There's only one voice, only Caruso, and the rest might just as well not sing. Double Scotch, and Coca Cola for the young gentleman. Are you another Caruso?"

"I will be," I said.

David drank his Scotch.

Afterwards he remained absolutely still. His eyes were fixed straight ahead. I was afraid to move even the slightest bit, afraid he might smash his hand on the table or cough blood.

I saw Jack come in through the swinging doors. A rush of cold air swept across my face. "Close that door!" the bartender yelled. "Oh, it's you, Mr. Cohen. Here, I'll get it," he said. It was hot again.

Jack stood by our booth. He took off his rich blue double-breasted overcoat. "Freeze your balls out there," he said.

"Excuse me, I'm gonna be sick," David said, rising and walking to the men's room in the back.

"*Shikka* like a *goy*," Jack said and, sitting down, he asked me how much money I had garnished for my Bar-mitzvah.

By midnight, The Merchants' Café was crowded. Someone dropped a quarter into the juke box. I could hardly hear the conversation, and my eyes teared because of the smoke. I was sitting in the same booth with Jack, and there were two other men with us: Herman Winer, son of Moishe Weinstein, both of the dress manufacturing firm of Weinstein and Winer, and Max Kling, court jester to the kings of the dress business. A man in his fifties, whose mouth frothed like a mad cocker spaniel as he talked or laughed, Max Kling was a particular friend of my uncle Larry and a partner in my uncle Sol's dress business. David had not returned from the men's room. Jack was holding forth:

"Gentlemen, today, or should I say yesterday, was the day on which my young cousin Sam became a man. Gentlemen, to look at that boy who sits so quietly in a corner, you would hardly know what kind of blood runs in his veins; you would think, 'Ah, a stupid boy.' It is not so. He is the son of Colonel Isaac Starobinetz, a Russian war hero, and also of Esther Kagan, from whose liquor store—she's Dave's partner—you'll buy your liquor. She, of all women, is a cook. Her *gefilte* fish, her *blintzes,* her *knaidlach* . . . gentlemen, to her cooking there are no comparisons. But even more important, she is the sister of Jacob Kagan, that boy is his nephew, I am his son."

"Ach!" Max Kling exclaimed. "Again? You know no other stories, can't you tell us about your latest fuck?"

"Max, the last time I was in bed was exactly like the time before, and the time before that was also just the same. One woman is like another, but Jacob Kagan is like no other man."

"That iss a good answer," Max said to me, and I wiped my face when he again looked at Jack.

"Mr. Winer," Jack said, "you have a college education. You shall tell me if you have ever before heard a story like this."

"Mr. Cohen, to be of any assistance to one of your stature, to one of your enormous stature in the world of high finance, to be perspicacious enough to exercise my critical acumen for such a gentleman as yourself, will be my greatest delight."

"Thank you, Mr. Winer. And you, Mr. Star," Jack said to me, "you have certainly heard this story before, and I shall count on you to correct me, to verify the truth that I speak."

I nodded my head.

"Gentlemen, I shall tell this story just as the great Yiddish author, Shmyola Bernstein, sometimes called the Yiddish Shakesberg, has immortalized it in his tales of Old Russia. Sometimes though, I shall add a bit of spice, that being a necessary ingredient for men not so kosher as Shmyola Bernstein."

"A good beginning," Max Kling said and nodded his head.

"You should've been a writer," Herman Winer said.

"To have to invent?" Jack exclaimed. "I know enough to

write a hundred books. It's only those who don't know enough to write a book who write."

"You should write and make money," Winer said.

"My nephew Jess, he makes money writing," Max said. "He lives in Paris and uses the pen," he said, looking meaningfully at his lap.

"A good pen's worth a thousand typewriters," Herman Winer said.

"Please, no interruptions," Jack said, "for now I begin." He brushed his long, soft blond hair back with his hand and said, "You have no doubt, gentlemen, heard of Prince Alexi Alexanderovitch?"

"He iss a Rusky?" Max Kling asked.

"A Russian?" Jack repeated and shook his head in mock amazement at Max's question. "He was uncle to the Tsar, to Nicholas himself! He owned most of White Russia, his forests extended hundreds of miles about his palace, and a palace it was that none of you have ever seen the likes of. Every tree he owned was untouched by human hands . . ."

"A virgin forest," Winer said.

"Exactly."

"And how iss a tree not a virgin?" Max asked. "In life I have heard of many things . . ."

"Shut up," Jack said, smiling, "and if you open your mouth again, I'll drown you in your own spit."

I did not listen to the story. Today was my day. I sensed a competition. Jack had identified me with my father's family, the Starobinetzes, and had, by calling me Jacob's nephew, cut me off, made me more distantly related to Jacob than I thought I was. Jack identified himself with his father and left no room for anyone else, not even his brother David. When he talked about Jacob Kagan, whom he had hardly known, he exaggerated a great deal and gave to his father all the fine analyzing capabilities that he himself possessed, as if his father were nothing more than a brilliant business man, an appraiser, a shrewd calculator. My eyes followed Jack's facial expressions: the smile that followed the planned job, the questioning look that someone in the story might have, the poker face of his father. Watching Jack, I believed that Jacob must have been just like him—proud, ambitious, confident. I looked away and glanced for a second at Herman Winer. Then my gaze caught a calendar hanging on the mirror behind the bar, on the other side of the room. It was of a girl wearing a two-piece bathing suit, lying on a beach, smiling. A caption beneath her asked: "Wish you were here?" At the top of the calendar, in bolder type, was printed: "Manhattan Dyeing Corporation for Never Fading Dyes."

"Where's David?" I interrupted Jack.

"What?" Jack asked.

"Where's David?"

"Young man, I'm in the middle of a story."

I wanted to get up to look for David. I was sitting between Max Kling and the wall, and I was afraid to interrupt Jack again. I watched a woman leaning on the bar, sitting on a tall, red leather cushioned stool. She was smoking a filtered cigarette and talking to a man who was sitting next to her. A black woolen coat hung from her shoulders, partly covering the stool; her thigh, pointing down, was covered by a tight fitting, knitted dress. I could see her knee. A giant of a man walked slowly past our booth, for a moment blocking the woman from my sight. He limped slightly, and the limp was almost graceful, not seeming to be a defect at all, as some men who limp seem to be neither limping nor walking, but dancing. This man's stiff right leg extended his straight bearing, made me conscious that every inch of his at least six-feet-three-inch height was all military. His cap and coat were frayed; his hands were immense.

"Ivan!" I exclaimed.

He turned around. "Samuel Yitzhocovitch," he greeted me smiling.

"Gentlemen," Jack interrupted his story, "may I present to you Ivan Ragushenko? And this is Max Kling and Herman Winer. Will you join us?"

"I'm supposed to meet David," Ivan said. "Is he here?"

"Indeed he is," Herman Winer said.

"He certainly iss," Max agreed. "And you will find him in . . ."

"The men's room," Jack finished Max's sentence. "You'll find him in the men's room, sitting on the pot."

"Excuse me, then," Ivan said and, leaving his cap on the table, walked to the back.

"A soldier," Jack said in explanation. "A soldier and then my father's servant."

"A bodyguard he looks like," Max said.

"That also," Jack added. "My father had many enemies."

"But you forgot your story," Herman Winer said.

"Well, listen. The Prince Alexi had sent the Tsar's engineer to my father. He wanted the engineer to take all my father's lumber . . ."

Ragushenko could not have been a servant. Not someone to wait on others. He was a friend. What could he say to David? David would be standing by the window, looking out into a backyard, or sitting, holding his head. What could Ivan say to David? How beautiful the opera had been. I would give anything to sing so beautifully. My right arm, yes, even my right arm. Out of the open window of a men's room in a café, what could he see? Could he see the stars?

The bartender brought a hamburger to the woman sitting at the bar. The man who had been sitting next to her had left. She stood up and shook her shoulders so that her coat should hang evenly; then she walked to our booth. For a moment she stood, listening to Jack. Her hair was brunette, and a thick wave curved down over her forehead. She smiled when Jack looked at her, and she asked, "Can I have the pepper?"

"Why sure, honey," Max Kling was quick to reply. He reached in front of me to get the pepper. She held the shaker in three fingers, the other two fingers holding a cigarette.

"Thanks," she said. "What a' ya talkin 'bout?"

"Mr. Cohen, the international financier, is telling us a story," Herman Winer informed her.

"Do ya mind if I listen?"

"Of course not," Jack said. "Please join us. This is Max Kling, Herman Winer, and that's my son Sam."

"Whose is this?" she asked, picking up Ivan Ragushenko's cap.

"No one important—just a wall painter," Jack replied.

"Oh," she said without enthusiasm. "He has a big head."

"He has big hands," I said.

She looked at me and then back at Jack. "My name's Arabelle. Please don't stop your story."

"As I was saying," Jack continued, "when they went into the forests of Prince Alexi Alexanderovitch, uncle to the Tsar, they cut down almost every tree, and, according to Shmyola Bernstein, the Prince got very angry. If I remember correctly, this is the way Bernstein concluded his famous story, *The Bear:*

'Alexi Alexanderovitch interrupted the officer who stood at attention facing him, "Whom did you say?"

' "Kagan, my lord."

' "Kagan!" Alexi screamed. "You fool, how did he do it?"

'The officer pulled a slip of paper from his tunic pocket and offered it to Alexi. "The engineer is authorized by the Tsar. He takes your timber to build fortifications for the river Berezina—to Kagan he has given the job of getting timber."

'Alexi read the paper and after a moment he smiled and said, "At least I am not the only one the Jew has outfoxed. He sued Nicholas." Alexi laughed and continued. "The Jew, Jacob Kagan, sued him, the Tsar, and he won. A single Jew against the Tsar, the father of all the Russians." Alexi looked at the stony face of the officer and stopped laughing. "Idiot!" he screamed. "Get the hell out of here! Go to my forests and watch the Jew steal my timber." '

"Ach!" David exclaimed, standing by the booth, his face quite pale and his eyes red. "Bernstein's story. He's a sentimentalist, our Bernstein. A sentimentalist—he knows nothing of the world; he lives in a dream."

"So, philosopher," Max Kling said, "tell us what you know about the world?"

"I shall. I shall tell you about the world of business, the real world, the real world of business, and without sentimentality, just facts, the way things happen, one fact following another like the wheels of an express train. Ivan," David said, "I shall tell you the story of the new Jacob Kagan, the American Cohen of Kagan," and he smiled at Jack. "My brother, the American version of Kagan, who will certainly make a million, and after that many millions more. Eh, Max? How? Only a minute, just a minute. How did it all start?"

Ivan took David's arm and said, "Why don't we leave now?"

"Ivan, Ivan, talk is good, it releases the soul, the imprisoned soul. Listen to the story and maybe you'll learn how to make a million."

"Well then, talk," Jack said, smiling condescendingly, "but sit down first. You have a long story?"

"I'm Arabelle," the girl said, when David had sat down and glanced at her.

"Arabelle?" David repeated and, eyeing her suspiciously, he declared, "I know Arabelle and you're not her—you're a spy."

"She was sitting at the bar," Winer said.

"She's a spy for Henry Ford," David said. "She'll report everything I say."

"I'm no spy and I don't work for Henry Ford."

"Of course you don't," David persisted.

"Don't be ashamed of working for Ford; he put America on wheels," Winer asserted.

"He did that," Max Kling agreed.

"And he sent us speeding down the highway to death . . . love your neighbor indeed. 'Spy on him' is Ford's motto; we know that anti-Semite. What are you spying on us for? It's on Jack; you have to watch him, eh?"

Arabelle looked at Jack and Jack shook his head as if to say, "It's only a joke." She smiled at him gratefully.

Max leered at Jack.

"The Greek, Stelios," David said and nodded seriously at Ivan, "it all began with the Greek, Stelios—he was the intermediary. A short dark man, a cutter in Sol's factory, a mysterious man whom even that judge of men," David said, pointing at Max, "never fully understood. He walked out of the small noisy factory into the small dirty showroom and said slowly, 'Boss, I want talk you money.' 'What kind money?' Sol asked, thinking the Greek, a shrewd customer, wanted a raise. 'Big money,' the Greek replied, 'I talk you big money.' So they talk, and then Sol takes him to the large office of Larry Cohen. Larry, he sits behind a desk, two telephones on it. Ben sits on the leather couch, Mendel and Sol sit with Ben. Jack paces by the bar. Me, I drink at the bar, and the Greek, Stelios, he talks:

" 'I come from old country many years go. I make living, so-so living, but I friends, many friends. Mitropoulis my cousin, Theodorokulus, brother-in-law's uncle. Greek, from time boy, he sailor. Sails small boats, many islands Greece, many beautiful islands and no buses, not like big city, like New York City. Small towns. You listen, Greek, he always love water, many Greeks, seamen, good seamen. Work hard, seamen get money, buy small boat, later, big boat; later he own many big boat. Greeks best shippers in world, smart. Theodorokulus, he very big man, own twenty boats, freighters, liberty ships. Understand? He want sell some, he tired, want to rest. You buy boats, make big money, very very big money. Understand?' "

David scratched his nose. "So Stelios finishes. The big businessmen, they sit. Ben's scared; how much money has he got anyway—and all of it's invested in insurance. Sol, he wonders what it would be like to have a million dollars. Mendel doesn't say anything; he'll go along with any decision. Larry, he slams his hand on the desk and says, 'What are we wasting our time for? You know, you can't do business with a Greek.' "

Jack laughed and agreed with David's account. "That's what he said, 'You greenhorns,' he said, 'you can't do business with a Greek.' "

David paused and pointed his finger at Jack. "He, he said he wanted to meet Theodorokulus, and the question is, gentlemen, why did he say it?"

"A smart cookie," Max Kling answered.

"Like any man with sense, he wanted to see what the proposition was. You never lose by investigation, is always a true saying," Herman Winer said.

"Sayings we don't allow," David said.

Arabelle smiled at Jack and Jack said, "I did it for my son, to be able to send my son to Harvard."

David looked at me as if he had just noticed me. "Are you the son of the great Khan?" he asked. "Why, then tell us your thoughts on the subject."

"I don't know," I said, and I was embarrassed.

David looked back at Ivan and said, "This is not the blood of my people, this is no heir to the father of Genghis Khan. Is he, Ivan?"

Ivan smiled at me reassuringly. "He is the son of Isaac and Esther, the grandson of Abraham Kagan."

"He's none of those things, he's the son of Jack Cohen, an American, a fifth generation American."

"He's my son," Jack said, "that's right."

"Son or rain, who cares? But why wass it only Jack who went to the Greeks? Tell us the real reasson," Max Kling asked David mockingly. "Smart boy, why wassn't it you?"

"Ah," David sighed, nodding his head, "there you have the question. There, in just a few words is stated everything. Why wasn't it me? It's simple, because I'm not Jack . . . I'm someone else."

"Who are you someone else?" Max persisted.

"I am. I don't know," David said and now shook his head from side to side. "I'm not a philosopher, not a singer, maybe," he said and he smiled, "a mimic or a story teller, but, above all," and his face became impressively sober, "I am on the *in*."

"Whose *in?*" Herman Winer asked. "Henry Ford's?"

"The Greeks," David answered.

"The Greeks?" Max Kling asked.

"The Greeks!" David affirmed.

"Which Greeks?" Herman Winer asked.

"Ask him, ask Cohen-Khan-Kagan," David said and looked menacingly at Jack. "Eh, Yitzhoc, what difference if I tell?" He looked at Arabelle and asked her, "Right? You know them, the ones who pay you, who finance Ford. God, what power! Ivan, you'd never know, how could you know? There's a conspiracy, the largest cartels—businesses you think are owned by stock holders, all owned by the Greeks."

"Which Greeks?" Max Kling asked.

"Above them, there's only one man," David continued.

"Who? Who iss he?"

David looked at Max. He screwed up his eyes and said in hardly more than a whisper, *"Him,* the Armenian, the Director of the conspiracy."

"Nonsense!" Jack exclaimed, exasperated that David was controlling the direction of the conversation. "There are no Greeks and no Armenians. Why don't you talk sense?" Jack looked at his older brother and shrugged his shoulders. "Why don't you tell us why I went to see the Greeks?"

David looked for a moment at his brother and said, "Fuck you."

Jack's face flushed.

"Stupid!" Ivan exclaimed. "Brothers should always fight, in front of strangers, yet. In front of a boy."

"Me no stranger," Max Kling said, "me old time family peasant from Old Country."

Ragushenko reached suddenly across the table and with the flat of his hand he slapped Max Kling solidly across his cheek. "You shut up," Ivan said.

"You God damned giant," Max said, looking down at the table.

"Good night," Ivan said. "I'll drive Sam home. Good night."

Max Kling stood up and I slid out of the booth.

"Wait," David called to Ivan. "I want to talk . . ."

"I'm still here," Max Kling said smiling and sitting down.

Ragushenko drove me home in his pre-war Chevrolet. It smelled of paints and turpentine; there was a sheet of white canvas covering the rear seat and floor that was stained in many places. In the car even Ivan seemed to smell of stale, dry paints. We drove crosstown to the East River Drive. There was snow remaining only on the sidewalks and steam billowed from around manhole covers. Ivan drove slowly, he shifted gears often. I watched his hands. They were covered with hair, even around the joints of his fingers. He gripped the wheel lightly with his left hand and his right just touched the wheel and played over the horn and the gear shift. "It is no good," Ivan said, and I knew he was apologizing for David.

2

Several years after the Second World War, I was shown photographs taken at a concentration camp immediately after the liberation of the Jews from Dachau, Auschwitz, Belsen: the bodies of naked, fleshless men and women. There was one photograph of a uniformed man, dropping as one might drop branches on a fire, the body of a woman. She is in mid-air, facing the camera, falling into a hollow filled with bodies like her own. When I had looked at the photograph for a moment, I gasped involuntarily and thought suddenly of the agony of my father.

Six months before my Bar-mitzvah, my father suffered a heart attack, and he was permanently disabled until his death four years later. Every month, he received one hundred fifty dollars from an insurance policy, and with that he tried to support his family. He concluded, a year after his attack, that only a miracle could restore his health, and he sold his automobile and office, selling with his office the nameplate that for twenty years had been fastened to the outside brick wall: Isaac Star, M.D. Sickness and death had plagued him all his life. Near the end of the war, he received a letter from his brother, who had escaped the Nazis, informing him that his parents, his three sisters, and almost all his cousins were dead. They had been branded, starved, and gassed; never resisting, never having learned to resist, they found dignity in the monstrousness of the crimes perpetrated against them. It was with the receipt of the letter that all my father's fears, the same fears he had expressed to his parents in 1932, when they had paid him a short visit here in the United States, were materialized as exaggerated reality. When he was sick, a cancer eating an already sick body, he knew without anyone telling him—he had always been an accurate diagnostician, pessimistic and correct—that he was dying. He could not resist the diseases of his body, and he was a prophet of illness who could not reconcile his hopes with his diagnoses until, finally, he lapsed into coma. I remember him one morning, standing by the dining room window, wearing his blue woolen robe and a black skullcap, a Bible open on the marble-topped bureau in front of him. He had learned that during the night a friend of his had had a heart attack; for several hours, my father repeated aloud the Psalms of David. His pride, the pride my family had in him, was the pride a Jew has in a doctor, knowing him, not as a businessman, but as a professional, an educated, liberal, and expertly efficient doctor. He was short and slight, but when I walked by his side down Hunts Point Avenue to the park, or to the orange brick synagogue off Lafayette Street, I felt the respect the passersby had for him, and I tried to share in the pride of his straight bearing.

And then suddenly he was no longer a doctor but a prematurely sick, old man. He could hardly walk a regular city block without stopping twice to catch his breath. He resigned himself to sitting out-of-doors on a folding chair like a grandmother, sitting right next to the street entrance of our apartment and the adjacent medical office that had once been his. He nodded his head at many people and sometimes had short conversations with former patients. "Yes, doctor, I have stones in my gall bladder, and my liver, doctor . . ."

Horowitz, the vegetable store man, made a point of passing by our apartment each time he was out making a delivery. He pushed a large wagon with metal wheels that made such a noise on the coarse sidewalk pavements that my father could tell he was coming when he was still a block away. And he would sit there and think of something to say. "Hello, Wendell Willkie."

"Why Willkie?"

"Willkie was too liberal and too smart to be a Republican, and you, you're too liberal and smart to be a vegetable store man."

Through most of the afternoon he sat in the straight armchair by the dining room window, reading his newspaper and journals or listening to the radio. He read the New York *Times*, the *Herald Tribune*, the *Journal of the American Medical Association*, or *The National Geographic Magazine*. He read mainly to be informed, and when he read for pleasure, he read mystery stories or reread Pushkin and Bernstein. He also spent two hours every day listening to the soap operas. When caught listening to one, he invariably complained about the things he was forced to listen to because he had to rest his eyes. And, of course, he played cards, if not with his very dear friend Deutschman, then with my mother or me, or anyone who might be visiting him.

During the four years that he was sick, he carried a notebook in his trouser pocket in which he recorded every expenditure made by himself, my mother, and me. On the last pages of the notebook, he recorded his debts, how much money he had been given by each of my mother's brothers. When, after his death, I found ten of these notebooks, and searched through them, hoping to find I don't know what, I discovered figures and dates set down in a very legible print, as though he had wanted to be especially sure that these books would one day be read. I found, at the same time, an envelope containing forty cancelled checks of fifty dollars each, made out to my grand-uncle, Louis Cohen, and dated from 1927 to

1929. My father had borrowed two thousand dollars from his uncle in 1921, when he had come to this country, and though Louis Cohen was perhaps not even concerned about the loan, my father, when he began to earn just a little more than was necessary for him and my mother to live on, had paid his debt. Perhaps he hoped, in this later instance, in some way to repay his brothers-in-law. The monthly insurance payments of one hundred and fifty dollars could hardly keep his wife and son going for two weeks; his savings were exhausted a year after his attack. It was then that he began to accept the money my uncles Larry, Mendel, Sam, Sol, and Ben had been offering him from the time of his attack.

Me too. Ben gave me a dollar and sometimes five, every week, and I selfishly guarded my money with the same anxiety that my father kept accounts of his debts. It was my money, spending money, and it was not to be budgeted in my father's notebook. That notebook, with three pencilled lines running down each page—date, amount, reason. Reason! How generous my uncles were, but how my father suffered! And then my uncles did something else; they set my cousin David and my mother up in a liquor store. My father was afraid; he could never repay the initial expense of the store, nearly thirty thousand dollars—an impossible sum. When my uncle Larry visited us just the day before the store was to open, and said confidently to my father, "Assoc, if all they do is get ten percent of my friends to buy from them, they'll make more than enough," my father said in reply, "I hope so, but I know nothing of business."

"Who ever said you did?" Larry asked. "If you knew something, if you'd been a little smarter, you wouldn't 've ruined your health here in the stinking Bronx. You'd 've been in Long Island, relaxing, not working twenty-four hours a day, not climbing five flights to see one lousy patient for two lousy dollars."

"That's right," my father answered, "but then I wouldn't be a doctor. I'd be you and not me."

"Smart doctors make money," Larry said.

"Good doctors die early," my father said. "They work hard . . ."

"And some only get sick and can't make a living."

"They're unfortunate."

"Your friend Lessner makes money," Larry said.

"When he treats hypochondriacs like you, he does," my father said, smiling.

"Hypochondracs? I can't move my neck, so all of a sudden I'm a hypochondrac."

"Hypochondriac," my father corrected.

"You're an idealist," Larry exclaimed, "that's what's the matter with you. You were always too smart to make money, and now that you can't even make a living, you ought to thank God for the liquor store."

My father's face was pale when he stood up and said, "For my brother-in-law Larry Cohen, I thank God; for his success and generosity, and if you don't mind, I think I shall lie down."

I identify the liquor store with the cancers that killed my father and my mother, and that I once thought were destroying my family. The history of the liquor store, commencing just after my father's heart attack and ending immediately after my mother's death, has seemed to be a highly intensified and highly focused history of the hopes and failures of the family Kagan-Cohen after its arrival in New York City. The store was financed and backed by virtually the entire family; during the first few months, many of my aunts and cousins helped out in the store, cleaning and delivering, taking inventory and keeping the books. The purchase of the store was a family enterprise, but the original idea had been Larry Cohen's. Of all her brothers, my mother loved Larry the most. Of all the Cohen brothers, he was the most successful, the most extravagant in personal spending and personal affections, and the most conservative in the way of business. He had never lost his good looks—he had been handsome as a boy, and now, much later in his life, when he was known throughout certain sections of certain cities in the world as the prosperous dress manufacturer that he was, he was still referred to as Larry the *shaneh,* Larry the pretty one. Pretty indeed! He was tall, his features all regular, and he stood straight. In the New York City garment section, a man whose nose was not broken was regarded as pretty. Larry was a beauty.

It was Larry Cohen's idea to buy a liquor store for my mother, and it was Jack Cohen's idea to make David a partner. Then the family invested money, and my mother and David were launched on a faulty construction that eventually collapsed, sinking the partners, but hardly affecting the builders. Oh, Larry was a handsome man, and nothing, nothing at all ever hurt his good looks. At the age of nineteen, he had arrived in New York City, a steerage passenger on a cattle ship and, taking long, healthy steps, had walked down the gangplank, first in a long line of crouching, huddled ghetto Jews to be admitted to the United States of America. He came to this country with a little money and much ambition, the money permitting him several months without work, and the ambition sending him to school to learn English. When the money was gone, he went to the Jewish Immigrant Relief Organization and applied to them for help in obtaining a job and in locating his uncle, Eleazar Kagan. The J.I.R.O. put an advertisement in the Yiddish newspapers and one week later, Laban received a telegram: "I am your uncle. Have job for you tomorrow morning. 323 W. 18 St. Signed, Louis Cohen Enterprises."

"Louis Cohen?" Laban repeated the name many times. He could be an impostor trying to cheat a greenhorn. The J.I.R.O. had warned him. And even if he really was Eleazar, he was most probably still a thief. Hadn't he stolen all Abraham's money while Abraham had slept, and then when he was only a boy? No. Laban decided he would not go . . . but to send a telegram. This Louis Cohen might even have a large automobile. In the morning, Laban went to the offices of

Louis Cohen Enterprises. He waited longer than an hour, and was finally directed to an office whose hard wooden door had stenciled on it, "L.C.," and beneath those initials, the word, "QUIET!"

When he opened the door a heavy man, seated in a cushioned swivel chair, wearing his jacket open—showing a large expanse of vest crisscrossed with three silver chains—said, "You speak English, eh?"

"Yes. I speak English very well. I study three months. You look very much like my father, you know?"

"Your father?" Louis Cohen mused.

"Abraham, son of Yitzhoc Kagan."

"My brother," Louis said and smiled. "How is he?"

"Very good when I leave."

"That's fine. Does he make money?"

"He is an advisor to Jacob. Jacob is very rich."

"Who's Jacob?"

Laban stared a moment and then explained, "Jacob Kagan."

"Yeah?"

"Well, I leave Russia," Laban began his story thinking that Louis had finally recognized the name, "because me not very good with government."

"A bolshevik?"

"Me, not Jacob," Laban said proudly. "I come here to land of freedom, but now I have no money."

"So you want a job?"

"Very much want job."

Louis stood up and walked to Laban. He felt Laban's biceps and nodded his head. "Cutting trees," Laban said, and smiled.

"Trees?" Louis asked. "What sort of work did you do in Russia?"

"I work with Jacob, Jacob Kagan. We lumbermen."

Louis looked at his nephew and burst out laughing. "Peasants and bolsheviks!" he exclaimed. "Well, look. You'll work hard for me, and unless you work hard, you won't hold your job. One other thing: I don't like your name, it's too much like the old country. This is a new start. It was for me and maybe it'll be for you."

Laban changed his name to Lawrence Cohen and went to work for his uncle. He was given a job as floorboy and worked six days a week from seven-thirty in the morning to seven-thirty in the evening. He lifted and carried heavy rolls of material, delivered goods from one building in the garment district to another. He swept and mopped and opened windows when the factory was too stuffy, and closed them when it was too cold. Larry Cohen's first American winter was lonely, cold, and gray. But how much worse it would have been if he had not made the acquaintance of a fellow employee, a man of many talents, Max Kling! This short, lean, and nervous man was younger than Larry, but had emigrated to America years before him. And he knew the ropes. He knew where to buy a suit of clothes for three dollars, where to eat for a fraction of a dollar, and where to get laid for slightly more than the price of a cheap dinner. After a short while Larry and Max took a room together on the lower East Side. Max saw more in Larry than his good looks; Larry was a nephew of Louis Cohen. He attached himself to Larry and stuck to him like a leech the rest of his life. Every morning, they walked, rain or snow, the three miles to Louis' factory. Larry spoke bitterly of his uncle, but looked longingly at his chauffeur-driven automobile.

"One day," Larry said, "that money will belong to all of us."

"If it is just for the two of us it will be very nice."

Larry talked and Max listened, and joked, and waited.

Louis Cohen's factory occupied an entire floor in a large building. There were two rows of men working on sewing machines, a table for embroiderers, a table for cutters, and another for designers. There were no partitions in the factory, and the floor was uncovered concrete; there were no shades on the windows, and there was no heating. The sewing machine operators worked in their overcoats and sometimes had to stop their machines in order to warm their hands. All of the workers were Jewish immigrants from Germany, Poland, Russia, Roumania, Hungary. Only a few of them spoke even a little English. They spoke Yiddish and forgot their original native tongues. They lived in tenements where all their immediate neighbors and all their shopkeepers were Jewish. Their children spoke English only at the public schools. Most of the men and women who worked for Louis Cohen had run away from Europe, not because they were hunted, but because they were poor and because they were Jews, as if being a Jew meant being poor; wanderers, with the single responsibility of never forgetting the fact of their more recent history, persecution and no resistance, they came to this country hoping not for even the smallest freedom, but for a job, for meat once a week. As their children grew up (and none of them resembled their parents), being a Jew came to mean something entirely different. Those children who had gone to *Chedar* and had been Bar-mitzvahed, who had gone to public school and maybe high school, exchanged small crowded tenement apartments for larger, more comfortable apartments in elevator buildings; had two children and not ten, ate meat six times a week and dairy dinner once (more as a reminder than as an economy), planned for their children, my generation, to be accountants and lawyers, doctors if studious, businessmen if clever. They gave up the history of their fathers, hardly knew in which countries their fathers had been born, and, in place of this knowledge, in place of the real faith of their fathers, were Jews only in the ways they made their livings, residing in comfortable Jewish communities, working in Jewish businesses like the garment industry, where they dealt with Jews like themselves and were concerned wholly with their middle-class comfort.

The Old Country Jew, resettled in New York City before the First World War, was underpaid and exploited. He worked hard and respected his employer, often took pride in his employer's wealth and craftiness: "Ach, that Cohen, he is a smart one! Imagine, to stop the entire shop just when the union wanted to organize! Now everyone is afraid for his job, and Cohen can even cut our wages if he wants!" And Louis Cohen was a prince when he took all his workers back at their old salaries. He was seen by his workers rarely, but when he did walk through his factory, he made an impressive appearance. He smoked a Havana cigar and kept his thumbs in his vest pockets, fingering as he walked his silver watch chain; he looked around sharply, sometimes felt the material someone was working on, sometimes asked about a wife or child, and always, just as he was leaving after having consulted his watch as if he had a pressing appointment, he yelled at someone whom he declared to be doing the job improperly, who was wasting material, or who, he said, was plain lazy. On one of these periodical tours, he yelled at his nephew Larry. For more than six months Larry had been working as floorboy and his uncle had never, after their first meeting, spoken to him, had seemed to have forgotten his very existence. This one time Louis Cohen noticed a pile of dust underneath a cutting table, and he pounced on Larry. "Is this the way you keep my factory clean? Is this what you're paid for? You're a lazy boy, a lazy boy," he concluded, without giving Larry a chance to explain. Then he turned and left, flicking ashes from his cigar in disrespect on the otherwise clean floor.

"Who is he? Is he God?" Larry exclaimed loudly in anger when Louis had gone.

"Mr. Cohen," a worker informed him. "He loses at poker sometimes ten thousand dollars in a night."

"My own blood," Larry said in Yiddish and addressed himself to the workers. "He is truly my grandmother's son and my father's brother, but he is as bad as the Tsar, as black as blackest Russia. I came to America to be free—very free I am! I've hardly enough to eat. Is this freedom? Say no! It is slavery like niggers in the south, in Atlanta, Georgia. In Russia we tried a revolution, and my brother was killed fighting for liberty and I am in exile. We can revolt in New York City as well as in Russia. Do you hear?"

"That wass a good speech, but in Russia the revolution failed, no?" Max asked.

"Haven't you any courage? Listen, Patrick Henry said, 'Give me liberty or give me death!' "

The following day, Larry was called into the front office. A management spy had informed Louis that his nephew was an agitator. Louis, without offering Larry a chair, said, "Against your uncle you speak? By you that's smart?"

"By me," Larry said and paused, "I believe to fight for right."

"But against your uncle?" Louis said shaking his head. "That's a shame."

"I speak against something very larger than you. I speak against a system."

"Labelle," Louis said calmly, "don't be a *shmuck*. You speak out of anger to anger me. If you want to be a bolshevik, be a bolshevik, but not in my factory, someplace else maybe, but not here."

"You are firing me?" Larry asked.

"No," Louis said, clipping the end off a cigar, "I am giving you a job as a salesman if you are forgetting you are a bolshevik."

"I am a socialist. In Russia I was a Social Democrat," Larry explained.

By 1914, Larry was managing Louis' dress business. Never too close to his uncle, who no longer even visited the factory, having become a big real estate man, an owner of horses and backer of Broadway musicals, Larry made his own decisions involving loss or gain for Louis, drew a large salary, and waited only for an opportunity to go out on his own. He did that in 1917, when the United States entered the war, taking his brother Sam, who had arrived in New York in 1908 and had worked since then in Louis' factory, and Max Kling with him as junior partners. They started a new business—manufacturing overcoats on a government contract for the army—and within a year they had made a small fortune. When the war was over, they re-equipped their factory and mass-produced cheap dresses. They manufactured a dress for a dollar and sold it to retailers for two. In the wake of his success, Larry married a New York City-born Jewish girl, bought a house in Yonkers, joined a Jewish country club—(he knew many Gentiles but never trusted one)—and invested his profits in only the safest securities. Sam played the stock market. He worked eight hours a day in the new factory, supervising and patrolling, and in the evening he put on his white, belted camel's hair overcoat, drove a Packard, went to shows and nightclubs, and though he hardly ever thought of the wife he had deserted in Russia, he was often reminded of the disease he had taken along with him. Louis, Larry, and Sam were the founders of what Max would one day call, half in jest and half in seriousness, "the Cohen monopoly on wimminss' dresses."

3

In the winter of 1920, Larry Cohen received a cablegram from Russia: "Jacob killed. Need money to get family out. Ben." Larry read the cablegram several times, then placed it on his desk in front of him. He remained silent for a moment, and then suddenly yelled to his secretary in an adjoining room, "Get my brother, right away, you hear?"

When Sam entered the office, Larry said, "You're going to Russia."

"And you're crazy," Sam said. "Why should I go to Russia?"

"Here," Larry said and handed Sam the cablegram.

Sam read it and shook his head sadly. "Jacob killed? Ach! Who would do such a thing?"

"You'll take a couple of thousand dollars and bring them out."

"He was a big man. One bullet could hardly kill him. It was a machine gun."

"No doubt it was a machine gun," Larry said in mock

agreement and then looking at his brother, asked, "Sam, are you listening? I'll make preparations for you to leave in a week or two."

"A week," Sam repeated distractedly. "To murder Jacob Kagan?"

"A week. And don't spend all the money in Paris."

"What Paris?" Sam asked placing the cablegram on Larry's desk.

"Paris, France. On your way to Nishkovitz."

"Ah, you're crazy. How can I go to Nishkovitz?"

"Your wife's already forgotten you; maybe she's dead," Larry suggested.

"I guarantee that she won't die as long as I am alive!" Sam said emphatically. "There are women like that . . ."

"Listen!" Larry interrupted impatiently. "We can't send money—to whom should we send it? That's impossible. We must get papers for them and *you* must go there and bring them out."

"I refuse."

"You refuse your family?"

"I love my family, I am afraid of my wife. *You* have never met her. What a horrible bitch! Oh, the things she did to me . . ."

"Sam, I insist that you go."

"Definitely, I refuse! I refuse definitely!" Sam lit a cigar and while Larry stared at him, he paced in front of his desk. Finally Sam stopped, and facing Larry, he said, "There's only one solution."

"What's that?" Larry asked suspiciously.

"*You* go."

Larry considered Sam's proposal. "I'm a married man."

"And so am I," Sam said significantly.

"And to leave the business with you?"

"Max will keep the books."

"Enough!" Larry said. "I'll go."

"Ah," Sam sighed, and then, smiling, he said, "I left my

wife in Russia, and you can leave yours in Yonkers. You'll have a good time in Paris?"

"I may stop to see the styles."

"You'll certainly have a good time," Sam remarked.

The cablegram that Larry received had been sent from Warsaw, and several days later, Larry received a long letter postmarked from the same city. The letter was from Ben, and it informed him that the Bolsheviks had left Nishkovitz—that the area about Nishkovitz was a no-man's land. Corniloff, Sligorin, and Ratuski—the Bulgarian mercenary—had decided that their decimated armies were useless as independent forces. The three generals were massing their armies in preparation for a final push against the Reds. "If you meet me in Warsaw," Ben wrote, "I can return to Nishkovitz with the money necessary to bribe the Poles to get the family out of Russia."

One week later, carrying an American passport, and wearing beneath his shirt a silk money-belt containing five thousand dollars, Larry left New York City. From Antwerp, where the ship docked, he went directly to Warsaw where he was met by Ben and Sol.

Warsaw was a feverbed of activity. Agents of all the Western powers were noisily observing the progress of the Whites. Red Cross Stations feeding thousands of refugees were being continually photographed by foreign journalists. Pawn shops were running a thriving business—silver crosses, pearl necklaces and all kinds of jewelry were sold by emigrées for a fraction of their worth. The Jewish ghetto of Warsaw doubled in size as Russian Jews settled there. Ben and Sol brought Larry to the crowded apartment of Chaim Eliah Starobinetz, who had left Russia several months before, and there they made their plans. The two youngest sons of Abraham Kagan were engaged in smuggling activities. They obtained flour and leather from Chaim Eliah and then ran great risks in getting it back into Russia. Three times they had been caught, twice by the Whites and once by the Reds, and three times they had bribed their captors for their freedom. This was to be their last trip, and Larry, rather than wait for them in Warsaw, insisted that he take Sol's place. "I've come so far; I should see Nishkovitz once more." But when he and Ben departed, leaving Warsaw the morning of one day and thereafter travelling by night, his desire to see Nishkovitz faded in the darkness and cold of embattled Russia.

The water was frozen near the banks of the Berezina and at the center of the river the current flowed quickly. Esther threw a stone into the water. She could not see a house or a person, just the lumber mill Jacob had built years before that stood, burned and scarred, a relic of a former age. She sat down on a stone and rocked back and forth. She heard the noise of a sleigh and turned around.

"Eshka," Motke Bulba called when he was still some distance away. He slowed to a stop next to her and said, "Tonight I'll eat at your house."

"If you like," she said.

"I think tonight you'll cook like you cook only on Passover."

"Because of you?" Esther asked laughing. "I'll cook pig for you."

"In truth, because of me you'd cook pig, but because of Laban?" Motke Bulba said with a grin.

"Laban?"

"Yes, Laban."

"What about Laban?" she asked. "He's in America."

"He's an American," Motke Bulba said.

"That's right."

"In truth, he's an American, but he's here in Russia."

"Laban's here?"

"Not here," Motke said looking all around, "but in your house. I saw him there myself."

"Motke, has he come to take us out?"

"He comes as another Maishe Rabaine. In truth, he comes to take his people out of the land of the Pharaoh."

Esther ran to Motke and clasped his hands. "A Passover

dinner," she said. "The best." She climbed onto the driver's bench and they began to go towards town. "He's dressed well?" she asked after a moment. "He has nice clothes?"

"A prince," Motke replied, "could not be more handsomely dressed. He's a picture . . ."

"He wears a fur coat?"

"A fur coat and a derby. In truth, he's a real American."

She smiled reminiscently and said, "You know, I hardly knew him, but I think he was more like Jacob than any of us. He was beautiful. I've always loved him."

"For his looks and not for his wit," Motke Bulba interrupted.

"He's smart. Why, he's very smart. He once made speeches."

"He's an American—yes, he's smart. But I say you love him more for his looks than for his wit."

"Motke," Esther said impatiently, "you must have studied Talmud. Your reasoning works in circles. Everything you say, you repeat."

"A line has a beginning and an end. In truth, my wisdom is like a circle, now here, now there. I say your brother has little wit, for when he saw his father he said, 'Papa, you look as good as new.' "

"Is that all he said?" Esther asked. "He didn't embrace him?"

"And I said, 'If new means old and old means new, then he looks new. But if new means new and old means old, why then he's not even newly old.' In truth, a saying of great wit."

"You should've been a writer. Listen, go to Paris and study with Shmyola Bernstein."

"That man is a genius, but he too has no wit."

"No wit? Why in truth," Esther mimicked, "you said he was a genius."

Motke scratched the corner of his mouth and, smiling, said, "You have a genius for cooking chickens, Isaac for being a doctor, Laban for being an American, Shmyola Bernstein for writing stories, but . . . Look!" He exclaimed, interrupting himself and pointing to a bird flying over them. Motke watched the bird as it passed them, flying quickly in the darkening sky.

"Your wisdom," Esther said, "I can do without. But I wish you'd get me home."

Motke looked at Esther seriously. "He's going south. There's a genius to that, but in truth," Motke said and smiled, "there's wit in remaining here."

"Now you speak like a Rabbi," Esther said, and smiled.

"Like a Rabbi? A Rabbi would say to follow the current."

The sons of Jacob Kagan, David, thirteen years old, and Yitzhoc, seven, were playing with a group of boys who stopped their game as Motke's horse and sleigh approached them.

"The two boys have divided the corpse of their father," Motke said. "One speaks like a tyrant, and the other has the ambition to be a tyrant. Together they'll be a good American."

"Today must be Saturday, for you to give so much free philosophy. David," she called. "Yitzhoc, your uncle from America is here in Nishkovitz."

"Is it Laban?" Yitzhoc asked.

"Your uncle Laban's come to take us to America. Come home and see him." Yitzhoc ran from the group of boys to the sleigh. "David," Esther called, "aren't you coming?"

"I'm busy," David replied. "Give him my regards."

Esther shook her head, and Motke smiled and touched the reins of his horse. David watched the sleigh go towards the town and said to the boys standing about, "Laban's my uncle from America. He arrived with two black servants. He wears a sable coat, (I bet none of you have ever seen sable or even ermine), and the blacks wear nothing. In the dark you can never see them. They could sneak up on you and . . . ffft!" David said, whipping the edge of his hand against a boy's neck.

"I don't believe it," a boy said. "Americans don't have servants since Abraham Lincoln."

"What do *you* know of America?" David asked. "Have you two uncles there? Of course not; you're just a fool."

"Is he rich, David?"

"He has money," David said casually. "But when he lived in Russia, he worked for my father."

At dinner that evening, Abraham sat at the head of the table. He had brought out a bottle of wine, and now he poured six glasses: for himself, Larry, Mendel, Ben, Esther, and Isaac. Five of the Kagan brothers who had married and had moved with their families to cities, where they lived in small apartments, were absent. Abraham was the only one at the table who wore a hat and, before he drank, he repeated a prayer. Then he listened to his children as they asked Larry questions about America. Esther served hot soup, and Abraham bent his head towards his plate and let the steam mist his eyes. "It's very good soup," he said in Yiddish, when he had tasted it.

"In America they'd call this *delicious,*" Larry said looking at Esther. "Maybe we'll start a restaurant in New York."

Abraham smiled and formed the English word *delicious* in his mouth. There is hope, he thought. Again there is hope. *"Delicious,"* he said aloud and, pointing at his soup and smiling at Larry, repeated, *"Delicious."*

Motke Bulba, sitting alone at a small table at the side of the room, belched once and exclaimed to himself, "God bless you!" Though he often ate in the Kagan house, he never sat at the regular table. He felt that he had to preserve a proper distance from his benefactors. Eating was for him a solitary business; he never talked while he ate, and the only noises that emanated from his table were those of chicken bones being crunched between strong teeth, and loud, rumbling, digestive sounds. His stomach sometimes sounded like a subdued organ.

"The soup's not that good," Isaac said. "As a matter of fact, I think it's not nearly as good as last week's soup."

"I agree," Ben said. "Eshka cooks by accident, and when she wants most to cook best, why then she cooks worst."

Motke Bulba belched.

Each time Motke Bulba belched, Larry looked up, startled, from his food. But the others did not even seem to hear Motke. "It's good soup," Larry declared. "You're too used to good cooking. You should come visit me in Yonkers," he said, nodding his head seriously.

"Your wife's a bitch?" Ben asked.

"She's a fine woman," Larry said, "but she's no cook."

"Ah," Esther sighed.

"No Americans cook," Larry explained. "But that's all right. There are cans for everything, more vegetables than you've ever heard the names of, and there are the niggers to put everything together."

"Black people," Ben said. "I want to see one of them."

"They all look alike, and they smell alike," Larry added, smiling. "You can't tell one from the other."

"Pushkin was a Negro," Isaac said. "Dumas also had Negro blood."

"So?" Larry said.

Motke Bulba belched.

"What's the matter with him!" Larry exclaimed.

"He likes to be rid of gas," Abraham explained.

After dinner, while Motke helped Esther clear the dishes, the others went into Abraham's study. Larry passed around a package of cigarettes and said, "I don't want to stay in Nishkovitz long. In Warsaw, they say the Whites may attack any day."

"In America we'll all be rich," Ben said.

"First, let's get there," Larry remarked. For a moment no one said anything and Larry asked, "How are we going to do it?"

"Maybe we should wait a few minutes," Isaac suggested as Esther entered the room. Motke stood in the doorway, smoking a pipe.

"Why wait?" Larry asked impatiently.

"We must wait for Ragushenko," Mendel answered, tapping his sewn-together fingers on the arm of his chair.

"Who's he?" Larry asked. "Is he coming along too?"

"He was my orderly during the war," Isaac said. "Now he sells to the Bolsheviks. He'll know what's what."

"We can get out without him," Larry said. "The same way that Ben brought me in, we can go out. Don't you know that everyone who comes will cost me a couple of hundred dollars? Dollars and not rubles!"

"Laban," Esther said and leaned on her brother's shoulder, "one day we'll all be together in America. Does your daughter look like me?"

"And Jacob's children? We'll take them, eh?"

"Of course," Mendel answered.

"The oldest one is spoiled," Larry said.

"He sings like an angel," Esther said.

"Where is your orderly?" Larry asked. "We must make plans." He was nervous, not really afraid of the possibility of being in the center of a battle, but restless to return to a place he understood, where he could buy what he wanted.

"Every day for three months, the Whites have been saying they'll attack tomorrow. There's nothing to fear," Mendel said.

Isaac stood up and walked across the room. He wiped the mist off the inside of the window and looked out. After a moment, he said, "Ah, here's Ivan now."

Ragushenko limped into the room and said without greeting, "They'll be here in the morning."

"Didn't I tell you?" Larry asked quickly. "Didn't I say they would?"

"The Whites are even now retreating into Poland."

"The Whites?" Larry asked.

"We'll have to hide the linens," Esther said.

"We can bury them behind the house," Ben suggested.

"Linens? To hell with your linens, let's get out tonight!" Larry declared. "Before they arrive."

"What are you afraid of?" Mendel asked. "*You* are an American."

"They can't shoot an American," Isaac said.

"The Bolsheviks would shoot me *because* I am an American."

"We'll take guns," Ben said.

"I'll shoot all of you!" Larry exclaimed. "We're leaving tonight."

Motke Bulba smiled and Ragushenko walked over to Larry and asked, "My friend, why don't you relax? Now," he said looking at Esther, "I should like some tea."

"It shall be tea," Esther said.

"And for me," Isaac added.

"Even for Laban," Esther said.

An hour later, they decided to leave before morning. Motke Bulba, who had remained silent all during the discussion, was asked to drive them nearly a hundred miles to a Polish town. He held his pipe in his hand and replied, "Such a trip has many dangers. It will cost you a sack of flour for each of you, and one sack for both children."

"If you are afraid," Isaac reasoned, "refuse. But do not charge friends."

"We have no flour," Esther said.

"It can be bought in Poland," Motke said looking at Larry.

"All right, then!" Larry exclaimed. "You take us out, and you'll get paid."

Esther packed silverware and linens and then woke David and Yitzhoc. Isaac took only a cloth bag filled with medical instruments. Abraham packed three suits, his Bible and prayer books; he kept the silver-knobbed walking stick Jacob had given him years before tightly grasped in his hand—he could not leave that behind. He walked through the house, and while the others were still packing and talking, he put on his overcoat and went outside. It had begun to snow. He walked behind the house, and for a moment he thought he heard his wife chanting prayers. He looked up at the sky and feeling the snow fall on his face, closed his eyes and said aloud, "Oh, Merciful, All-powerful, help us! Oh, merciful Creator of the earth, give us safe keeping. Oh, merciful Savior of my people, do not let us forget your gifts." He looked back at the house, and he began to cry. "What a family is come to," he thought. He wiped the sleeve of his coat across his face.

"Abraham," Motke Bulba called from behind, "do you believe the Bible?"

Abraham turned abruptly at Motke's call. He approached him and asked, "We'll have to walk all the way, eh? There's room in your sled only for our packages."

"There's strength in my horse only for an American. But I asked, do you believe in the Bible?"

"I believe," Abraham replied.

"As of this night, perhaps I shall too," said Motke, "for, in truth, if the Berezina opens up like the Red Sea, I shall be convinced."

Abraham said, "It can be done," and seeing in his mind's eye the Berezina running swiftly between banks of ice, he thought suddenly of summers on the river, on huge rafts with big men. "There'll be a way."

"A miracle?" Motke Bulba asked, smiling. "There's wind enough tonight to blow a path in the waters."

"With rafts," Abraham said.

"Then it'll be a miracle if I don't lose my horse and sleigh," Motke said and laughed.

Shortly after midnight, everything was ready. David and Yitzhoc, covered by blankets, lay in the sleigh with packages all around them. Abraham sat with Motke Bulba on the driver's bench and the rest stood about the sleigh. "We should burn the house," Larry said. "The lousy Bolsheviks!"

"No," Abraham said, "we shall not burn the house. Let's go, Motke."

They set out. The wind-driven snow bit into their faces. When Esther turned around to look back at the house, she saw only a dark blur. They stopped at the river for longer than an hour while Mendel, Ivan, Ben, Larry, and Isaac tied together the heavy planks of wood they had carried from the house. They had to unload the sleigh and make many trips before everything was transported to the other side.

"This was no miracle," Motke Bulba said to Abraham when everything was put back into the sleigh. "This was no miracle and perhaps . . . I offer as a suggestion . . ."

"It's too cold even to listen," Abraham said. "How can you talk?"

"In a day, we'll smell fresh bread and eat hearty. With dollars, there is no suffering. You'll go on, but I'll have my flour and return to Nishkovitz with something to make even more profit with."

"What are you talking about?" Abraham asked impatiently.

"Only that I don't believe in the Promised Land."

Jacob could not move his hands; his face hurt where one of the soldiers had hit him. Funny. Several hours before, his prospects had been good. The jewelry might already be in Berlin—out of reach. Everything! Sligorin was insane, no question about it. There was nothing to do. He had been taken to Sligorin's headquarters, a log cabin surrounded by mud huts. Sligorin had offered him a drink and then thrown it in his face. Yes, that madness would pass.

Sligorin entered the hut. Leaning down, he slapped Jacob hard on the cheek. "Look," he said. Jacob's face burned, and his hands strained against the ropes that bound his wrists. "Your last sun, see it, *Zhid!* Tonight, when it gets dark."

Jacob inched himself to a wall and rested his back against it. The redhead Bernstein. Nishkovitz and Abraham and Eshka, his son David. "God!" he suddenly exclaimed aloud. He felt hundreds of things crawling through his hair and under his clothes. Lice. He threw himself flat on the ground and rolled over and over, hoping to throw some off. Then he sat up straight in the center of the hut and clenched his fists.

FIVE

AFTERNOON

I

My hair is long; it is the strength-giving hair of Samson, and it is the gray flowing hair of the prophet Samuel. The features of my face are large, Jewish. I have not the beauty of grace of David, but my dreams have always been to be a David, a singer to God, a Blessed Son of God. Perhaps what has always led me towards the image of David is the joyous and glorious, the sad and beautiful period of youth of the second king of Israel. From the time of my father's heart attack, I lived in an atmosphere of dependency and sickness. During that time, death was an intimate acquaintance. I saw death first when my grandfather Abraham died, then again, and then once more, until the lights of my life were all extinguished.

Abraham died in his bed a year after my Bar-mitzvah. Sweet death, coming to a man in old age, who has lived and had many children and seen much and loved much. Abraham had been my teacher; it was he who taught me to want to sing from far inside me. When he died and all the elegance of his religion, of his black and gray striped trousers, his gray waistcoat and black coat, was covered over by the sod of a Brooklyn cemetery, I knew that though my desire to be a singer was greater than ever, I would not, because of my father's dependence upon the family, because there was no Abraham to insist that I get lessons, be allowed to study voice. My youth had none of the quick joys of childhood. Rather, it was crowded with portraits of failure and guilt. Dear God! I put a piece of scotch tape on the back of my bed-board and caressed it every night before I fell asleep, telling myself that if the scotch tape ever loosened and fell off, my father would die.

That I would not be given voice lessons was an enormous disappointment to me. I suppose that I am now adjusted to the fact that I will never sing professionally, yet, when I think of the immediate and inordinate beauty of great voices, a sadness comes over me that only the joy of listening to recordings by Caruso or Gigli can alleviate. Certainly I shall always regret that I am not a great tenor. Of course, I cannot truly say that even with lessons I could have become a great singer. My cousin David studied voice for years and years and then stopped singing (never singing even in private) when he realized that he was not as perfect as he wanted to be. Who can say but that that might have been my case? I do think, however, that if I had benefited to the full from study and practice and found that I had not developed and could never develop all the greatness I desired from my voice, I would still have gone on. I find it satisfying in the extreme just to sing, and most disconcerting (though not to the point of silencing me) to be told, as I often am, that perhaps I once sang well. Music has always been necessary to me for the pleasure I derive from it, and when I find a theme that intrigues me repeated and expanded until it is transformed through its construction and spirit into a feeling that controls me, why then music is as important to me as my very life.

David, whose single aim for many years was the attainment of perfection in his own singing, identified his voice with wealth and prestige. When he realized that he could never be a successor to Caruso, or even a replacement for Nelson Eddy, that though he might sing phrases as beautifully as Caruso, he could not sustain that beauty even through an aria, and when he realized that further study and practice could not help him, he threw everything to the winds and with family assistance started a small business in which he went bankrupt after several bad years. A month before Pearl Harbor, he was drafted into the army and, five years later, discharged as a sergeant. He went to work in a minor capacity for Ben Cohen and Company, where his brother Jack was already a partner. From the time that he gave up singing, his history became that of a failure. He had once had a great ambition, and having failed in that, he failed in everything else he tried. Because of my desire to sing and David's experience as a singer (his voice was always referred to by my family in the most extravagant terms—their reason for his giving up voice training was what they called, variously, artistic temperament, laziness, and lack of ambition), I began to think of myself as another David, as one who had tried and had failed.

I went to work in the liquor store when I was sixteen. It was like being inside a box eighty feet long and fifteen feet wide. A yard-wide counter ran the length of the store, and under the counter and on the wall behind it was kept the stock. The desk, telephone, and books were at the rear, near the staircase leading to the balcony. My mother did most of the work behind the counter, selling individual bottles, packing and unpacking, dusting and cleaning. David had installed an extension phone in the balcony, and he sat upstairs a great part of each day. In the first year that they had had the liquor store, he had made phone calls for hours at a time, trying to get business from his own friends, friends of the family, and friends of friends of his. He would be out the remainder of the day, seeing those people who had, in even the slightest way, responded to his phone calls. But later, when there seemed to be no solution to the poor state of the business, he made shorter outside visits and fewer phone calls; he spent his time in the store relaxing in a beach chair on the balcony. Every afternoon, I went directly from school on the lower East Side to the liquor store in midtown. I often delivered liquor to Larry's, Ben's or Sol's place of business. Each of my uncles kept large selections of expensive Scotch whiskeys and domestic bourbons; buyers from department stores all over the country enjoyed my uncles' hospitality. I would sit in their offices and listen to the never-ending streams of gossip of the models and bookkeepers until my mother would phone. A fifth of Cutty Sark for Mr. Schwartz in the Exchange Building. Hot crowded streets. Street corners with unemployed men standing about, talking among themselves. Small businessmen arranging deals two feet from the gutter. Mr. Schwartz would take the bottle and pay cash, or write out a check, but most often just sign a carbon of the bill and shrug me off with his signature. Me? I was a kid to whom one might or might not give a tip.

Back in the store, David would ask me to get him a package of cigarettes. A Negro, staggering, peering into the store through the window, was a vulgar reminder of the trade we were in. I was the son of a doctor! I felt trapped by the liquor store and by my father's sickness. The Cohens' air-conditioned showrooms were cathedrals of success, and I did suddenly want success. When I heard stories of my cousin Jack, or when he came on a Sunday to visit us in the East Bronx, I considered it a particular treat. His success was not the success of the City College accountants and lawyers, but the success of the millionaires, the real conquerors!

Sundays were special days for my parents and me. In the morning, neighbors, former patients of my father, or friends visited us. Horowitz, the vegetable store man, came every Sunday morning, wearing his one dress suit, and stayed until shortly before lunch. He had discussions with my father in which he passionately revealed himself as he did at no other time. They might be talking about Israel, communists, or Harry Truman, and though there hardly ever was any difference in their opinions, Horowitz had to make it seem as if there were. Then, when in the course of half an hour, he had restated what my father had originally said, or had agreed with, Horowitz would ask, "So, do you see why I say Truman is a wizard?" My father would nod his head once or twice but then ask, "But what do you say about his sport shirts and fishing trips? And Margaret, you might say she has a pleasant voice, but she's no singer." Horowitz would then have to go through long and involved explanations of just how Truman's sport shirts and fishing trips, and even his daughter Margaret, bore out his opinion that Truman was a wizard. There were two other men who sometimes visited us on Sunday mornings: Mr. Matter and Ivan Ragushenko. Matter was a pinochle player, and one might have thought that that was his sole occupation. He had started playing cards regularly with my father twenty or twenty-five years before, when he had been a friend of one of my father's colleagues who was now dead. What pinochle games they had had then! They had played three-handed pinochle one night every week. During the playing of a game, if anything was said by an onlooker or a participant, the violator would be fined fifty cents. All of the players, except Matter, who was a jeweler, were doctors. Once, one of the doctors had a heart attack during a game and died before the evening was over. The following week, another doctor had been invited to take his place. My father, afraid now of overexciting himself, generally played only a two-handed pinochle, a much slower game, during the progress of which he could even talk to Horowitz. But if Ivan Ragushenko visited us, as he sometimes did on Sundays, why then there would be no pinochle and only talk. Matter would invariably leave a short time after Ragushenko arrived, knowing that my father had finished with pinochle at least for the morning.

There were strong ties between Ragushenko and my father and even Horowitz. They spoke in Russian, and that language was more than a means of communication—it was a source of pride. No matter how much my father protested that he was an American, nor how much he believed in the Zionist cause, his strongest feelings of nationalism were associated with Russia. For him there was only one literature, that of

Pushkin, Gogol, Tolstoi, Turgeniev, Tchekov, and Dostoievski. If he read a naturalistic French or American novel, he would compare it unfavorably with Gorki, whom he admired far less than the others. My father was a Jew in his feelings of identity with the victims of persecution, but when he felt uplifted, why then he was a Russian. While the three men sat in the dining room and talked, I kept the door of my bedroom open and listened to their voices, to hear their language which I did not understand but whose strength and beauty I loved.

After Sunday lunch, there was a respite for several hours. My father listened to the radio and rested, my mother visited a friend and I went cycling. No later than four o'clock, the family visitors would begin to arrive. Nearly every Sunday my mother's family came to see my parents. Morris (Mendel), Ben, Sol, and Sam, and their wives and children were regular Sunday visitors. Larry and his wife came once in several weeks, as did David and Jack. I left the apartment in the early afternoon before anyone had arrived. A Puerto Rican had opened a bicycle store on Lafayette Street next to Zack's candy store, and I rented an English racer from him.

I walked the bicycle to the gutter. Then I rolled up my cuffs and got on. Lafayette Street, after it crosses Faile Street, slopes down in a series of short steep hills that ends only a little before the Bronx River. I started down. The wind swept past me, whistling as the bicycle picked up momentum. I did not apply the brakes until I reached the street that ran parallel and adjacent to the river. Then I coasted for several blocks. Later, I stood by the river. I saw flames spurting out of the huge brick chimney of the Gas Company and dissolving into smoke. Everything was still. Behind me there was a metal works and two scrap depots, all deserted. The afternoon sky, except for a few stray clouds, was pale blue. I stood the bicycle against a tree and walked onto an obsolete, crumbling dock that jutted out several feet over the river. I sat down on the far edge, my legs hanging in the air, and began to hum a song Abraham had taught me. I dreamed of soft riches. Distantly I heard the sound of automobile horns. I lit a cigarette and looked at my reflection in the water beneath me. I saw a rubber prophylactic suspended on the surface of the river and then I saw others. The water was filled with wastes. It suddenly seemed to me as dirty and as crowded as all of the East Bronx.

When I returned to the apartment, my uncle Morris' Buick was parked outside. "So, what's new?" I asked Morris and Rebecca as flippantly as I could.

"What should be new?" Morris asked, turning to face me.

"The state of the world. The communist menace."

"Sam's a smart aleck," Rebecca said to my father.

"An aleck he may be," my father said and then asked me, "Don't you have any homework?"

"Did it," I answered. "All done 'cept for current events, which I s'pect to get now."

"Read the Times," my father said, "it has all the news."

"That's fit to print," I added.

"Dope!" my father exclaimed. "What's got into you?"

"The end of summer," my mother answered for me. "I think he's learned to drink whiskey in the store."

"He's learned to smoke, I know that," my father said. "If you're going to smoke in the bathroom, at least don't burn the plastic on the hamper."

I blushed.

"It's bad for your health," Rebecca said sharply. "He smokes to be a big shot."

"All the boys smoke," Morris remarked placatingly. "Leave him alone, he's a good boy." My embarrassment grew.

"When he sleeps, he's a good boy," my father rejoined. "When he sleeps, he's quiet, he doesn't snore, he doesn't joke, he isn't moody, he doesn't even sing."

"If he could," my mother said, "he'd sing even while he slept."

"How stupid!" Rebecca exclaimed. "He's no singer."

"His voice was good," Morris said. "When he sang his portion at his Bar-mitzvah, he sang fine."

"He's not a baby any more," Rebecca said to her husband.

"No, I'm not a baby," I declared forcefully, like a man, I thought, and walked out of the room. I shut my door. Maybe Jack would visit us today. I would wait for Jack. I lay down on my bed and clenched the bed sheets. Then I listened to recordings of *La Bohème*. Rebecca could not compare to Gigli.

By five o'clock, all my mother's Cohen brothers and their families, and David, who was a bachelor, had arrived. The children were in my room and the others, the elders, sat in the dining room around the large table, under whose glass top they could easily find pictures of themselves. In one photograph, taken in 1921, when my uncles and parents arrived here, Larry, Morris, Sol, Ben and Sam, and my mother posed about their father. In that photograph, I saw unmistakable indications of each of their characters. Abraham so stiff and elegant; Larry looking directly and belligerently at the camera; Morris, the biggest of them all, taller even than his father, unable to smile as if he had already known what kind of woman he would marry; Ben, handsome in a careless way; Sam, smiling thinly to the left of the camera; Sol, looking for all the world like a gangster, or gambler at least; and my mother smiling, with her hands on the shoulders of Abraham, as if life would be nothing without touch.

Jack and his wife Gloria were the last to arrive. Gloria was wearing a mink stole that she did not take off until it was roundly admired. I hung it up and brought out two folding chairs. Jack smoked a cigarette in a silver filter holder and said (when he had entered, all discussion had been immediately transformed into greeting), "So I tell you, things are looking up." He grinned and waited for a leading question.

(Jack's rise in the shipping business had been by no means meteoric, nor did Jack ever reach the pinnacle of success that would have established him as a great shipper. Those great men, virtually all Greeks, each owned fifty to a hundred ships. When rates were low they put their ships in dry-dock and brought them out only when there was a chance to make sizeable profits. Whatever success Jack achieved came through endurance, patience and subtle struggle. In the course of the four years after the family's purchase of the ships at outrageously low prices, to the time of the Korean crisis, Jack developed a set of ulcers that made it painful for him to indulge even in light social drinking. During those four years, he had a small cubicle in the headquarters of a Greek who ran, sometimes with Jack's advice and more often without, the family's three ships as well as perhaps fifty that he himself owned, and another twenty whose owners had, like my family, made contracts with him to run them. This Greek, who was called John by everyone who knew him, not so much for democratic reasons as for the sheer impossibility of anyone but a Greek being able to pronounce his last name, was not only a captain of the shipping industry, but a cultured patron of the arts. This was clearly indicated by his fastidious appearance and the cocktail parties he often gave in his Park Avenue apartment that were attended by Greek symphony orchestra conductors, Greek sopranos (there were several in this country) and visiting dignitaries. He once said to Jack, "I tell you Jack, you worry too much. Business is business, but friends is for pleasure. You, Jack, I like you and I want you should enjoy life. You come my apartment and meet my wife, she sings like to no one, like bird. I want you, Jack, should trust me. Maybe," he said sincerely, "if you see me home with friends you should like me like friend."

"John," Jack replied, "I not only like you, but I admire you. But to tell the truth, I wouldn't trust you as far as my nose."

John laughed and said, "Jews should not be so smart. Always afraid even friends should cheat you."

Until the Korean War, Jack remained as a partner in Ben's firm and worked there afternoons. Mornings he spent in his cubicle at the Greek's headquarters on Broad Street, examining expenditures and contracts. Often he found purchases charged to his ships that the Greek had bought for his own ships, and when he would go into John's office and tell him, John would shake his head and say, "A mistake, sorry." Jack never told John that he thought these mistakes were intentional. The men played a game, with Jack always on the receiving end; he had to discover the mistakes. Business was not very good during those years and, because of that, even when Jack thought that he knew enough about shipping to run the family's ships himself, he kept his ties with the Greek, knowing that though the Greek took a percentage of the money the ships made, it was only through the Greek's domestic and international connections, his uncanny ability to get freight, that he, Jack, could break even. But when the war began, Jack broke with the Greek and, on easily obtained government contracts, started to make a fortune to be measured, not as it had been with Larry, who was the wealthiest of my uncles, in tens of thousands or fifty thousands, but in half-millions!)

My mother looked across the table at Jack and said in response to his first remark, "Things have looked down for too long."

"America's a great country," Sol said. "Just think of when we came here," and, looking at me, he said, "We had nothing, greenhorns."

"America's fine, but watch those cut-throat Greeks," David advised his brother. "They'll give you a screwing while you aren't even looking."

Gloria laughed embarrassedly and Rebecca looked at David with distaste.

"A screwing's not so bad," my mother said, "but I don't want your throat to be cut."

"When do we start getting dividends if everything's so good?" Rebecca asked. "That's what I want to know."

"No dividends for you, you frigid bitch," I said under my breath.

"My dear aunt," Jack said, "you're impatient, and though impatience may prove profitable to some, I prefer to use my head. Logic!" he exclaimed. "Logic," he repeated slowly and adoringly.

I smiled at Jack.

"You have all our money and all we get is logic," Rebecca

insisted, staring at Jack. She spoke precisely; she never had any difficulty expressing herself, and the quality of what she expressed was equalled only by the way she expressed it. "Morris gave his insurance to the bank. What would happen . . ."

"The shipping industry's on the way up," Jack interrupted. "I'm going to make every one of you rich, even you and Assoc," he said making a sweeping gesture with his arm and addressing himself for a moment to my mother. "Understood? I want to use the recent profits to buy a new ship. It'll cost close to a million. We can put up two hundred and fifty thousand, borrow two hundred and fifty thousand from the bank, and the government gives us a mortgage on the rest. Two hundred fifty thousand for a million dollar ship," he concluded smiling.

"You can't buy!" Larry exclaimed.

"Wait a minute," Jack said. "Just a minute, and listen. Do you remember? Logic? Logic! Relax and let me tell you." He spoke easily, referring every so often to notes he carried in his coat pocket. He explained the picture facing the shipping industry and said finally that only if the war was brought to an immediate end could they stand to lose. Sol, of all the brothers, seemed convinced. He whispered something to Ben, and when Ben didn't answer, he looked around the room and announced, "Yitzhoc, I'm with you. I've always been ready for a big gamble. America's a place for gambles."

"It's no gamble," Jack said, "it's almost a sure thing."

"Almost a sure thing?" Morris repeated. "How sure is almost?"

"Mendel, it's sure enough for me," Sol insisted to his brother Morris.

"Me," Ben said, looking from Jack to Larry, "I think this way. Jack knows his business better than any of us. He's a smart boy, and he knows what the chances are. All of us elected him, we chose him to make his own decisions."

"But not to lose our money for us," Larry said.

"Ach, you've another hundred thousand in the banks," Sol said. "You'll always have money."

"I do have, and I don't want to lose it," Larry said fiercely. "My money is from forty years of work, forty years!"

Ben smiled and said, "Jack hasn't lost it yet."

"Too much money's bad," David said. "What can you do with money in your pocket? Here's a chance for money to work."

"But it's my money, not yours! What money have you at risk in the business? None!" he exclaimed, answering his own question. "You're just a nephew."

"A brother," David said. "A brother," he repeated, "without money. If I had a million dollars, everything I said would be gospel, but as it is, you don't even listen."

"You talk enough," Rebecca said.

"Enough or not enough, he's my nephew and I'll listen to him," Morris said, tapping his sewn-together fingers on the glass table-top.

"Sing?" Larry asked. "Is he going to sing?"

"Have you forgotten whose sons they are?" Morris asked angrily.

"No!" Larry exclaimed. "No! No! No! I haven't forgotten, and neither has he," he said, pointing at David, "nor he," he said, pointing at Jack.

"You all spoiled them," Rebecca said. "Do they know what real work is? Any of them?"

"Now listen to me," Jack declared, "if I hear another word, I'll leave. Do you hear? Just another word." He paused and said, "I came here with a victory. Through the shipping business, each of you've made more money in a month than you'd make in a year. I want to make more money, and I know how to do it. Are you afraid of money? Do you hate me because I'm like my father?"

"Oh, my God," David thought. "He is. No. But he is."

My mother said, "Well, I like money and even though I've none, nothing at all in the ships, I want my brothers to have money. Maybe they'll buy me a new store."

"All right," Ben said to Jack. "It's your decision, and we'll go along with it, but take a warning. In thirty-five, I overbought, and the same year I had to raise money. What good was all the material I had when there were no orders for dresses? What good? Remember Yizhoc, I travelled all over the U.S.A., from left to right, north to south, Chicago, Los Angeles, New Orleans, Texas; each place I went, where I thought I had friends, I had to cry, me, a grown man, a manufacturer, in front of people whom I'd been friendly with, who wanted only to cut my prices, to get my goods at half of what they were worth because they knew my position. Remember that."

"Sure I'll remember," Jack said, "and you remember who it was who advised this new purchase. You remember it and keep it in mind, and say it was Jack, Mr. Jack Cohen, for because of it, you're gonna be millionaires, and I'm gonna be as big as the Greeks."

Everyone except David had left. He sat with my parents in the dining room and addressed my father. "Assoc, every now and then I get headaches, in the back of my neck, as if all the muscles were stretched taut, tighter than they can bear. Always I know it's psychological, that if only I could solve some problem, even a small one, the tightness would ease up. But I never can do anything; there never seems to be anyone around to help me."

My father looked reflectively at his own hands and my mother shook her head and said, "You need a wife, a woman who loves you. To rub your neck," she added, laughing.

"A wife? Who should I marry?" David asked. "Someone like the beautiful women my uncles married? Someone intelligent like my brother married? I leave that to a stronger man. I have enough as it is." He nervously smoked a cigarette and putting it down in a glass ashtray, he said, "How can I love someone else, when I hardly know myself? Who am I?"

"Philosophy you talk," my mother said. "Speak of women, not philosophy."

"It may be a question of relaxation," my father suggested. "Do you sleep well?"

"Hardly ever," David answered. "I can never stop reliving the day."

"Maybe in music," my father said. "You always loved music."

"Music?" David repeated. "Assoc, do you know what happens to me each time I hear music. Do you see the agony of my name? Cohen," David said disgustedly. "Ah, what beauty there might have been."

"If you don't sleep, at least you dream," my father said sympathetically. "You're a romantic."

"No I'm not!" David exclaimed and looking around the room he spread his arms and said, "There they sat. Every one of them. All my uncles, their wives, those women. Oh, my God! Oh, Assoc and Eshka, oh Assoc and Eshka, I'm lost!"

"You speak like an idiot," my father said firmly. "You still have the liquor store; there's some hope there."

"No hope, Assoc. Eshka knows. Listen, without money I'm worthless. When I'm with the family, I'm sick. There's only one way to live with the rich or the secure, and that's to be rich yourself. Every time I see a chauffeur-driven car, every time I hear of the stupid ways my brother spends his money, the stupid trips they all take, I ache inside."

"It's not for them that you ache," my mother said, "it's for yourself."

"Yes. That's true, but so what? How else can I think of them? They're my bosses. Everything I do is open to their criticism. They sit around your table like a jury, the elders who can do with me whatever they like, whose wives despise me. Yes, they do despise me, I know that. Oh, God, what am I to do?"

"Learn to live your own life," my father said. "That's what. You're young yet . . ."

"My life's over," David protested.

"Shut up!" my father exclaimed angrily. "I'm sick. I can't leave the apartment even to take a walk. You still have a life.

Learn to teach. You can teach Russian. Try harder with the liquor business. Do something, but do it, and if you can, do it well."

2

After his attack, my father often considered the possibility of opening an office in which he would work only a few hours a day. Colleagues of his suggested that he become a diagnostician; they had full confidence in him. In the autumn of 1950, he felt comparatively well—(he could walk a block or two, or stand on his feet for an hour)—and went ahead with plans to open a new office. He wrote to the insurance companies that were sending him disability payments every month, to ask for permission to have a trial peiod to see whether or not he could work even the few hours he planned to work every day. A colleague located a medical office with an adjoining apartment in uptown Manhattan, and my father arranged to take the apartment and office in two months, months in which he wanted to build up his strength. Then he ordered equipment, but that was as far as he got. His period of feeling well was the calm before the storm, for suddenly, near the end of the year, he found himself unable to retain his food; he had sharp pains in his stomach and frequent palpitations about his heart. Gradually, he was weakened, until he could hardly leave his bed. All his plans and hopes were forgotten; he was sicker than he had ever been.

One day, my father was visited by three doctors, one of them an internal specialist. They talked with my father for a short while, and then the specialist gave him a rapid examination. "It's a liver condition," he announced. "Nothing more." When the doctors left, my mother accompanied them to the street door.

My mother worked in the liquor store now every day only

to noon. The responsibility of running the store fell to David and partially to me. In the mornings, my mother and I travelled downtown together on the subway, she getting off at Thirty-fourth Street, and I continuing to Fourteenth Street, where I went to school. Sometimes, on the express train, my mother might see the narrowest space between two seated people, and she would excuse herself and make them push apart until there was enough room for her to sit down. Then she would take her knitting out of her bag and smile at me. I rarely returned her smile. Sometimes she read the Yiddish daily "Forward," and then if she would smile at me, I would look in another direction, at an advertisement.

The morning following the visit of the doctors, my mother and I went downtown together. At Eighty-sixth Street, when the train had come to a stop, she said, "It's cancer." The train started, and all the resolution that had kept that knowledge secret even for the one day, dissolved under the awful roar of the subway. "Nothing can be done. Don't tell anyone, Sam. Don't tell him. He said he'd kill himself if he knew."

MOLDED TO PERFECTION . . . FILTERS YOUR SMOKE . . . THE GENTLEMAN'S GIN, GO SEE . . .

She was crying.

"Nothing?" I was finally able to ask.

She began to sob, and she put her arms around me and leaned against my side, her body shaking.

When I got home that evening, I went into my father's room. He had always been thin, but he seemed especially so now; his elbows made sharp points in his pajamas. He lay on his bed with three pillows propping him up. "How was school, Sam?"

"Okay."

He spat into a basin on the floor.

"Lucky you're not outside; you'd be fined five dollars each time you spat," I joked.

"Maybe you can find something more convenient for me than this basin," my father asked. "It's uncomfortable to have to bend over every minute."

"I'll go and look," I said, having hardly any idea at all as to what my father wanted, but thankful for the opportunity to leave the apartment. I walked outside and, without thinking, went down the Lafayette Street hill towards the Bronx River. Solitary electric lights hardly penetrated the darkness; cold winds blew scraps of paper spiraling in the air. As I stood by the river, I looked up at the sky, then slowly lowered my gaze until I stared at the water. I was shivering. I would be able to talk with my father all right, but how would I be able even to look at my mother? I walked back up the hill to Hunts Point Avenue and entered a drugstore. After I had tried to describe what I wanted, the pharmacist brought out a small tray and then a plain glass cup. I bought neither of them and went from drugstore to drugstore. More than a mile from the apartment, off Southern Boulevard in a Puerto Rican neighborhood, an elderly pharmacist nodded his head. "Cancer?" he asked. I hesitated a moment and answered, "No, T.B.," not knowing why I should reveal my secret to him. He showed me a dusty, conical cup. Its nearly circular rim was indented in order that the cup might be pressed into the cheeks and chin. There was a small handle on the side of the cup and at the bottom of the handle there was a device that when pressed down, drained the cup. The pharmacist explained that to clean the cup all that was necessary was to keep the device pressed down and to run water right through it. "Just the thing, eh? They don't make items like this any more," he said proudly.

"How much is it?"

"Two-fifty," he said. I paid him and he took the cup to wipe off the dust. He came back in several minutes. He had polished the cup until it shone. "Like new, eh?"

I brought the cup home. My father inspected it and spat into it. He kept it at his side continually.

It was cancer of the liver. Because of the advanced state of the cancer and his heart conditon, the doctors would not operate on him. No one ever told him, but he knew. He knew he was dying. How long? I wanted to ask the doctors. One, two, six months? And if I asked, would it help? Help whom?

Not him. My father could sleep only a few hours at a time. He was always under the influence of some narcotic, and most of the day he was only semi-conscious, rarely recognizing or speaking to visitors. There were too many people. They pitied his wife and they invaded his bedroom, but their claims of love and sympathy were made fraudulent by their numbers. My mother's brothers and their families came often to visit. They sat around the dining room table and as usual talked of business and drank tea. They all knew that he was dying, but accepted the knowledge only on the level of fact. To understand would have meant commitment to despair and sorrow. As individuals, some of them understood, certainly Ben and Morris, but in company or at business, there was no room and no time for such understanding. The final day, the day of the burial would be time enough. With sad faces, friends and relatives came from all the boroughs. They entered the apartment, and when they met cousins or friends they had not seen for a time, they smiled and talked about themselves and said, "Isn't it a shame we never see each other except on sad occasions?"

I wrote a letter to my father's brother, Grisha, in Paris, informing him of my father's condition. Four days later, I received a cablegram that he was flying with his wife Olga to New York. Ben made reservations for them at a hotel and, when they arrived, Ben and I met them at the airport. What a far cry from their last reception! Then, in 1945, immediately after the end of the war, they had come here for a short visit, and over a hundred happy, crying relatives and friends had crowded the airline waiting room. Now they were both tired; Ben drove us directly to the apartment. My father and Grisha wept as they greeted each other.

One night, I was awakened by my father's coughing. I got out of bed and went to his bedroom. My mother was wiping his mouth and, when he saw me, he brushed her hand away and said, "Sam, Sam, what do you want to say? What do you want to say?"

"Oh, Dad," I wanted to answer, "oh Dad, Dad, Dad, I'm

with you! I'm with you!" I stood there and said nothing. His eyes seemed to be staring straight through me, seeing everything.

Grisha slept at his hotel, but otherwise he was constantly at our apartment. One Saturday morning, when my mother, who had not slept during the night, was trying to sleep in my room, and Grisha and I were sitting in the dining room, Jack and Gloria came for a quick visit. They had a luncheon appointment in Great Neck and stopped in on their way to the Whitestone Bridge. They went into my father's room and stood for several minutes, watching him. He spat into his cup and Gloria drew back. "Don't worry," my father said, "I'm not spitting at you." Jack laughed and asked him if he were feeling any better. My father did not answer; he had lapsed into the coma-like state he was in most of the day.

"I'd want someone to kill me," Jack said when he came into the dining room.

Grisha nodded his head. "I don't know," he said. "Bernstein often says that life is a process of dying."

"Bernstein's a fool!" Jack snapped. "To lie there like that," he said pointing to my father's room.

"Mercy killing," Gloria said.

"Right!" Jack exclaimed. "Seeing him, I believe in it."

"He's so helpless," Gloria said.

"Not so loud," I warned, thinking that my mother might hear.

"Yes. We've got to get going, anyhow," Jack said.

That afternoon, my mother, Grisha, Olga, and I listened to the Metropolitan Opera broadcast of *La Traviata*. With the same fervor that I had wanted to sing, I believe that on that day I wanted to be an opera composer, if only to be able to listen to something I had created given voice by great singers. "Isn't it magnificent?" I asked at the end of the first act.

"Wonderful," Olga said. "In Paris, you know, they rarely sing Italian opera."

"But what other opera is there?" I asked.

"There's Carmen, Manon, Wagner . . ."

"No," I interrupted, "I mean opera."

"Regardless of what you mean," Grisha said, "this is beautiful opera."

"Do you think Dad might listen?" I asked my mother.

"If he's awake, why not?" my mother replied.

I opened the door to his room and tiptoed to his side. His eyes were closed. His right arm lay by his side, his hand holding the cup tightly, as if the cup were attached to him. As I stood by him, the second act of the opera began, and I could hear it faintly. My father opened his eyes and I asked him if he would like to listen. He did not answer and I repeated my question. He slowly bunched his legs up, his knees bent close to his body, and brought his cup to his mouth. He racked his body trying to spit, but could not. He coughed and began to cry.

I could hardly stir, and then I ran out of his room and out of the apartment. Without an overcoat, I walked outside. No more opera; I cried softly. "God! Don't make him suffer. God! Don't make him suffer!"

It was his spitting and his breathing and the horrible reptilian bright-yellow color of his skin that made him, more than a week before he died, become hateful to me. He was no longer my father. I never admitted my hate to anyone, but I believe that my aunt Olga knew and understood it. One morning, Grisha came to the apartment alone and told me that I should get some air. I had not worked in the liquor store for a month and had stopped attending classes a week before. He suggested that I visit Olga at their hotel, thinking that a change might do me good. "Besides," he added, "she's painting, and you can watch the artist at work." The idea amused him and was very agreeable to me.

Olga was wearing a paint-smeared smock when she opened the door. Her dull red hair (she was forty and not unattractive) was uncombed, and she wore no makeup. "Ah, Sam!" she exclaimed upon seeing me, "I thought you were a delivery boy. I must look a wreck," she said, and I smiled. I sat down in a chair facing the back of her easel. "Sam, you never say anything; you have no gift for talk, eh? It's a pity. What weather! Is it freezing?"

"It's not so cold."

"Yes, look there," she said, pointing out the window. "There's a break in the clouds. The sun may come out yet. Maybe we'll take a walk." I smoked a cigarette and she sat down on the window sill and, looking at me for a moment, she said, "Your father was a wonderful man. But, you know, Sam, the one in his bed is not really him."

"What do you mean?" I asked.

She paused and seemed to be thinking. After a moment she said, "Words are really quite impossible."

"I wonder," I said, almost belligerently, and she laughed.

"You see, there are words that cannot communicate—life, death. When you speak those words, they mean different things to everyone. I have my own understanding of life," she said stressing the last word, "because physically I breathe and eat, and esthetically I try to understand it through painting. But death, ah, that is another matter. I can understand death only as absence of life, and without life I am quite lost. I am afraid of death, the dying man frightens me." She paused again, then smiled and asked, "Would you like to see what I'm doing? But do not be too critical. I really dislike critics very much."

At first sight, the canvas seemed to be composed entirely of fusing colors of all shades. I stood embarrassed and unable to say anything until I suddenly distinguished flowers in that mass of colors. I nodded my head in premature approval and then noticed that, almost completely buried beneath brilliant flowers, slightly to the bottom and right of the canvas' center, was a dull white rose. It had three petals that were shaded by the flowers about it, as if the red, yellow and violet colors had been washed into white. In the center of the white flower there were several tiny, dull black spots. It was difficult for me to look away from the white flower. The initial sense of wildness, formlessness, and sheer exultation from brilliance of color that I had felt about the painting, I now knew to be wrong. The white flower, tainted slightly, was, at its center, a denial of color. "It's very fine," I finally said without understanding why I liked it so much.

Two days before my father died, he lapsed into a state of complete coma. His loud breathing sounded like moaning. The doctor said it was due to an obstruction in his throat. It was a continual moan, and the sound permeated the apartment. My mother tried to sleep, as she had from the beginning, in her own bed in my father's room. She walked about during the day, her eyes red, hardly recognizing anyone, all her nerves rebelling against sleepless nights, twitching, collapsing her into a never-consummated hysteria. She cried several times and was then able to sleep, but never for more than a few hours. On the last day that my father was alive, the apartment was filled with relatives and friends waiting for him to die, as if their waiting was an all but final act of love and respect, or as if there were great honor in being present at that specific instant. But by midnight all the visitors had left except Grisha, Ben, and David. One of us was always with my father; David stayed with my mother. At one in the morning, he insisted that she lie down on my bed. She was up in half an hour and went into my father's room.

Every so often there was a longer interval between breaths. My mother and David sat on her bed. She took a wet cloth and gently applied it to my father's forehead. I stared at him. The cup I had bought him two months before was on his night table; no one had taken it away. While we three were in the room with him, he made a gasping sound and then stopped breathing.

From the cemetery my mother, Grisha, Olga, and I were driven directly to the apartment in a hired limousine. The cemetery was in Queens, an hour's ride from the funeral parlor where we had all been that morning, where a rabbi (hired by Ben from the garment industry synagogue) who had never known my father, had never even looked upon his living face, had only seen the powdered white waxen image filled out with fluids which gave the impression that he might have been fat and even jovial, had spoken of *our* loss, and had consoled us with the fact that my father had lived a good life, and had been respected and loved. We had followed the coffin out of the funeral parlor, and my mother had cried. At the cemetery, when they had lowered the coffin into the ground and thrown the first spadeful of soil onto the coffin, she had cried again, and did not stop until we were halfway home. We hardly talked at all. We watched the dull streets we were passing through and I felt cold.

3

For a week following the funeral, my family sat *Shiva*. The custom of sitting *Shiva* seven days was, I believe, originally intended as an observance of a period of mourning.

Certainly, though the same customs are observed by German, Polish, Spanish and Russian Jews, each of these peoples has different interpretations of the traditional customs. At one point in the Passover service the outside door of the house must be opened. The custom originated, no doubt, in the Middle Ages, in the times of the earliest pogroms, when it was widely thought that during this celebration Jews murdered Gentile babies. The door of the house would be left open in order that any suspicious person might see that no one was being murdered at all. The custom was revised when it was discovered that while the door was open someone might steal into the house and hide the mutilated body of a dog or child, leave the house, and then return to discover the body. Today the custom involves opening the door and, shortly thereafter, closing it. In the text of the Passover service the opening of the door is to allow the prophet Elijah to enter and partake of the feast, but the text was written as an answer to four childish questions. In my family this custom denoted in the old country, a show of hospitality: that on the night of Passover above all other nights, everyone was welcome to enter and to join the celebration.

The Russian Jew was unlike all other European Jews; he lived in a large geographic area, a Pale, and within that area had relative freedom. To live in a large city a Jew required wealth, and then he lived almost like his Gentile neighbors. Most of the Russian Jews lived in villages and small towns, rarely experiencing the life we most associate with European Jewry (perhaps because of the horrible and recent history of the Warsaw Ghetto), that of being closeted in a small and crowded section of a large city. The Jewish customs I know, transmitted to me through my grandfather, my parents and uncles, are all social and hardly religious.

The week that we sat *Shiva* provided a transitional period for my mother to adjust to my father's death. It was not a period of mourning, though we did observe the rituals of the custom. Twice a day we repeated prayers, none of my uncles shaved, and we all sat on low wooden boxes—fifteen vegetable crates borrowed from Horowitz.

During this time, we were visited by a continual stream of relatives, friends, and former patients of my father. Ivan Ragushenko was one of the many people who visited us. He came late one afternoon and greeted my mother and Grisha and Olga, and, glancing at me and then back at my mother, he said, "Sam even looks a little like his father, bigger, but his features are honest. He will be a fine man, that is a certainty." My mother served tea, and then the four of them conversed in Russian. Later, Horowitz came in. He was wearing his Sunday, double-breasted, blue serge suit.

"Hello Willkie," my mother greeted him, calling him by the name my father had given him.

"Ah, Willkie," Horowitz repeated, and speaking Yiddish, he reminisced sadly for a moment, shrugging his shoulders the while. Ivan told of his experiences as my father's orderly in the Tsar's army, and Olga translated from Russian to English for me. Once when, during the course of the story, my mother and Grisha laughed, Horowitz smiled wistfully and interrupted in English to say, "Sam, you'll never know what a fine man your father was. Now that he's dead, all you have are memories, that's all any of us have." He looked down at the glass-covered table and added, "Photographs and memories."

Ten days after my father died, there were virtually no more visitors at the apartment. Grisha and Olga sailed for France, my mother returned to work in the store, and living assumed a new routine. For me, the routine began at five-thirty in the morning. I was awakened at that hour every day for eight months by the violent ringing of an alarm clock. Still half-asleep, I switched the alarm off. Then all was silent and, rising from bed, I walked barefoot to the bathroom and washed my face in cold water. Dim, gray light filtered through the Venetian blinds. In the streets, there were a few people waiting for a bus or walking towards the Hunts Point Avenue subway station. When the sun came up, I was sitting on a wooden bench in the orange brick synagogue, my eyes wandering, watching every day the same people recite the same prayers, old country men with white stubbled beards, wearing black skullcaps. A small man in a blue suit, another dressed in torn clothes. None of the men spoke much with each other. After the prayers, they might nod, but then each went about his own business. Castoffs, tolerated in the homes of their sons-in-law or daughters-in-law, unable to get work, doled out an allowance if they had no savings, they had nothing left them but their orthodox Jewish faith.

Photographs and memories.

There was one tall and thin old man who one day, in the middle of the service, cried out and collapsed. The *Shamus*, the caretaker who opened the synagogue every morning, laid him out on a bench and then went downstairs to phone a doctor. The old men did not stop praying, but continued as if nothing had happened or was happening. None of them even glanced at the sick man. I sat anxiously awaiting the doctor. "He might die right there," I thought. When it was time for me to say the *Kaddish,* the prayer for the dead, I stood up and nervously stammered it aloud. "Why don't they look at him?" I thought, and it occurred to me that they all knew death too well. "They are waiting for death," I answered myself. "They all meet here and wait for death," and suddenly I hated them. The doctor arrived and gave the sick man an injection of adrenalin. He died, still in the synagogue. And while the doctor packed his instruments, and the old men finished their prayers, I said to myself, "I shall have nothing more to do with prayers! God, I don't want your charity. I am not a beggar. Strike me with a bolt of lightning! I have pride, at least enough to be a man. Understood?"

And I heard no response. There was no lightning, no sudden gasping—just void. I could no longer go to synagogue, but I never told my mother. I awoke at five-thirty but went directly downtown. Often I did not even go to school, but saw four full-length films before it was time to be at the liquor store. The movies, the Hollywood school of social hope, became my salvation, and, once in a theatre, I found it difficult to wipe my face clean of that idiotic, dream-inspired, half-grin of pleasure. I sat smiling for hours until my muscles ached, and I walked into twitching sunlight.

"Hello, Sam!" The voice of Max Kling. I turned around. "This is the nephew of all the Cohens," Max said to a younger man standing with him. "And this is my nephew," he said to me, "the writer, Jess Kraut."

"Sam Star," I said, introducing myself. He was very thin. His eyes bulged and his lips were almost Negroid. There was a fishy and potent look about him.

"No school, huh?"

"I'm cutting," I said.

"Good for you," Jess Kraut said. A sperm. A veritable sperm!

We taxied downtown together and Jess spoke of Europe. His novel had just been accepted for publication, and he was returning to Paris where he had already lived for three years.

"A mad world," he said. "Max, the only time I really eat well is when you come over. No money for starving geniuses, huh?"

"For a stupid better than for a lazy."

"That's the ticket," Jess said. "But you come over soon, will you?"

"For you I'd never come to Paris, but for the styles . . ."

"And for the women," Jess said, and laughed.

"And what are you talking about? You are the real fucker," he said proudly. "Sam, there iss no vun who der girls like like him."

We parted in front of the building where Cohen and Kling had their factory. On the same street was Larry Cohen, Inc., Ben Cohen, Inc., and the liquor store.

"See you, Jess."

"Sure."

"Where?" I asked myself as I walked alone towards the store. "Where would I meet Jess?" I was on a one-way street, with only a single exit, and that leading into a subterranean straight and narrow road. The road of the Cohens. Silently, inwardly crying, I walked into the store. "I cry for you, mother, for everything that's gone and, yes, I cry for the Cohens because they are the sons of Abraham Kagan and the brothers of Jacob Kagan, and they were and are not now lumbermen. I cry sweetly for us all. Photographs and memories, that's all!"

Friday evenings, my mother and I generally ate at some relative's home. One Friday, several months after my father died, we ate with my uncle Larry and aunt Lily in their large and expensively furnished apartment on West End Avenue. There was a grand piano in the living room, whose single function seemed to be as a table-top on which to place ash-trays and lace. There are homes and there are homes. In our apartment in the East Bronx, if one piece of furniture had been rearranged it would have required weeks to adjust. Everything had its position, its human use. Larry's apartment was as barren as his marriage. The one interesting thing in the entire apartment was a button, a slight bulge under the carpet, that, when pressed, rang a bell in the kitchen. Each time we finished a course, down went my aunt's foot and, seconds later, in came the maid. What a miracle of invention! Snap your fingers, and they run. My uncle Larry was in an expansive mood this evening. He had an arthritic condition that made his neck joint very stiff, and when he spoke to me he turned his entire body sideways in order that he should see me. "What am I to do, Sam?" he asked me laughingly. "When I see a pretty girl, I only see her for a second. Now you see her, now you don't. If I was your age, they'd never be out of sight."

"Maybe you should watch movies," I suggested.

"Ah, movies aren't half so good," he answered.

"Always there's one conversation," Lily interrupted. "Girls! Three models he has all day long, and still at night, that's all he can talk about."

"That's all he can do is talk," my mother said.

Larry nodded his head in mock agreement and Lily said, "Enough already. How was business?" she asked Larry.

"Business is all right."

Lily pressed the button and the maid came in and cleared the dishes.

"Pretty ingenious device, that," I said pointing.

"Oh, everyone has them," Lily said.

"But don't they mind?" I said nodding towards the kitchen.

"Why, they wouldn't work for someone who didn't have one," Lily said.

"Hm," I said and my mother smiled at me. "So tell me all about Paris," I asked Larry.

"What's to tell? Paris is Paris. I like New York. It's crowded and dirty and no work gets done. You go to school, Sam; you know about French politics, it's all a mess. They got styles that women want, so I go for the styles. Believe me, if they had no styles I wouldn't go at all."

"Grisha and Olga want me to visit them," I said.

"Paris is for a man with money. Maybe when you're making a living," Larry said.

"Paris is for bohemians," Lily said.

"Bums," Larry corrected. "They sit all day at bars. I've seen them. American bums."

"In Montmartre?" I suggested.

"Who knows names? All over."

"Pretty girls?" my mother asked.

"Some pretty," Larry answered critically, "some dirty. They don't bathe, not all of them, but in general. I've always said the American girl is the prettiest in the world; her clothes, she's taller and better built. The Paris girls are too thin."

"Girls! Girls! Girls! Girls!" Lily exclaimed. "I went to Paris once, and I went to all the museums. Larry's been there a hundred times, and he hasn't ever gone."

"The museums are for school teachers," Larry said.

"I'm no school teacher, and I enjoyed them immensely," Lily said.

"Me, I enjoy good food, and I enjoy my business," Larry answered his wife. He turned to me and said, "When you're smart, you know what you want."

He left that statement hanging, as if it were a question and I said, "Yes, I guess so."

"What do you want?" he suddenly asked me.

"I don't know," I answered after a moment. "I want to go to college."

"Why?" Larry asked.

"To get an education," my mother answered for me.

"Everybody goes to college," Lily explained.

"Study business?" Larry asked.

"I don't know," I answered. The New York City success story: City College at night and a lawyer or accountant in ten years.

"Study business," Larry said. "Then you can always make a good living. Life's hard when you've no money. That comes first. A good living. Jack may not be smart, but he's got ambition, and look at him and look at Dave. Jack lives well, Dave's not even married."

When we left the apartment and were walking to the subway, I said to my mother, "I hate West End Avenue Jews. They're all fakes."

"So what's real?" my mother asked.

"I don't know. People who sweep the streets; you know, laborers. They work with what they have . . . or maybe a person who works for an ideal, like a doctor."

"And everyone else?" my mother asked.

"Not everyone," I said impatiently. "No, sure there are some others, but these people," I said spreading my arms dramatically until I felt that both spiritually and physically I had encompassed all of West End Avenue, had seen the truth of it, "they don't do anything real. Why, they don't even make the dresses they sell!"

He heard their drunken shouts. He was not sure whether or not he had slept. An automobile engine was started and then switched off. Waiting. Who would know? Not a newspaper in all the world would record his death; everything was too late. A millionaire acquaintance of his had lost most of his fortune during a depression and had died before he had a chance to recoup. What a legacy he might have left his children!

"It's time." Two soldiers came in, lifted him up and cut the bindings on his ankles. His legs were cramped and his body stiff. His nerves twitched even when a garment brushed over his skin. He tried not to think of the insects. He wanted a bath and he thought about that for a moment.

Suddenly a spotlight was shining in his eyes. He turned around and saw his shadow in the brilliant stream of light. He wanted to run.

"Run Jew!"

He walked towards the spotlight. It was suddenly switched off and another light flashed on behind him. His shadow grew enormous before him. He was a giant walking upon the earth.

SIX

EVENING

I

The new office of the Transatlantic Shipping Corporation was located in a skyscraper near the downtown tip of Manhattan. The office was a single room on the eighteenth story, and its one window faced New York Bay. It was an extraordinary view and it was not lost on my cousin Jack. When he had a problem to consider, he turned around from his desk in his swivel chair and watched ships entering and leaving the harbor. He might stand close to the window and, looking down, see incredibly small people and automobiles on the streets below, as if life down there were all in miniature. The office was partitioned, and each half of the room was little more than a cubbyhole, with just about enough space for a desk and chair. The partition did not fully divide the office; there was room enough to walk from one cubbyhole to the other. On the unbroken wall running the length of the office, there was hung a giant Mercator projection map of the world, with all the shipping routes and their mileages listed. The office, like the map, seemed to be drawn to scale—every inch of space representing not miles but thousands of dollars and enormous sources of power. Jack stood on his side of the partition nearest the window and, tracing a line on the map with his finger, crossed into the adjacent cubbyhole where his secretary was working. "Two thousand six hundred and fifty miles," he said aloud.

"Yes, Mr. Cohen?"

"Two thousand six hundred and fifty miles," Jack repeated reflectively and then looked down at his secretary who had been making out checks. "Get me Washington," he said suddenly, and walked back to his desk. He sat down and picked up the receiver of his telephone. "I want to be connected with . . ." Jack said to the operator and gave her a number. "You there?" he asked after a moment. "Listen. The Victory's gonna be in port without future contract in two weeks. How's it look? Are rates going up?" Jack pressed the receiver to his ear. "Righto," he said, and hung up. He jotted several figures onto a pad and then, picking up the receiver, dialed a number. "Gregory? I'll take it at fifty thousand per for three months . . ." He tapped his fingers on the pad. "No. I said three months." He began to print his name in large block letters beneath the figures he had written down a moment before. "Send the papers to my lawyer. Righto." He put the receiver back on the stand and then called to his secretary. "Aren't those checks ready yet?"

She stood up and, just reaching around the partition, dropped the checks onto Jack's desk. He examined the checks and signed them rapidly, his J and C large capital letters and the rest of his name written almost illegibly. The phone rang in the other office. He folded one check and put it into his wallet.

"Your cousin Sam's on the wire, says you have a liquor bill you haven't paid."

"Tell him I'll see him tonight. Wait, tell him I'll take him and his mother out to dinner, that's if he has a tie."

Jack looked back at the checks. "Pay to the order of Lawrence Cohen, fifteen thousand dollars. $\$15{,}000.\frac{00}{00}$. Signed, Jack Cohen, President Transatlantic Shipping Co." Their first dividends. There was a check to that amount made out to each of his five uncles. The money, Jack thought, would come to them as gifts from heaven; the imaginations, the wildest dreams of none of his uncles could equal the facts of where and how this money had been made. He alone, by secret meetings with small Greek shippers, renegades who no longer wanted to be led by the big Greek ship owners, by weekends on hired yachts stocked with Scotch, caviar, and ham, had fomented a rebellion in the ranks of Greek and American ship owners. He had started and was now chairman of an organization of one hundred and sixty-seven shippers, none of whom owned more than five vessels. He was often in Washington and spoke over elaborately laid tables to Admirals and Senators, Congressmen and self-styled underpaid Government officials about the unpatriotic and selfish, sly machinations of the big Greek shippers. And if he was unable to do much for the members of the organization of small shippers, he was at least always in a position to know the market and to get the best possible deal for himself. "One day," he thought, "I'll write my memoirs. A good idea, it'll sell millions. Money interests everyone. The Memoirs of a Millionaire. No. From Ellis Island to Wall Street, From Nishkovitz to President of the . . ." He called in his secretary, abruptly dispensing with his reverie, and asked her to put the checks in envelopes. "I'll deliver them myself," he told her putting on his homburg. "And call the long distance operator and tell her she can reach me at Larry Cohen's until six-thirty, the Excelsior about eight, and the Mogambo Club after ten."

The brothers Cohen were gathered in Larry's private office. Utter silence had surrounded all of Jack's recent activities, and they wondered why he had called this meeting. The dress market was in a seasonal slump; none of the Cohens had yet received even a single dividend from the shipping corporation. Jack entered and laid his homburg down on a desk.

"So, what's new?" Ben asked.

"Good news," Jack said, and started to reach into his inside jacket pocket.

"Always good news," Sol said. "If I had been smart and bought a farm and invested in chickens . . ."

"In what?" Jack asked.

"If I had invested in chickens," Sol said hopelessly, "at least now I'd have the eggs."

"How do we know our money isn't all lost?" Sam asked.

"This is how," Jack answered, and he gave each of them a check.

Looked good for them; of course I had a tie, and a Parisian tie at that. It had come to me as a gift, along with one hundred dollars, from Grisha, and had been delivered to me by Larry after his last trip to Paris. There were small, dull red designs woven into the rich blue fabric of the tie. I wore it every day for months, its elegance making up for the fact that neither of my suits, one blue and the other gray tweed, both bought for me by Morris, had been made with vests. Ever since I had seen Richard Conte as the lawyer son of the Italian-American banker, Edward G. Robinson, in the film, *House of Strangers,* I had longed to have a vest. Conte was Robinson's one son who was sure of himself, who had the rudeness and strength of his father and sometimes the polish and idealism of a hard-hitting American, and, he wore a vest.

"A vest is for an old man," Morris had said when we were buying the suits. "Everybody'll laugh at you if you wear one." I had not insisted, and I tried to replace that lost item of apparel by always wearing a suit, a button-down or pin-collar shirt, and my one elegant tie. I was then a freshman at Columbia College, and I had recently become a serious student and avowed future journalist; discovering the facts of intrigues and the truth of facts was to be my life. I saw myself as the man in the trenchcoat and tweeds, standing behind the scenes, covering the wars and revolutions, photographing the flag-raising at Iwo Jima, sitting on the aisle—attending first night performances.

In the liquor store one day, David and I had been discussing great philosophers (rarely doing more than mentioning names and attributing to any number of philosophers our own ideas about the state of the universe), and David had declared that Spinoza was a Jew, which statement I had immediately refuted. "Why, he was expelled from the synagogue. He was as much a Jew as Plato was . . . well, a Scandinavian."

"Mr. Edgewater!" David had exclaimed, thereby establishing a new identity and coining a soon-to-be-family-wide-known name for me. "You're just a bystander; you've never dared wade into the sea of life. All you're good for is random facts, and even then you're still uneducated. An American education!" It was very difficult for me to sustain any kind of discussion with David. He would get angry, say something insulting, and then retire to the balcony, where he fell asleep in his beach chair.

My mother rarely took part in our arguments. Just as some members of my family had begun to think of David and me as being equally distressing, my mother found us equally amusing. She was a neutral; but, living off the time she spent in a store where, except for David and me, there was no activity or even noise, as if when the outside door was closed we were quite entombed, she listened to us, sometimes laughed at us, and scolded us when we got angry at each other.

When Jack got to the store, my mother had already left. She had wanted to go to dinner with him but, in the late afternoon, she had had pains in her stomach and had gone home to rest. It was more than a year since the spring that my father had died. The still failing liquor store, the loneliness of being a widow when thirty years of her life had been spent as a wife, the season, her frequent internal pains—all things conspired to make her suspect, to believe so prematurely, that she had the same disease that had killed my father. A month before, she had had a thorough medical examination. Nothing had been discovered, and my mother, angry that she had had fears, angry at herself even for the pains that she continued to have, tried to live as she had recently become accustomed to live; working and visiting, cooking and cleaning, always busy, if only knitting, her fingers always in motion. She ate with relatives often, baked cakes for the people she visited, for birthdays in the family, but found that her pains did not disappear, were not psychological as suggested to her by a doctor, but grew steadily worse. There was hardly a day that she did not suffer. When she left to go home, I offered to accompany her, not wanting to at all, excited by the prospect of dining and perhaps doing the town with Jack, and she said, "Mr. Edgewater, you wouldn't ask if you really wanted to."

"I'm not Mr. Edgewater, God damn it!"

"God has nothing to do with it."

"With what?"

"With your being Mr. Edgewater."

She left and I turned around angrily and walked to the desk at the rear of the store. David leaned over the railing of the balcony and said, "Wake me before seven." An elderly Negro elevator operator from a building down the street came in and bought a bottle of cheap muscatel.

"Sonny," he said to me, "the world's a wicked place, sure as I'm standin' here, but listen to me, the men that has it, them that's richest are the wickedest of 'em all. I jes' drink and mind my own business. I don't bother no one or nobody, but when one of those Jews can come over to me and say, 'Boy, get some seegars,' and give me five lousy cents when I come back . . . I knows you'se a Jew. I'm a Jew also. We're all Jews, but he's the wicked kind. No sonny, it's no way to live like that—automobiles and classy seegars; it's no way to live."

When he left, I did not have to get up from my chair by the desk until Jack arrived. I tried to think of where we would go, of the people Jack might introduce me to, but each time I saw myself so quietly intellectual, so at ease in the company of men of power and women of beauty, I thought suddenly of my mother and what she had said. "We're all Jews," the Negro had said. I was her son. I understood that I had no father and that I was unique among my contemporaries for that fact. I was a college student and almost unique in my family for that fact. Surely. But sometimes, with my mother, I felt that I was nothing more than a clown and an impostor. Whatever beauty and fulfillment I had was in my dreams, less of opera then, but still of singing, of somehow confirming in life the reality, the love and beauty of my dreams.

Only once, when my mother and I went to hear Tagliavini in a performance of *La Traviata,* did we feel that we were in love with each other, that we were lovers feeling neither embarrassment or amusement about each other. It was on a weekday and the Opera House was nearly full. We had balcony seats two tiers above the dress circle, on a side, so that we had to bend our legs and twist our bodies to see the stage. But the music, the voices, the velvet and the warmth made us unconscious of everything and everyone.

"Let's go Shmoel," Jack called, entering the store and, by his call, waking his brother. "Where's Dave?"

"Up here," David answered for me.

"How are you, Sam? The lapels are a little too wide," he said feeling the material of my tweed suit.

"I'm fine. How's Gloria?"

Jack nodded his head and, looking around, he asked, "Where's mother?"

"She went home. She wasn't feeling well. I think she was sick or something."

"I'll be down in a minute," David called from the balcony, and I heard him go into the bathroom where he kept an opened bottle of Scotch.

"What's the matter with her? The doctor said there was nothing there, didn't he? I don't understand it. Does she feel pains all day, or just at certain hours?"

"I don't know. Just sometimes."

"I think it's an allergy. I'll call my doctor and speak to him. As a matter of fact, I'm sure it's an allergy. Does she have any rashes?"

"I don't think so," I answered.

"It could be. Doctors don't analyze enough. If they can't give a shot of penicillin, they don't know what to do. No imagination. Even Assoc never believed in allergies, and you know, they may very well control the whole human system. You react badly to one thing, a smell, a flower, and then everything turns sour."

"I don't believe in it," David said coming downstairs. "She's sick."

"I didn't say allergies aren't sicknesses."

"She's sick inside, either here," David said, pointing to his stomach, "or up here," he said, tapping his head. "There's no question about it," he said definitely. "She's depressed; the store's like a cemetery, and she's forced to come here every day like a widow, like a young widow all dressed in black bringing flowers. If she needs medicine, it's nothing the doctors can give—it's a good-riddance party for the God damned store. It's driving everybody bankrupt anyhow."

Jack nodded his head over his brother's last words and said, smiling, "Dave, you're just looking for an excuse to get out. Personally, I think that the store needn't lose money. This, of course, I've said before, but if I were running this business, there'd be a profit."

"A profit?"

"Brother, I guarantee it!" Jack exclaimed, still smiling.

"First you're a doctor, you diagnose a rash as cancer and cancer as a rash. Yes, she has a cancer and if it's not there yet, it'll be there. The store's eating her up. What would you do?" David exclaimed. "Could you put out a magnet and draw people in from the avenue like flies, could you do that? Like hell! You couldn't do a thing."

Jack faced the shelves of liquor and then turned his head and, smiling, looked at his brother and said, "Patience, David. Patience. I simply meant that I'd be out making contacts all day long, the whole day, and not be sleeping like this was Coney Island. Eshka and Sam could take care of the inside. I'd bargain and pester until people avoided me or bought from me."

"Haven't I done that?" David asked.

"It doesn't look like you have."

David looked fiercely at his brother. Then he walked over to the desk chair and sat down. Jack gave me cash for the bill he had not paid and, while I was ringing it up on the register, David said, "Jack, I have done it, but I'm no good. I'm no

Yiddel salesman. I can't crawl for a dollar, I'm really not a salesman at all."

Jack put the change in his wallet and said, "You haven't given it a real try."

"Jack, I'm sick of it. I'm physically sick. It's no good. Sell the store, Jack. Sell it."

We locked up the store for the day and took a taxi to the Excelsior. Gloria was late, and we waited for her at the bar for a good twenty minutes. I sipped a Scotch on the rocks and nibbled a piece of cheddar cheese. The bar was circular and made of heavily shellacked, rich dark wood. A young and good looking man came over to Jack, shook hands with him, and was introduced to David and me. I forgot his name a moment after it was mentioned.

"She went to Reno," he said to Jack. "A real bitch. I don't know, Jack, but when a *shiksa* marries one of us, she's after something."

I cut another sliver of cheese and wondered what she could be after.

"He's a lousy gin player," Jack said.

"Who's that?" I asked.

"You don't know him," Jack said over his shoulder.

David ordered another drink and looked at his watch.

"No. Eddie owns a couple of movie houses up in Harlem."

"Didn't realize that," Jack said. "I thought he was strictly in underwear."

Jack's acquaintance left us to join his party a moment before Gloria came into the restaurant. She wore a mink coat over her shoulders and was with an attractive girl.

"Hy honey," she said to Jack and kissed him on the cheek.

The girl, whom neither David nor I had ever met, was introduced to us as Sandy Goldberg and she was back in New York from Chicago, celebrating the annulment of her marriage to a furrier.

"This is my brother Dave, and his son, Sam," Jack said to Sandy.

"Is your wifey at home?" Sandy asked David.

"She's been dead the last five years," David answered. "Tuberculosis of the lungs."

"Oh, I'm sorry."

"You needn't be," David said. "It was a marriage of convenience."

"Oh, they're just joking you," Gloria said. "Sam's a cousin, and David's just a bachelor."

We sat in a leather-cushioned booth and ate shrimps and clams, garlic bread, salad, and roast beef and steak. For dessert we had the Excelsior's specialty, shortcake surrounded by strawberries, covered by ice cream and peaches, and everything buried under immense quantities of whipped cream. "Oh, it's too much," Sandy said. "Just imagine what Freud would say . . ."

"What who would say?" I asked.

"Freud," she answered, and then, laughing as if at a very funny joke, she picked up a spoonful of cream. "It's all very anal," she said, looking down.

"Anal?" Jack said.

"What's anal?" Gloria asked.

"Oh, you know," Sandy said and she looked from David to me.

I nodded my head and kept my silence.

"I'll tell you some other time," Sandy said to Gloria.

"It's a dirty joke," Gloria said and giggled. "Let's go freshen up, and you can tell me there."

When they had left the table, Jack said, "She's like Sam; she thinks she's intelligent, but she's all right."

"Intelligentsia?" David said. "She'll be a good wife for Sam; she'll teach him to screw."

"*That* she may not be intelligent enough for," Jack said and laughed.

"Mr. Cohen," the headwaiter, standing behind Jack, interrupted, "there's a call for you."

"Will you bring the phone over?"

"Yes sir," the headwaiter said and, snapping his fingers once, dispatched a busboy to the office. A phone was brought out and connected to a socket in the wall near the floor of the booth. Jack picked up the receiver.

"Yes, that's me." He pressed the receiver tightly against his ear, and made notes on the white tablecloth. "Hold on." He added two figures, divided them by another and pondered over his result for a moment. "Hello. Cable back—Proceed at own discretion. Do you have that? Righto." He gave the receiver back to the headwaiter.

"Who was that?" I asked.

"Western Union," Jack answered. "The S. S. Peter's in a storm and the captain's afraid to go on to Tokyo."

"Why did he cable?" David asked.

"You mean he sent a message right now?"

"An hour or two ago," Jack said, and immediately I saw in my mind's eye a storm at sea, a ship in distress. The captain was pacing in the wheel-room, looking in on the radio operator. Where was his answer? The ship was thrown thirty degrees to each side. And here, at this very table, my cousin Jack was in direct contact with the terrified captain. "If he doesn't make Tokyo and goes someplace else without asking me, he loses his job," Jack said. "He wanted all responsibility off himself."

"And now he can go someplace else," I said.

"Like hell he can . . ."

"But you told him . . ." I began to say.

Jack explained impatiently, "What I said meant go on as directed. Proceed at own discretion means proceed per orders. The cable's for the insurance people so I don't get blamed if anything happens. That son-of-a-bitch's got enough bunkers, he's just scared. If he doesn't make Tokyo on time, I stand to lose twenty thousand dollars."

"It's a big business," David said, as if he were speaking to himself. "It's the whole world."

Jack snapped his fingers and said, "That sort of money's nothing. I've got a deal that'll give me five ships under the Liberian flag, and that, my brother, will be sheer profit."

David saw Gloria and her friend entering the dining room and, leaning over the table towards his brother, he said, "Take me in, Jack. Take me in!"

Jack impressed designs on the smooth, white tablecloth with his fork, and then smiling at David, he asked, "What's the matter with the liquor store?"

"God damn the store!" David exclaimed.

"Oh, it wasn't very funny," Gloria said as she sat down.

2

Evening! the time after day that precedes night; an in-between time that is neither day or night. Images of the darkening grandeur of a sunset, of a terrace overlooking a city river. It is a prelude to sleep, the shutting out of day and entrance of night. It is an end. It is also the first barely discernible star. The evening of my family was prefaced by my father's death, and the acquisition by one cousin and five uncles of large sums of money. Enormous success brought a ten-year-old photograph of Jack Cohen into the pages of Fortune Magazine. He was described as an immigrant who was a captain of industry, a poor boy who now controlled millions of dollars. But the evening of my family arrived, not with success and wealth but, rather, with my mother's dying, the absolute bankruptcy of David, and, with a certain persistent man whose acquaintance we had just made. Jake Levine! It would be almost scandalous to pronounce his name during the day; he was a creature of the night, for me an emissary of darkness. Who was he? A friend of Max Kling, a companion of Larry and Jack Cohen, a retired garment manufacturer, a sometime poet and correspondent for the Ladies Wear Trade Journal. And, at a party tendered him upon his retirement by the most respected businessmen in the garment industry, he had been unanimously voted the title, "Public Schnorrer Number One."

"So tell me, Shmoel, what is a schnorrer?"

THE AUTHOR, ASKED A QUESTION, REPLIES BY WAY OF A DIGRESSION

There are several interpretations. In the old country, a schnorrer was most often something of a beggar; he went from house to house, getting chopped liver here, soup there, bits of meat and bread from all over, collecting everything until he had sometimes a seven course meal, and certainly never less than a full meal. He did nothing for a living but, strictly speaking, he was not a beggar; he never asked—he demanded! He was an adventurer who met all onslaughts, verbal or physical, with a wit that was as sharp as a thorn. All schnorrers were definitely clever, but not all were poor and itinerant. There were some who were famous and even highly respected. Such a one was Chaim Zlotkin of Berlin. Who can ever forget the story of how Chaim, on behalf of the starving Jewish community, went to the palace of the wealthiest Jew of that city, the bachelor, *Reb* Ginsburg, known throughout Germany as a miser whose avarice was equalled only by his wealth, and obtained from him a fortune of five hundred thousand marks?

Chaim Zlotkin presented himself at *Reb* Ginsburg's door every day for two weeks but was not once allowed to enter. *Reb* Ginsburg knew that Chaim was a schnorrer and would ask for money. If Chaim would ask for money, *Reb* Ginsburg would refuse, so what was the point of seeing him? Chaim was about ready to admit defeat, when he had an inspiration. *Reb* Ginsburg was a superstitious man: he observed virtually all of the Jewish rituals and customs. He never touched money on the Sabbath, and if business had to be transacted on that day, he dispatched an assisitant. His kitchen was kept Kosher by a rabbi (who had never been able to find a congregation) who had been hired specifically for that purpose, and it was every day at dinnertime that in his kitchen *Reb* Ginsburg performed his single charity; it was his custom to allow poor Talmudic scholars into his kitchen to be fed. If there was any way to get into heaven, he had been advised, it was through the scholars, the holiest of his people. This last superstition gave Chaim his idea. He disguised himself as a scholar. He obtained a shiny and worn black silk coat frayed at the collars and lapels; he pasted a false beard onto his shaven face. He regarded his image in a full length mirror for hours and, finally satisfied, he walked out of the house where he was staying, his head bent and his shoulders hunched, muttering sounds that might have been prayers. Appearing thus at one of the rear entrances of *Reb* Ginsburg's palace, he was, along with several proper scholars, admitted into the kitchen and seated at a rough wooden table. Chaim sat before his plate and with the scholars made preparatory prayers, but when they began to eat (and they fell to viciously and ate voraciously, consuming thick slices of doughy white bread with everything else that was put on their plates), he continued to pray. When the others had finished eating, Chaim was still praying.

"Eat," one of the scholars said. "Where in all the books does it say you shouldn't?"

"Indeed," another said, "if there are rules on how to eat, on what to eat, and how to prepare food, then the law can certainly be interpreted as saying that you must eat."

"Perhaps you are afraid that the food isn't Kosher?" a scholar asked sarcastically. "You know this is not the Day of Atonement."

Chaim did not say a word. He rocked back and forth on the bench he sat on, and even after all the scholars had gone, he continued to pray. It grew late, and the rabbi in charge of the kitchen spoke to Chaim. "My son," he said, "you must eat now. You cannot stay here all night." Chaim did not answer the rabbi, and when the rabbi snuffed out the candles, Chaim stood up and left the palace. He went home (he stayed with relatives), ate a nine course meal, and the following day at dinnertime, again entered *Reb* Ginsburg's kitchen. For five days, Chaim presented himself at *Reb* Ginsburg's kitchen table and ate nothing.

The rabbi informed *Reb* Ginsburg that there was a scholar coming to his house every day who never ate and only prayed. "An ascetic, a holy one," the rabbi said, describing Chaim. "His eyes are red with hunger."

"Then I must speak to him," *Reb* Ginsburg said. "Perhaps he will die soon and speak well of me."

The following evening *Reb* Ginsburg had Chaim brought from the kitchen to his own dining room. Two places were set. Chaim did not greet his host. He sat and prayed all through the meal; it seemed as if he never even noticed the servant who several times put different foods before him. After *Reb* Ginsburg had finished eating, he offered Chaim a bit of brandy. Chaim did not acknowledge him. "A cigar?" Still no answer. In exasperation, *Reb* Ginsburg slammed his hand on the table so that the silver clattered and the glasses shook and exclaimed, "Why don't you eat?"

Chaim slowly brought his gaze up to the ceiling and said, "Oh God, Oh God, how can I eat when my brothers are starving?"

"Ah," *Reb* Ginsburg exclaimed in apparent relief, "is that all!" And thrusting his hand into an inside pocket, he took out a small purse and threw a coin across the table to Chaim.

"For my brothers?" Chaim asked.

"For your brothers," *Reb* Ginsburg answered. Chaim fingered the coin speculatively and *Reb* Ginsburg exclaimed, "Are they elephants that that isn't enough?" And he threw a bill across the table. Chaim looked at the money.

"Will you eat now?" *Reb* Ginsburg asked.

Chaim looked away from the money, and then again up at the ceiling, and said, "Oh God, oh God, how can I eat when my sisters are starving?"

"There," *Reb* Ginsburg said, throwing another bill. "There," he said and threw another.

"But my mother . . ."

"Is she starving too?" *Reb* Ginsburg asked, and reluctantly threw another bill.

"My father . . ."

"Everyone!" *Reb* Ginsburg exclaimed. "Must I feed your whole family before you eat of my food?"

And at this question Chaim Zlotnick stood up and, leaving the money on the table, calmly shaking his head, walked towards the door.

"Wait!" *Reb* Ginsburg cried.

Chaim turned around and, looking from the ceiling to *Reb* Ginsburg, he said, "You cannot give me enough money. It is too much for a soul like yours. I will fast as long as one Jew in Berlin is hungry."

And in this way, Chaim Zlotnick, afterwards known as the king of the schnorrers, received a draft for five hundred thousand marks, of which he kept ten percent.

Of course there were no other schnorrers quite like Chaim Zlotnick.

Jake Levine was a schnorrer and, according to the financial donations he received, he was more like Chaim than like the poor itinerants, but actually, he was of an entirely different sort—he was a New York City schnorrer. He solicited within the garment section for Jewish charitable organizations. In one year, 1949, when Israel was at war, Jake Levine collected close to a quarter of a million dollars for the United Jewish Appeal. Earning nothing in the way of money for his efforts, he did appropriate to himself the authority of the cause he represented. He went to Israel, his Rome, and was given an interview with David Ben-Gurion, his pope. Never a very wealthy man, his work as a schnorrer gave him quick access to the inner offices of the large firms. If Jake Levine found a manufacturer stingy in his donation to any one of ten causes that

Jake might be representing, rumors would start that that manufacturer was cheap, or, much worse, that he was about to go bankrupt, and soon the entire garment industry would have heard. In certain ways, Jake Levine was a powerful man.

He came to the liquor store one day, several weeks before my mother was told that she had cancer, to ask for money for a Jewish home for the aged in Denver, Colorado. He spoke with my mother for nearly an hour. He told her that he knew that business was very bad, but that this was an important cause. My mother gave him ten dollars and spoke to him about her mother, Heika. They agreed that it was horrible for an old person to have to be put in a home. Several days later, Jake came again, this time just to rest—he said. Then began a serious and high-pressured courtship.

Retired from business (though still active as a schnorrer), a widower living on a small income, Jake Levine thought that my mother, a sister of the Cohens, would be a perfect wife for him. I do not impute dishonest motives to Jake; the fact that Larry, Ben, Sol, Sam, and Morris, if not all acquaintances of his, then all known to him as successful manufacturers, were her brothers, made it simple and inviting for him to conceive of her as his wife. He knew that her brothers' money was not hers, that the store was losing money, and that by now it could only be regarded as having been set up by my uncles as a charitable institution for the benefit of my mother, David, and me. These facts were obvious, and Jake, even if he had not the perception to see them (which perception he most definitely did have), still would have been informed of them, if not by my mother or David (the latter most frank, even anxious to divulge the state of the business), then by anyone of the Cohens' acquaintances, or certainly by his own friend, the manufacturer Max Kling. No. Jake was not thinking of marrying for money, but perhaps the same authority he so naturally appropriated from the charities he represented, he thought might accrue to him from being a brother-in-law of the Cohens. The courtship itself took place in the liquor store. He came by every day at exactly five o'clock, a half hour before my mother generally left, sat with her, and then walked with her to the subway. He was a short, heavy man, with a face the texture and nearly the color of dried, raw leather; he wore bow ties, and every day, in the lapel of his double-breasted jacket, a newly cut rose. One afternoon, more than a week after he had begun courting my mother, I was sitting on the balcony of the liquor store, reading, when Jake opened the door of the store and called out, "I'll take five cases of Chivas Regal; wrap it up and send it out tonight." He always made grand entrances. David was in the bathroom having a cocktail and reading poetry. I lowered myself in my chair, hoping that Jake's stentorian voice would perhaps pass over me and not interrupt my reading. David cautiously opened the bathroom door and leaning out, whispered, "Romeo?" I nodded my head and David locked himself in the bathroom. I began to read again and wished that there was another bathroom. But then, suddenly, I closed my book and sat up; I was a witness to the remarkable culmination of the romance. Jake said, "Estherella, you're a beauty, oh, not like these *shiksas* with cold red lips and cold eyes—your warmth is a fire where I warm my hands. Your heart is made of gold. I know it. Estherella, will you marry me?" he asked, and seeing my mother's amused smile, added, "If you say yes, we'll drink only fizzle water," and pointed to the shelves where we kept champagne.

My mother laughed and said, "Mr. Levine, why should you want to marry me? I have no money, I'm sick, and I have a son to support."

"Ah," Jake said smiling, "a little money I have, and the rest, well, a schnorrer can find from all over."

My mother laughed again and said, "In Russia, when I was a girl, we gave bread to schnorrers, not our hearts of gold."

Jake did not take no for an answer. He persisted in courting my mother, and it was for him, now, a kind of adventure whose progress he kept the entire garment industry informed of. For the time that he courted her, business improved. He made his friends buy from us at regular prices. They did it as a favor, but only as long as Jake played for them the role of lover. The romance ended just before summer, after my mother went for another medical checkup.

I was to meet her at the doctor's office on the East side in Manhattan. A moment after I got out of the subway station, it began to rain lightly. Thinking that it might let up soon, I waited in the doorway of a building. It was very warm and the rain made everything sticky. I felt hot and uncomfortable and wiped my forehead with a handkerchief. The cars going uptown had stopped at a red light, and I saw my mother crossing the street. She had not waited for me. She was walking slowly, and she did not see me. "Mrs. Star," I said, stepping towards her. She stopped and turned, and seeing me, she began to cry. Without her saying it, I knew it was cancer. Three weeks later, she had her first operation.

During the ten months that she was dying, David and I were manipulated like chess pieces in an incredibly slow game. The five brothers of my mother, in reacting to her illness, had become a perfect functioning single engine, sending out emissaries to find new doctors, refusing to believe that death could touch their sister. After several months, when it was apparent that if my mother's death was not imminent, at the least she would be unable to run a business, my uncles decided to sell the liquor store. David had been given up as hopeless, a prodigal. His experience in the liquor store confirmed him as a failure, as a family charity case. I was asked to leave school, to work during the day, and take courses at night.

Ben took me to lunch one Saturday and, while my mother was lying sick in a hospital, proposed to me a future, a future bright with the lustre of silver. "First you stay in the store, only until it's sold, then you work for me, learn a trade, then sell to customers. And, if you're good—the shipping business." Training, a sound basis in the industry in case I was not bright enough to be a salesman. He was gentle, Ben was. He was the gentlest of my uncles and I refused him gently. Dear uncle, there are things I want to do. Dear uncle this is not the time. I sat with him, drinking steaming coffee, and I sensed the coldness that had descended over our table. Afterwards, I came to be regarded by many members of my family as worse than David, a singer without a voice. Those ten months were agony, not simply because my mother was dying, but because I was chained to the store, could hardly breathe in its quiet and vacuity. What a wonderful release it would be if the store were sold! Some days, we had four or five prospective buyers come in to look the store over: widows, retired druggists, fathers looking to provide for their sons-in-law. They came with their accountants, glanced through our books and, shaking their heads, they left. David and I learned to explain our failure by apology, by shifting the blame to my mother. "No," I once said sadly but almost proudly, "she was not a businesswoman."

"Women stink in business," the gentleman with whom I was talking said, not catching my tone, surmising that I was excusing stupidity.

We tried to convince the prospective buyers (and succeeded only in convincing ourselves) that we had failed because of lack of business sense, initiative, and ambition. We gave them access to our yearly books, but withheld from them the frightening figures of the initial investment of my family—nearly fifty thousand dollars. My uncles were asking only twenty-five thousand for the store; they were prepared to take a hundred percent loss, but the price was still too high. It seemed hopeless until the schnorrer again appeared upon the scene.

Jake Levine came, this time as a buyer, a new man full of the vigor he perhaps had had in his younger days. He had plans. My uncle Larry and Jake had been standing outside the store, and Jake had been pointing to the neon sign above the display window, and then at proprietors' names printed near the bottom of the window.

"What do you suppose he's doing?" I asked David.

"What do you think?" David asked as if he knew.

When they came in, it was perfectly clear. Jake Levine was surveying the store as if it already belonged to him. He seemed to be making mental rearrangements of the stock and the counters.

"Here they are," Larry said to Jake, and, looking at me, remarked, "if they had your guts, they'd have made enough money to retire for the rest of their lives. They'd 've been able to read, or drink or do anything . . . but they don't have that one thing."

"They tried," Jake said magnanimously, looking from David to me, but speaking to Larry. "You need foresight, you know. A couple of tricks, some good sense, and lots of confidence—that's the secret."

Lawyers were set to work preparing papers to consummate the sale and for the next month, Jake was in the store every day. Without yet owning the store, he took it over. He received phone calls and visitors all day long; he gave away miniature bottles of brandy to all his friends. Several times every afternoon, he sent me out for sandwiches and coffee, informing me that he kept his weight down by never eating lunch. He occupied the downstairs desk and, sitting there, a cardboard container of coffee near the phone, making notes or studying the books, he looked like a misplaced and harassed bank vice-president. David stayed on the balcony whenever Jake was in the store. "That's the way to make a success," Jake said about David, lifting his eyebrows and nodding his head. "With all the opportunities he's had, I'd be a millionaire. Here," he said after a pause, handing me a letter he had been writing for the last two hours, "this is how to make money."

At the top of the paper he had written: JAKE LEVINE, SCHNOPS-OLOGIST. And then, in almost a full page, he declared that Jake Levine was staking his fortune, his life's savings on the generosity of his friends in the garment industry, and, to quote: "If you have no relations in the liquor business, I'll be happy to fill your order for a case or even for a bottle, be it Scotch, rye, vodka, wine or schlivovitz. Also, I have a special in Bourbon mixed with a little arsenic, particularly good for some of your resident buyers who gave you ulcers this season—God forbid!"

I laughed and handed it back to him.

"A sense of humor," he declared, "that's the way you get business. You see, Sam, I know everyone in the market and they like me. If they don't give me business, who then? They can come in here, listen to a couple of jokes, and spend even as little as five dollars."

For some time, Jake Levine seemed to me to have that extra something. I was firmly convinced that Jake's confident manner and his prestige within the garment section would win for him hundreds of manufacturers who had never bought from us, and that he would make the liquor store a thriving success; indeed, if one can judge by the business he did during the time we were waiting for the actual transfer of ownership, he would have tripled the gross income. But, on the day that he and David were to sign the papers, Jake did a remarkable thing. By this time, of course, we knew him to be quite capable of achieving the remarkable, even expected it of him, though this in no way minimized our present surprise. On the morning of that day, Larry Cohen received a phone call from Max Kling who informed Larry that Jake had gone to Miami Beach, Florida.

"Right now?" Larry asked incredulously. "What does he need in Miami? The papers are all ready."

"Schmuck," Max Kling said, "where did you think Jake would get the money?"

"What money?"

"Money!" Max exclaimed and then laughed. "Money to buy the store with. He hass *kein* money."

"What are you saying?" Larry asked. "You're crazy."

"If I'm crazy, it's because you live in another world, where people without a cent can spend twenty-five thousand dollars like that," he said, and making a strange quick sound over the phone, he hung up.

Jake's hurried departure left us with the store, with a five hundred dollar lawyer's bill, and with an inventory discrepancy of seventy-eight dollars and fifty-six cents, accountable to the number of "free samples" Jake had distributed to his friends.

A month after my mother died, the store was sold for fifteen thousand dollars to a young Italian, the partially paralyzed son of a garment manufacturer. With the sale of the store, David went to work, for a short while, in Ben's dress factory. When Jack's plan for running ships under the Liberian flag materialized, it was decided to send David to Liberia to open an office and establish residence for tax purposes. In all probability, the ships registered in Liberia would never put into a home port. David's job, in spite of the fact that he was going to be listed as President of the Liberian Corporation, would give him no responsibility; the vessels would be run from New York City. He was to be an intermediary, to communicate and sign orders from New York City to the ship captains, to accumulate all profits that would eventually be divided among his uncles and his brother. Though the sale of the store exiled David in a final way, it gave me a new and long-wished-for freedom. I suddenly had time to do what I wanted. I had no commitments to anything but school, and I decided that in two months, during my school vacation, I would go to Paris!

3

David entered the large, modern, slightly curved showroom of Ben Cohen, Incorporated. There were framed reproductions from fashion magazines of Ben Cohen originals hanging as in an art gallery on one wall. The hidden fluorescent lighting, the curved walls and furniture, the wall-covering mirrors at either end of the room, the line of white pine tables, and the thick carpeting would have indeed made the showroom appear strange to anyone not familiar with the high class garment salons of New York City. The extremes in design would certainly leave our hypothetical stranger in a quandary about the function of the room. You obviously could not sleep in it; who would want to eat in it? You would not even want to sit in it, not with all those mirrors. Clearly, this was a special place. On this occasion, it being after five o'clock, its function was purely social. Max Kling and Larry, Sam, Sol, Ben, Morris, and Jack were seated about two tables at the end of the room nearest the entrance. There were three bottles of whiskey, several highball glasses and half-filled ashtrays, and many unsorted copies of Vogue, Harper's Bazaar, and Town and Country, on the tables.

"Here iss the white god," Max announced, his back to David, seeing him enter in the reflection of a mirror. "In Liberia with the niggers he will be king with a throne of gold."

"Ach Max," David said mimicking him, "what iss it you are doing here?"

"I come to say goodbye. Adeeyou."

"Monrovia's a regular city," Jack said to Max.

"With mud huts?" Max asked. "For Dave the mud huts will be like in the old country, where he wass with the peasants."

"Brick," Jack said. "He'll have a big house with servants. Living, you know, is very cheap in Liberia."

"Take a drink," Ben suggested when David was already pouring himself one.

"They want you should be well fortified—in Liberia there iss no whiskey."

"Tomorrow morning?" Morris asked and David nodded his head. "Are you all packed?"

"We'd never see our money if they had whiskey," Larry said to Max.

"I've got everything. Two suitcases and a bottle of Scotch . . ."

"That's everything," Max confirmed.

"And all the arrangements are made; his house is just waiting for him. My agent, L. Sprague Fiske, has prepared everything."

"An Englishman?" Ben asked.

Jack nodded his head. "He'll help Dave get acquainted. That's always the most important thing."

"So when are we going to eat?" Sol asked.

"A while yet," Max said. "Give us a while. When we go to eat there will be the wimmin and they will chatter—here, there iss only friends."

"My dear chaps," David said, "I rather like it here, bloody good. I say old cock," he said to his brother, " 'ow bout another Schweppes?"

"Immedchiately," Jack replied.

"Too happy," Sam Cohen said simply. "Why is everyone so happy?" he asked smiling.

"This iss obvious," Max replied. "Always at a party people are happy. Why not? There's whiskey and good humor."

"Still," Sam insisted, "he's leaving tomorrow; maybe he won't be back for a few years."

"It's necessary," Morris said.

Sam looked at David sadly and, shaking his head, said, "More than a year."

"It'll be a good year. With Dave gone, who's to go bankrupt? Life'll be too simple," Larry said.

David looked at Larry carefully, wondering whether Larry was going to condemn him or just laugh at him.

"We'll be doctors without even a patient," Ben said, and laughed.

Larry smiled at David paternally, and walking to him, put his arm around his shoulders. "You're just bad luck," he said seriously, "you can't help being the black sheep of the family."

"A black sheep goes now to live with other black sheeps," Max remarked.

"But a year," Sam said speculatively, as if he were considering the number of months and days in a year.

"It's not jail," Morris said.

David watched the faces of his uncles. Now he could hardly understand what they were saying. He felt Larry's hand squeeze his shoulder and heard him say, "Should be jail. He'll get fat, nothing to see, nothing to do but count our profits and loaf."

David shrugged Larry's arm off his shoulder and started to walk away from him when Jack said, "It'll be a good year, Dave. This year we'll all make money and retire. Right?" he asked, half smiling, but looking intently at his brother.

David finished a drink and nodded his head. "Right," he echoed.

I had been invited to join them at a restaurant and, knowing my uncles to be always late and their wives always early (as though my uncles in that way proclaimed mastery over their wives, and the wives, by waiting, their suffering loyalty to the Cohen brothers), I arrived fifteen minutes after I was supposed to. I was living alone then, in a furnished room near school; my mother's twenty-five hundred dollar life insurance policy, even after the large chunk taken out for the funeral, and the war bonds I had been given by my uncles on all my early birthdays and on my Bar-mitzvah, made me, for that year, a man of independent means. I visited relatives only when I cared to, and that was not too often. When I met my aunts at the restaurant, I had not seen any of them for three months, since the week after my mother died.

"Ah, you're so thin," my aunt Fanny said. "You're a scarecrow."

"Tomorrow night you're eating at my house," Gertie declared. "I get sick from eating in restaurants."

"Really," I answered, "I'm busy. I have an exam the day after tomorrow," I lied.

"Well, suit yourself," Rebecca said. "Your eyes are bloodshot," she observed.

"I read too much," I lied, and smiled.

The men arrived; Max, David, and Sam were in high spirits. I sat across the table from David, and was flanked by Gloria and Rebecca. Max was on Gloria's other side, and he was whispering into her ear. Every so often, she blushed or giggled. Rebecca was very proper, regarding the dinner celebration as a charity to David, who, she thought, would soon receive sufficient punishment for his laziness and degeneracy. She had protested to Morris when he had told her that Jack was sending David to Liberia, thinking that David was to be given great authority, but when Morris had told her what he would be doing there, and when she had consulted her atlas and discovered that Liberia was nowhere near Paris, she had been pleased; while her husband had deplored what he thought was the necessity of an exile decided on by all the brothers (and Jack being included, the decision was final), she had nodded her head in approval of this particularly fit and moral punishment.

"Always," Larry said, carving his steak, "doctors tell me my neck is finished, that they can't help me and nobody can. I say thank God for the Christian Scientists."

"Ach," Sol exclaimed, at the mention of the word Christian.

"They teach you to believe that you have no pain, to say, 'I have no pain, I have no pain,' " Larry continued, "and then suddenly you believe it and you don't."

David looked at Larry. "If you're sick here," he said, pinching the flesh of his neck, "it's because you're sick here," he said, tapping the left side of his chest. "There's no physical sickness. All sickness is inside, all scars and pimples come from the soul."

"That's exactly right," Larry said, finding philosophical support in David's words. "That's just what they teach."

"What's right?" Max asked, his face now emerging from behind Gloria's head.

"Christian Science," Larry answered.

"Ach, a *scientiste!*" Max exclaimed. "Which one of you *schmucks* iss a *scientiste?*"

"Science cures through knowledge," I said, "but faith isn't science."

"You play with words," David said, pointing an accusing finger at me. "You always play with words," he concluded and nodding his head, announced, "Sickness is never cured. I mean real sickness, when something begins to eat and makes you fall apart."

"You're stupid," Sol said. "If you're sick, you go to a doctor."

"They get new medicines every day," Ben said.

"God bless America and penicillin," David said.

"If you don't be careful," Max warned, "we don't give you the passport."

"I'd like to go to Africa," Gloria said. "There are beautiful flat trees . . ."

"And wimmin," Max said and laughed. "Black but . . ."

"Oh stop that," Lily said. "Why can't we talk about what David will be doing?"

"But there you are," Max said.

"They always end up talking about women," Lily declared.

"I want to sing," David said. "I want to sing a farewell song."

Ben and Sam looked up surprised, and, smiling as if David had just announced his forthcoming marriage to a wealthy, beautiful, religious Jewish girl, Ben asked, "Will you sing that song about the soul?"

"O sole mio?" I suggested.

"That's it," Ben said.

The others at the table had stopped talking. "He hass no voice," Max whispered to Gloria. "After that many years, he will sound like a squeaky door."

Jack said to his brother, "Don't be silly; we're in a restaurant."

"Let him sing," Ben insisted, remembering a youthful

David reaching with easy grace the high and beautiful notes of a lyric song.

"A farewell song," David repeated. "From *Trovatore*."

"Tremble ye Tyrants," I offered, and smiled.

"A love song," Max suggested.

"No songs," David declared. "No songs. Nothing."

"Oh, Dave's being temperamental," Gloria said.

For a moment David sat, quiet, while conversation resumed about him. "I'll make a speech," he said, and stood up.

"Hear! Hear!" Max exclaimed.

"He's a baby," Rebecca said to Morris, and Morris rubbed his sewn-together fingers over his dry mouth and looked straight ahead.

David put his hand up for silence and began: "The poets are a noble breed, not worried about anything but immortality, that supreme condition of the spirit existing through time. The thought of their death upsets them and obsesses them, and some poets can hardly think of anything else. Well, that's only half of it; there's something even worse, and I claim discovery of this understanding—money! Money! If you haven't got it, it's like you're dying, dying every minute with hardly a breath that's free . . ."

"That's enough," Jack said, suddenly angry. "You're like a broken record. We've all heard your speech at every one of your goddamn crises. Why don't you just relax and be a man?"

"How is one a man?" I asked.

"You wouldn't know," Jack answered.

"I guess maybe I wouldn't."

"Be still," Max said to me. "I wish to hear the rest of the speech."

"No speech," David said. He remained standing, his lips open and his head straight.

"If no speech, then I will take you home. I will take good care of him," Max said and winked at Jack, who did not acknowledge the gesture. Max said good-night and led David out. We all left soon after.

Max helped David out of the cab. "I want to walk," David said.

"Sure, we walk a bit."

"This isn't my house," David said, glancing at the tall apartment building they stood in front of. "Max, this isn't my house."

"I know," Max said, "but we have a gift for you here. A present from the family."

David held on to Max's arm. "What kind of present?"

"You will see."

They walked around the block once, and when they came back to the building Max said, "It's apartment 8C—you go there and take your time. I will wait here." David did not move and Max asked, smiling, "You feel all right?"

David rejoined Max in less than half an hour. "How wass it?" Max asked. He did not reply. They began to walk towards an avenue. All David could think of was that he wanted to be alone—where were they sending him, where was he going?

"Look," Max said, "a dead man."

"Oh my God!"

"I was only joking," Max explained as David stopped, his face white, his eyes staring blankly at a caved in cardboard box.

AN END TO DYING

I was hardly awake; my eyes were closed. Then, suddenly, a train going at breakneck speed in the opposite direction passed my train, a blur of light. I listened to the monotonous rhythmic noises of the wheels, the shrieks of steel turning and grinding against steel. The short man across from me was sleeping. He had folded his jacket and was using it as a pillow; his back was flat against the wooden bench, and his legs were up in the air, resting heavily against the wall and the window frame. We had both boarded the train in Brussels; he might be returning from a visit and have to be at work in the morning. I saw my reflection in the window, but all I could see through the nearly impenetrable darkness outside was here and there a shape or a solitary light. Europe. I was very tired. I slept through the dawn and, soon after, commuters crowded onto the train at frequent suburban stations, so that the short man opposite (with whom I had exchanged no words during the whole journey, though we had laughed at each other's attempts to find a comfortable position on the hard wooden benches of our third class compartment) and I had to sit up straight to make room for them. Then I saw Paris. It appeared from behind a hill, a sudden panorama of low lying buildings. I smiled at the short man, and he grinned back at me.

Paris! Four thousand miles away, I had left a scandalized family. Three times, I had asked my uncles to provide me with free passage on one of their ships. Three times, it was agreed by five uncles and echoed by five aunts that I should not go, that I should work and learn to "make-a-living," that incredible phrase that when used by members of my family referred not to specific earnings, but to a commitment demanding an apprenticeship and, finally, a lifetime. Five years, and I would be earning not less than one hundred fifty dollars a week, be married to a nice Jewish girl, and own or partially own a small house in Long Island, in which I would raise my two children named Michael and Joan, or Leslie and Stephen. My family instinctively blamed David's business failures on his alcoholism, his degeneracy on his artistic ambition; he had not been forced to "make-a-living" until he was almost twenty years old, and then it was too late. They feared that my life might parallel his—I was already nineteen years old. Besides, I was told, what could Paris offer me when I had hardly any money at all? Paris was a dream. Perhaps, some day, I might go there to buy styles. Styles? Ladies and Gentlemen, No! Paris was Hemingway drinking at the Select, waiting for the safari to be completed. Paris was Cézanne, Van Gogh, and Lautrec. It was the love of the Frenchman crying in the *Life* magazine photograph, as he watched the Nazis march down the Champs Elysées. It was the splendiferous city that Jacob Kagan had almost bought. Bitter, I searched five days for a shipping corporation that might give me a job which could get me to Europe, and finally found a Greek captain, short a hand, who signed me on as a workaway. I left New York for Antwerp, informing my family by the following message sent to Ben one hour before we left: "Will be in Paris in two weeks. Love and kisses to you all. Sam."

I got to Paris, and by my signing my name on the dotted line of a paper written in Greek, I thought that I had killed twenty, two hundred, two thousand, two hundred thousand, and two million Cohens. God bless your souls, family Cohen!

God bless all of you! I cry for all the sons and daughters sucked into the watered-down version of their parents' watered-down new world existence. God bless you and keep you all. I am Sam Star!

I taxied to Grisha and Olga's apartment building in Neuilly, and introduced myself to the concierge. I presented quite a picture; I had not shaved since I had left New York three weeks before, my tweed suit was unpressed and dirty, the leather of my cheap black suitcase was peeling and torn, and my rucksack smelled of dirty laundry. The concierge was suspicious of my claim that Monsieur Starobinetz was my uncle. "Sit there," he said brusquely, pointing to a straight wooden chair. He made a phone call, glancing at me every so often. I took out a package of cigarettes and offered him one. He shook his head and hung up the receiver. He made another call and I heard him mention my uncle's name twice. From the pleased expression on his face, I was sure that he had just reported me to the police. We sat silent, hardly stirring for fifteen minutes. Then the door was opened and an old man, his nose broken at the center, his short gray beard still showing traces of once violently red hair, entered and asked, "Starobinetz?"

"Star," I answered standing up.

"Welcome, Star," he said. "I was a friend of your father."

"You're Shmyola Bernstein!" I exclaimed.

"Just so," he said and embraced me.

My aunt and uncle had expected me (I had cabled them from New York), but not knowing exactly when I would arrive, had left instructions with the concierge to call Bernstein if I came while they were out. He lived only a few blocks away and had a key to their apartment. Bernstein and I went upstairs; he fumbled with the lock and finally opened the door to the apartment, then we both sat down and he asked me in the correct Parisian French I had learned to understand in school, "How do you think about the Rosenbergs?"

"The Rosenbergs?"

"Ethel and Julius," Shmyola said.

"Oh," I nodded, and then said, "Well, they are guilty."

"You know, it is another Dreyfus case," he said, "legalized anti-Semitism."

"That's wrong," I answered and felt myself for the first time pressured into a pro-American stand. "The judge himself was a Jew."

"Ah," Bernstein sighed, "that's exactly it."

I heard a key in the lock and the door was opened. "Sam!" Olga exclaimed. "What a wreck you look!" she said and then embraced me.

Embraced by the old man, by my aunt, later by my uncle, by the cafés, the museums, and finally by Paris itself, I forgot the bitterness of my departure and was in love. I lived in Grisha and Olga's apartment, four rooms cluttered with antique furniture, paper-bound novels, leather-bound art books, and paintings of flowers. The apartment had two tiny terraces, one off the bedroom and one off my aunt's studio where I slept. From the terrace of the studio, I could see the Eiffel Tower standing above all of Paris, and facing away from the center of the city, I could see huge tree-covered estates in Neuilly. Every morning, my aunt awakened me by gently shaking my wrist; I remained in bed a few minutes longer and listened to the exquisitely intricate piano pieces someone in the same building was learning to play. Once out of bed, I dressed quickly, had breakfast with Olga, and listened to her schedule my day, she asking questions about what I preferred to see, I smilingly acquiescent to all her suggestions. Together we visited Notre Dame, walked on the Left Bank browsing at the *boutiques,* visited the Luxembourg Gardens, the Invalides, the Eiffel Tower. It was her great pleasure to take me about the city and her special pleasure to take me to the art museums. Though she never accompanied me inside a museum, insisting that she was uncomfortable when she felt the presence of anyone at all while she was looking at a painting, she did, previous to our separation, tell me what I should not miss. And I did not miss a trick. I raced through the Louvre in two afternoons studded by rare discoveries, I searched through the Modern Museum and I burned through the Jeu de Paume. There, in that small museum, I saw Gauguins, Lautrecs, Van Goghs, and Cézannes competing for space and light but all bursting with color and energy.

Afterwards, my aunt and I sat in cafés and discussed what we had seen, but more often, talked of my family in New York, of Bernstein, Grisha, and ourselves. Her own paintings had been exhibited in a well-known gallery, and she was lately a creator of ceramics, nymphs united with trees in painted pink-and-green, hardened clay. The inseparability of man and nature was her theme, and each of her ceramics (all of her work was either of great power or quite ridiculous) was a portrayal of this idea. The one that I liked most was a tree that in its tense and gnarled trunk seemed to be an arm and a hand grasping for something unreachable, the hand of a drowning man, or an old man trying to hold on to life.

"But why don't you exhibit your ceramics?" I asked her one day.

"And why doesn't Bernstein show his new book? Because I'm not really finished, and I'm not sure I care."

"Is Bernstein writing another book?"

"Ah, yes. For seven years now he has been writing a book about anti-Semitism . . ."

"So that's why he's so interested in the Rosenbergs."

"Of course, his interest in the specific is enormous. His life has not been a happy one, you know. We are his only friends."

Olga never cooked, and we ate out nearly every evening. We would meet Grisha at a restaurant and afterwards have our coffee at cafés in the various *quartiers*. One evening, shortly after my arrival, we were joined by Shmyola Bernstein at Korniloff's off the Champs Élysées. We were already seated when he entered. Grisha waved to him, but Bernstein did not see. He was wearing a belted blue summer jacket that had no padding. What with his round shoulders and protruding stomach, the jacket was much too large at the top and seemed to be about to burst at the waist. "Here we are," Grisha called. "Over here, Shmyola."

"I was walking on this street," he said when he was seated, "and I must have passed here three times. You know," he said looking at me and scratching his ear, "I have cataracts and don't see very well." I nodded and he said, "But I thought of something quite unusual: a new theory. For instance, take my nose," he said, without explaining. "Everyone, you understand, lacks one thing and that is what makes a man what he is. Not what he is given, but what he isn't given."

"A very democratic idea," Grisha said smiling, "and what do you lack?"

Bernstein answered seriously, "Looks. I've always been ugly and, you understand, it's helped me to see the beautiful."

"And me?" Olga asked.

"I haven't developed my ideas yet. It's still a new concept," he answered.

"And me?" Grisha asked.

"You? You lack everything."

"I do not like your democracy."

Korniloff himself supervised the serving of our table. A tall and elegant expatriate, he drank a glass of Polish vodka with us, and warned me that my uncle would have me drunk in no time. When the hors d'oeuvres were served I was not yet drunk, but I was rather high. Each time Grisha poured a drink, I drained my own and refilled my glass. I fell one or two behind when I ate a piece of herring coated with sour cream. For a while, I just managed to keep my eyes fixed on the red caviar atop black bread, but then colors began to merge in horrifying combinations, and I felt very strange, then did not feel anything at all.

"You know," Olga said while I was trying to catch up to Grisha, "I have almost exhausted Paris. There are still some places to show Sam, but now we shall have to search for them."

Grisha suggested that I might visit the Folies Bergère.

Bernstein pondered a moment, rubbing his index finger against the broken ridge of his nose, and then said something in Russian.

Olga exclaimed, "I forgot entirely. That will be wonderful. Oh, you'll love that, Sam."

"What will I love?" I asked, nervously watching Grisha pour another drink.

"The Countess Sonia," Olga said. "You'll love the Countess."

"You're not speaking of my aunt?" I asked.

"Your aunt?" Grisha repeated, and I could not tell whether he was smiling at my question or at the unfinished drink I was holding in my hand at some distance from my mouth. "No. She's not your aunt."

"Then whose aunt is she?"

"She's an extraordinary woman," Olga went on. "You've never met anyone like her."

I could not follow the conversation.

The next morning, I awoke with a terrific hangover. Grisha had left for work hours before, and Olga was impatient for me to get dressed and have my breakfast. "We'll be late," she warned. "The Countess is expecting us in half an hour."

I had vague memories of something having been said about a countess the night before.

In the bus, Olga described the Countess Sonia: "She is of another age; I believe that she has more than seventy years, and with all the powder and rouge she wears, you cannot mistake it. You will think she has no taste, but before . . . Ah, Dior would have died to have her wear one of his creations. Her husband was a millionaire, no! a billionaire—director of all the enterprises of the Norwegian match king. To her house everyone came, the great writers, the aristocracy—Anatole France inscribed many books to her. Once she was a great woman, she wore hundreds of thousands of dollars worth of jewelry every night, she had paintings, everything, but you will see something else. She is desolate. Four rooms of her apartment are all that's left to her; she has no money and she lives by selling her jewelry and so little is left."

The countess lived in Passy in an apartment building whose front overlooked the Seine. The elevator was not working; we climbed three flights of stairs. The countess herself opened the door. It was very dark, the hallway and foyer were unlit. The countess stepped back (I could not distinguish her features in the darkness) and exclaimed in French, "My dear Olga, it is so good to see you." Then, kissing her and noticing me, she asked in English, "And is this your United States nephew?"

Olga said yes, and the countess asked me, "Do you speak French?"

"Je parle un peu," I answered.

"Ah, but you speak beautifully."

She led us into a sitting room where all the shades were drawn. I sat down, and my gaze was immediately attracted to a crystal chandelier hanging from the center of the ceiling. It was imperfect—I could see where pieces were missing—but it caught whatever light filtered into the room from around the shades and some few crystals sparkled. The countess said, "I should like to speak English, but it is so exacting a language and my mind is so old and used. Tell me," she continued in French, "you have been here several days, what do you think of our Paris?"

"It's magnificent," I answered enthusiastically.

"He's in love with Paris," Olga said.

The countess leaned back and smiled. "Ah, youth!" Olga and I both remained quiet as the countess slowly folded her hands and nodded her head. In that pause, I suddenly felt myself an intruder, as if I had just entered a deserted room where the sheets had not yet been taken off the furniture. "When I was a girl, I, too, loved Paris: L'Opéra, La Comédie, all the restaurants. But now," she sighed, "everything is different."

Of course—she was Jacob Kagan's countess. How many times had I heard that story? Had Bernstein mentioned it last night? I conjured up Hollywood-inspired images of the countess as she must have been. What a dark and dusty old room!

"But," she continued, "you like your home most?"

"I feel more comfortable here," I answered quickly.

"Ah? Yes. There is an ease to Paris, if one lives a certain way. I have seen a great deal of the world: St. Petersburg, Danzig, Rome, Cairo, London, New York, Rio . . . so many others. They are all nice, but I too have always been much more at home here in Paris."

"Perhaps because here in Paris there are no demands. In New York City you have to be always rushing about from one place to another making money," I suggested.

"I understand," the countess said. "You are an artist?"

"I like to sing," I answered, embarrassed.

"That's wonderful. A good voice is always a pleasure. Do you know the *lieder?*"

"No. I like opera."

"Charming," she said. "Always the artists find Paris a haven, a meeting ground. You know, I was once patroness to a painter. What has become of him—it was after the great war—I don't know."

"Probably he is a communist," Olga said.

"God forbid!" the countess exclaimed.

"That is what happens to successful artists; they become Catholics or communists, and sometimes both."

"But you say you like opera; have you gone yet?"

"I believe the season's over."

"Ah, that's a pity. A friend told me that their *Manon* is simply wonderful. The Opera is really our pride. I have heard Caruso, you know, but there are no tenors any longer."

We did not stay more than fifteen minutes, and once in the street, I exclaimed to Olga, "What an extraordinary woman! Imagine, forty years ago, Jacob Kagan went to one of her parties, and today I met her."

"She was a woman of importance," Olga said. "If she liked an artist's work, she would support him. Since then, art has made great strides. Today the governments don't allow the right people to have enough money. Ridiculous taxes! It is the middle class upon whom everything depends, and they have no taste. They think themselves to be artists; they copy, they paint in their spare time—a whole civilization of amateurs! They are quite impossible. To have lived in her time, when people had charm, when there was no fear of infernal machines, of atomic bombs!"

Olga and I went one day to the Palace at Versailles, where we were guided through fantastic corridors and ornate rooms: Madame Pompadour's bedroom, the libraries of kings and their counsellors, the marble-floored ballroom with twenty chandeliers where Marie Antoinette had danced. Later, we walked in the gardens and by the lakes where children were sailing model boats. I stood for a moment, my back to all tourists, and looked out over a closed garden. The sun was setting, and I thought that I was a monarch. Leaving the palace grounds, and the enormous cobble-stoned courtyard, we came upon an equestrian statue of Louis Quatorze. *"Le roi soleil,"* Olga said.

"Ah!" I exclaimed, *"c'est mon cousin."*

The summer that I lived in Paris was wonderful. The tourists were everywhere: German and Scandinavian boys wearing shorts; female English school teachers asking questions in French; Chinese and Indians in western dress, and Americans—American college girls on fifteen-hundred-dollar tours, businessmen and their families on fifteen-thousand-dollar tours. Like a victorious and generous army, they descended on all the *quartiers,* swooping down at night on the Latin Quarter in overcrowded buses provided by the American Express, shuttling from St.-Germain-des-Prés to Montparnasse and the *boîtes* in between. When I was not with Olga, I roamed the streets of the Left Bank, carrying a French literary magazine, *Le Figaro,* or the Paris edition of the *Tribune*. Invariably, I ended up at Les Deux Magots or the Café de Flore, where I would sit and smile condescendingly at all my countrymen in their button-down shirts, white bucks, gray flannel or seersucker suits. One afternoon, I read in an article by the celebrated columnist, Josh Reuben, that the fashion houses were about to have their summer openings, and that we might all expect something rather shocking from the drawing boards of Christian Dior. Exactly what, was not mentioned, but my inference, and I believe it was accurate, was that it was a topless evening gown. (Josh Reuben, whose column appeared in sixty-seven newspapers in thirty-four states of the union, and two provinces of Canada, was master of the style of flat statement loaded with ambiguous undertones). I in no way related the openings to my uncles in New York, but I was soon brought to realize, by the receipt of a cablegram addressed to Grisha, how closely connected Paris and Seventh Avenue really were. The cablegram was from Larry; he would arrive at Orly in two days. Larry and a thousand other New York City garment manufacturers, in preparation for their Fall lines, were flocking to Paris for purchasable inspiration. Already, in the lobbies, sitting rooms, bars, and restaurants of the George Cinq and even the Plaza Athénée, innumerable Mr. Levines were paging Mr. Goldbergs, and Mr. Bernsteins were greeting Mr. Cohens. At home, American women held their breath, awaiting the decrees of Dior, Fath, Balmain. Resistance movements were formed of women who anticipated changes in styles that might force them to reveal certain uncomplimentary features of their presently disguised or hidden anatomies. Paris and New York were waiting, and so was I. Jesus Christ, was I waiting! That messenger from hell was already winging his way across the Atlantic. Paradise was coming to a quick and untimely end. I would flee to Madrid? Florence?

"What's your answer?" Grisha asked after a moment. He had just invited me to join Olga and him on their summer vacation. They intended to leave in several days for a month's rest at a hotel near Lake Como.

"Of course," Olga said, "after Paris, it will be rather dull. We will not go about much, but you might enjoy it."

"No," I answered, "I don't think so."

"Good," Grisha said. "We'll find you a *pension*. You'll see

Paris much better living on your own, and Larry," he added smiling, "he may show you a good time."

On the morning that Larry was to arrive, we drove to Orly in Grisha's Citroën. We passed an airline bus going towards the airfield, and I thought that all the people in that bus would soon be flying across oceans and continents. How great to be able to buy, on the spur of the moment, any moment, a plane ticket to Lisbon, Ankarra, Shanghai, Johannesburg! To walk on the streets of any one of the world's capitals of intrigue, and if suddenly pursued, to buy a ticket and fly someplace else! And here I was, driving, in the protective custody of an aunt and uncle, to meet Larry.

"Say something," Grisha said, turning his head to look at me.

"U.S. Go home!" I said, and Grisha and Olga both laughed.

A four-engined Constellation circled the field and came in for a landing. Its curved fuselage was tilted up just the slightest bit, and the plane sank gracefully to the ground. It taxied on three wheels and, coming closer to where we were standing, roared deafeningly, and finally came to a stop. An aluminum staircase was rolled out to the door of the airplane. There were twenty or thirty people standing behind the gates with us. One man looked familiar. He turned his head slightly and I saw his profile. It was the nervous Jess Kraut. How could I ever forget that face and body?

"Mister Jess Kraut," I said.

"Who's paging?" he asked, and turned to face me.

"Sam Star," I said. "Remember me?"

"Sam Star, nephew of the Cohens—so you finally made it, and here you are in Paris, waiting for your uncle."

"What are you doing here?" I asked, but did not need an answer, for at that moment the airplane door was opened, and out popped Max Kling, followed by my uncle Larry.

In less than ten minutes, Larry and Max were cleared through customs. Introductions were made, and we all crowded into Grisha's Citroën. Larry put his hand on my knee and turning his neck as much as he could, and then only so far that he could just see my nose, he asked, "So how do you like Paris, Sammy?"

"I love it," I answered, my response to that question automatic by now.

"Sammy," Larry said by way of explanation, "wanted to go to Paris, and I said, 'Work for your money.' So he worked his way over. Not so smart, but he's got his mother's nerve."

That was that. Olga smiled at me. I had gone to the airport expecting abuse, and here I was being complimented. Yes sir, with Larry's hand on my knee, I could relax and enjoy life.

Grisha let Larry, Max, and Jess off at the Plaza Athénée; we were to meet them for dinner at seven-thirty. And when we got back to the apartment in Neuilly, Olga telephoned Bernstein and invited him to join us. It was Larry's first evening in Paris, and Grisha and Olga's last—they were leaving on their vacation the next day.

We ate on the glass-enclosed terrace of a restaurant in the Bois de Boulogne. About thirty feet away, a double column of trees separated us from a road, and every now and then I saw the blurred shapes of passing automobiles. It was growing dark. A small boy wandered onto the well-cut lawn that surrounded the restaurant. He stood for a moment, looking in, and then he began to posture; placing one hand behind his head and the other on his waist, he swung his hips to one side and stuck out his tongue. Max was telling a story: "A midget iss standing on a street corner when along comes this big blonde. The midget says in a squeaky voice, 'Hey lady, plees come here and help me.' " Bernstein lightly massaged his eyes with the tips of his thumb and forefinger; he did not understand Max's English. Larry was cutting his filet mignon into very small pieces. The boy sat down on the grass, his legs crossed beneath him. In a moment it would be too dark to see him.

Max finished his story and even Larry was shocked.

"What kind of stories do you write?" Jess asked Bernstein in French. The two men had been introduced to each other as writers, but neither of them had previously heard of the other.

"My stories are history," Bernstein said. "There is only one important study, and you know that it is history." He scratched his nose. "I am now writing a book on anti-Semitism; at the moment, I am working on its manifestations in the Paris newspapers . . ."

"It must be a great deal of work, gathering material," I said.

"Not only is it a great deal of work, it is bitter work. What our race has gone through, what sufferings we are subjected to, you in the United States can have no idea."

"I bet it'll be a monumental work," Jess said, and Bernstein, I thought, did not catch the trace of sarcasm in Jess's tone.

"Monumental! Of course, it's a study that . . . you know," he said, suddenly interrupting himself and then looking at Larry and continuing in Russian, "Kagan and I once had dinner together, with Tania, in a restaurant much like this one. Then we ate out of doors."

"What are you saying?" Larry asked in Yiddish.

"Ah, nothing," Bernstein said.

"He said that he once had dinner with your brother in the same kind of restaurant," Grisha translated.

"So?" Larry asked.

"It is only," Bernstein said in Yiddish, "if people would see what crimes they commit. That the crimes against the Jews must be understood by the Gentiles and by the Jews."

"But will they change?" Olga asked and sadly shook her head.

"Art is impotent," I said in French.

"If I believed that," Bernstein asked, "do you think I'd be working on this book?"

"But your book," Jess said, "is not art, but facts."

"What are they saying?" Max asked.

"They're talking about Bernstein's book," I informed him.

"He writes books?" Max asked. "What kind of books?"

"Facts," Bernstein said to Jess in French, "are nothing unless one understands them. Understanding is art."

"Interpretation, truly," Olga agreed, "is art."

"Sure it's art," Jess said, smiling.

I saw our reflections in the glass wall of the restaurant. Outside it was too dark to see anything.

"My undertaking this book," Bernstein went on, "was mainly a question of conscience."

"What iss he saying now?" Max asked me, and I translated for him.

"Conscience," Max said in English to Larry.

"If only to satisfy my conscience," Bernstein said, "the work must be done."

"Conscience," Larry said, and then continued in Yiddish, "I do not understand. Honesty? Yes. You must be honest . . ."

"Maybe once in a while you don't have to be, but in general . . ." Max interrupted, grinning at me.

". . . but you're either born honest or not, and if you're born honest, then you don't have to worry about it."

"You make it too simple," Grisha said in Yiddish. "There's more to it, even in business. There's conscience in treating your customers, in dealing with all people."

"That's what I said," Larry interrupted.

"But we were talking about another kind of conscience," Olga interrupted. "We were talking about artistic conscience. Every act of the artist must be directed towards a work of art, and the work of art must be moral."

"In business and art," Jess said in English, "it's the same thing. Right, Max?"

"Correct," his uncle replied. "You work to make money."

"That is conscience!" Larry agreed, looking now at me, and repeating Max's thought in Yiddish.

"That is not conscience!" Bernstein declared. "When I speak of conscience, I refer to the conscience of the Jew to his race; that is the most important. A Jew must always work with the knowledge that he is a Jew. He cannot forget it, and he must act accordingly."

"But we're not only Jews, we're part of humanity," I said in English and repeated in French.

"You're too young," Bernstein said in Yiddish. "You're still too young, and then you are also an American. Sam, first of all we are Jews, and if we do not want it that way, it is forced on us, and if we do not accept it, we are cowards."

"Who doesn't want it?" Larry asked angrily.

"We are of a great heritage," Olga said. "Moses and the Old Testament. It is all about us."

"Our sufferings," Bernstein said, "our people wiped out by the Nazis—seven millions! Will we ever forget that? And we are part of it all. My blood! No Jew exists alone; his history is the history of the sufferings of the Jews. It is a tragic and great heritage, something we must regard with pride and sadness. We are all Jews, Jews first, sufferers—the Chosen People," he said with great pride.

"No Jew is an island unto himself," Jess paraphrased in English, and winked at me. I smiled back.

When we had finished our coffee, Larry called for the check and, glancing at it, he stood up and extracted from his billfold a ten thousand franc note that he gave to the waiter. "So where to now?" Larry asked. "The Lido?"

"I don't know about you, but we are going home," Grisha said. "Tomorrow we shall be driving all day."

"Grisha, you don't know how to enjoy life," Larry said. "Sam, you'll come along," he said to me and I nodded my head. "And Shmyola, will you come?"

"Where?" Bernstein asked.

"The Lido. The nightclub."

"Oh, no. I think I will go home. I work best at night."

"Fine," Grisha said, "we'll drive you."

I asked Olga to wake me the following morning before they departed, no matter how late I got back to the apartment. Bernstein asked me to visit him soon, and then we separated.

Larry, Max, Jess and I taxied first to the Plaza Athénée where Larry went upstairs to change his shirt; the rest of us went to the hotel bar. A Negro attendant dressed in an elegant

Turkish costume, an artist's dream model for a semi-masculine simpering odalisque, salaamed to Max. "He looks like a prince," Jess said as we sat down at a table.

"Just because he comes from Harlem doesn't mean he's a prince," Max said.

"Yes sir," the Negro, standing behind us, said, "me prince."

"From Harlem," Max added.

"Yes sir," the Negro exclaimed, smiling broadly, "me prince from Hollem."

Larry entered the bar, and a middle-aged woman who had been sitting alone quickly adjusted her mink stole, stood up, and exclaimed, "Why, Mr. Cohen!" Larry faced her. "Don't you recognize me? I'm with Sol Bloom in Chicago, his designer."

"Oh yes," Larry said, and Max smiled at Jess.

"Will you join me for a nightcap?"

"I'm sorry, I'm busy, with some people," he said pointing at us.

"Oh," the woman said, waiting for an invitation.

"Yes, we've got an appointment," Larry explained.

"Well," she said, "I'm staying right here at the Plaza, and if you're not doing anything sometime, just call me. You remember, Emma. Emma Gold."

"Sure," Larry said, and walked over to our table.

"They come after you like you wass fly-paper," Max remarked.

"She's too old," Larry said.

"When in Rome, do like the Romans," Max said.

"She's a *miesse,*" Larry said, "at least in Paris . . ." he added meaningfully.

"Does that sort of thing happen often?" I asked, smiling.

"Once in a while," Larry replied. "In Paris, for them, anything goes, and anyone'll do."

"Even me?" I asked.

"Why sure," Max answered. "We'll fix you up, don't you worry."

We had several drinks and then taxied to the Lido. Larry

slipped a bill into the headwaiter's hand, and he led us to a table just several feet away from the large, rectangular stage that projected far into the room. Larry was hailed by a garment manufacturer sitting with an attractive woman. "A lively place," Larry said.

"It's all right," Jess said. "You know, back at the bar you can pick up classy girls."

"Shiksas?" Max asked.

"The real thing," Jess replied.

There were seven or eight girls dancing on the stage, kicking their legs out, it seemed, even over our heads. A fully dressed man came onto the stage and said, "My name's Sam Katz and I just blew in on a Chicago breeze," which remark earned him much applause. I looked at my uncle Larry. He was laughing, and I suddenly felt very warm towards him. I loved him. I loved him because he was my uncle, and because he was so rich that we were sitting at one of the best tables in the nightclub. "You're a good man," I said to him.

"Thanks, but to what do I deserve such a compliment?"

"To the whiskey," Max said, "what else?"

"I really like you," I persisted.

"Sam wants some money," Larry said.

"He's worth it," Max said, and laughed. "Jess, why aren't you so affectionate?"

"How much do you want?" Larry asked smiling.

I could not see too clearly. "Look," I said, pointing to a girl on the far side of the stage, "she's embarrassed."

"College you need!" Max exclaimed. *"Schmuck,* she'ss barassed, and no fancy trimmings."

"She doesn't belong up there," I protested.

"Did you see her just now?" Jess asked. "Look, Sam, she's winking at you."

"The boy should get laid," Max advised Larry. "For his mother's sake, you should treat him to a fuck."

They led me out of the Lido, and we taxied to Jess's studio apartment. Larry took out a little black book, found a phone number and made a call. Four girls soon arrived. The evening was very disorganized. Nothing made sense or had any order. I was introduced to the girls as Larry's son, and Jess told them that Larry's wife was his aunt. Larry did not want to go to bed with the girl who had attached herself to him, telling her that he could not, what with his son and his wife's nephew around. I said, "Papa, don't be a fool; it's all right. We won't tell mama." And Jess laughed and said that this evening certainly was off the record. Well, let it be. The evening passed in a blaze of whiskey and girls. The universal American passport signed by the Secretary of the Treasury burned quickly but brightly.

I was awakened by the sound of laughter. I opened my eyes and then quickly closed them; the glare on a large, slanting window blinded me. The window dominated one wall of what I vaguely remembered as Jess's studio. I was still in shirt and trousers; my shoes were on the floor beside the couch I was lying on.

I heard a woman's voice at the far end of the long room. "Who is he?" she asked in English.

"He? He's a great man, he's a hero. Sam Star—nephew of Larry Cohen." The girl was dark; her mouth was wide, without lipstick. I did not remember her.

"How old is he?" she asked.

"I don't know, old enough—just a kid."

"Where am I?" I said, pretending I had just awakened, and Jess and the girl both laughed.

"My apartment, seventh arrondisement, Paris, France."

I sat up on the edge of the couch and, rubbing my eyes and twisting my neck, exclaimed, "Jesus Christ!"

"Just Jess, Sam," Jess said, and laughed, "and this is my own Rosy."

"Hy," I said.

"Good afternoon," she said and, unable to control herself, she burst out laughing. "Are you a hero?" she asked.

"No. Just a Jew from the East Bronx," I replied.

"Welcome, brother," Jess cried.

Rosy prepared a cup of coffee for me and then left, saying

that she had a rehearsal. Jess explained that she was a vocalist with the great American Jazz-man, Sam Juvenal. When I finished my coffee, Jess suggested that we go for a walk. I put on my jacket and we went out together. We came to a cemetery in Montparnasse and Jess said, "This is it, kid, the most fantastic cemetery in the world . . . your uncle wouldn't understand it, but I think you will. Come on in. Just look at those old ladies sitting in black, Utrillos, they come here for picnics. They got family plots, and they set a tablecloth over a grave and break out the wine and cold chicken sandwiches—they all eat chicken, they think it adds to their sex potency. I was like you when I got out of school, the same sort of thing," he added, smiling at me.

"One on top of the other," I said, noticing the crowded tombstones.

"Sure. Catholics and Jews and even Protestants. You know, I come here so often, I feel right at home. When I think of those idiots who incinerate themselves . . . they're crazy. How could they want anything else, what the hell, this is the life, to be buried in a cemetery like this. So what if you've got troubles, relax, enjoy yourself. See this headstone, they quote lines of poetry, hilarious, they got family poets, every French family has a poet, sometimes two or three, budding young Eddy Guests who write the most unbelievable epitaphs. I once read this on a headstone, "Here lies just one John, murdered by the Boche near the Marne. Crazy!" Jess exclaimed. "They think he's the God-damned Unknown Soldier. It's a beautiful day, isn't it?"

"It sure is."

"So what I'm trying to say is, we're similar. Your uncle's a business machine, just like everybody seems to be a machine, he's a business machine. I suppose you got a family back there," he said pointing in the direction of Belgium, "and they're all machines. An auntie Lily, and an auntie Rosie, and a Tante Tilly . . . all Jewish families are the same. I'm gonna give you a word of advice, you're not asking me, but I'm gonna give it all the same."

"I wish you would," I said.

"Fuck 'em!" he exclaimed. "Stay here in Paris, sure if you go back—now, just look at me talk and you're saying to yourself where does this Jess fellow get off, talking to me like he was my best friend. Well, I'm not, but you're like me, and this is what I learned from experience and lots of it. If you go back, you'll find maybe a cave to crawl into, in that insane hectic world there'll be maybe one cave, but here you can be at peace, do you follow?"

"Sure," I said.

"Okay! Let's go get a drink."

We walked to the Dome and sat down. "Are you doing another book?" I asked Jess.

"I'm always doing a book," he answered. "I carry it around with me in my bowels. You see that guy?" Jess interrupted himself. "He knows me, respects me, my opinion, but he's nothing. Look how his pockets bulge. He wants to show me his photographs, photographs of all his lousy paintings. Like a guy with dirty pictures. No. I'm busy," he said to the astonished man without greeting him. "Thank God! These people don't know a thing about art. Really, not a thing. I saw a guy once painting white crosses on clear new windows in a new building. He painted blind, no thought, just power, just balls. He had more than any of these frauds. How about some billiards?"

We left the Dome and walked to another café. "If I were to stay in Paris, what would I do?" I asked.

Jess planned his shot, took it and missed. "What would you do? Just what I do—you have coffee someplace, come here in the afternoon, play billiards, pay one of the whores at the bar a couple hundred francs, and get laid. That's what you do."

"But where do you get money?" I asked.

"If you want money," Jess said, "you better go back to New York City—your uncle Larry will fix you up."

"But how do you live?" I asked.

"Here a job, there a job. I scrounge. Shit! What's money anyhow?"

"Money's everything!" I exclaimed. "What happens if I want to go to Spain?"

"Why then you go."

"How?"

"What do you want to go to Spain for, anyhow?"

"Oh Jesus," I said, suddenly remembering, "I was supposed to say goodbye to Grisha and Olga."

"Well then you better run along," Jess said looking back at the billiard table and positioning himself for a shot.

"Will I see you tonight?"

"If you want. I'll be with Rosy—Sam Juvenal's *boîte*."

I taxied back to Neuilly. Grisha and Olga had left. The concierge had my suitcase and rucksack in his office. He gave me an envelope and a small package that Grisha had left with him for me. I opened the envelope; there was a ten thousand franc note inside. The package contained a book. It was leather bound and on the front cover at the bottom right, was stenciled in small gold print, SAM STAR'S DIARY. I put the money in my wallet and, holding the diary, I asked the concierge if I could not leave my luggage with him until tomorrow. I wanted to walk. It was late afternoon. I walked on the shady side of the street, and then crossed over and walked in a park. I was sorry that I had missed my aunt and uncle. They had been very good to me and most probably I would not see them again. Just a little longer than twenty-four hours ago, I had known my Paris—had enjoyed it without thought. Everything, the whole world was now on my shoulders. I should not have missed my aunt and uncle. A cave to crawl into. I passed a man sitting on a bench and suddenly turned around. "Bernstein," I exclaimed. He was sitting with his arm resting against the back of the bench, his eyes closed, his cheek pressed against his hand. He opened his eyes and said, "Hello, Sam."

"What are you doing here?" I asked.

"I live just a short distance away," he said.

"And why aren't you home writing?" I asked. "At this rate your book will never be finished," I said jokingly.

"I am writing no book," he said.

"Your book on anti-Semitism."

"For whom should I write a book on anti-Semitism?" he asked. "For your uncle Larry—he has forgotten his own language. I am not a crusader; there is too much rudeness and violence as it is, there is an anarchy of will with as many horrors as there are people."

"They were having a good time," I protested. "They were drunk."

Bernstein ignored my remark. "You know, for many years I have doubted even the importance of art. I am convinced, certainly for me, well, I am really quite unimportant. I have told stories, thinking to entertain and to teach, but whom have I taught and *whom* have I entertained? I was a journalist, but the truth, the truth is too monstrous to report. Ah, no, one must retreat. Let me tell you that I find greatest pleasure in my dreams."

"In your dreams?"

"Yes; there is no form, but I can control my dreams at least in their selection, like a cinema that I switch on and off, picking which film I want to see, and they are all charming. Anti-Semitism? Sometimes I dream of St. Petersburg, of Kagan . . . no, they are my life. This world, this reality I shut out. Why suffer in the knowledge of horror and anarchy? I shall drink wine moderately, sleep well, and dream. I like Westerns you know; one can always see who is right."

"But your stories!" I exclaimed and stopped. "Surely," I finally said, "there is love, there is life."

"When I was younger . . ."

"You loved life?" I interrupted.

"Yes, but that was another time."

"You're wrong," I said.

"For me, Sam," he said calmly, "there is still nature," he said and gestured clumsily with his arm towards the trees. "But look," he said and opened his hand in front of my face. "There are blisters, infections, unnatural deaths. I fear that I will not die in my sleep."

"Oh God!" I exclaimed. "Is that all?"

"No more," Bernstein said. "I should like to be left untouched in my own world."

"Like the countess," I said. "Is my world so ugly?"

"Perhaps one can find peace in form and order, and that may be possible in art."

"But in life?"

"Life?" he repeated.

"Life!"

"Which one?" he asked smiling. "Who is to say which is the more real? Certainly I know the one I prefer."

"This one," I said and slapped his thigh, "the life of touch, of contact."

"Ah, I know that one. If you like, it is real, but you must watch what you touch."

We sat for a moment in silence and then he asked me, "But what have you got there?"

"A diary. Grisha and Olga left it for me."

"That's nice," he said and, standing up and straightening his jacket, he said, "You must visit me sometime," and walked away.

I walked from Neuilly to the Arc de Triomphe. Then I walked by the Seine. Ten thousand francs: twenty-five dollars. I did not want to visit Larry; I was too tired to go back to Neuilly to pick up my luggage. I went to a movie.

At ten o'clock I went to Sam Juvenal's *boîte*. It was on the Left Bank just across from Notre Dame. The moon was full and bright; the towers of Notre Dame seemed to be too low, as if the builders had erected a dwarfed cathedral without the great energy and aspiration of the originals. Jess was standing outside with Rosy and a short, bald Negro. "Hi, Sam," he said, "this is Juvenal, and you know Rosy."

I said hello.

"Juvenal's got the greatest tenor-sax in the world," Jess said. "Isn't that right?" he asked the Negro.

"Maybe it was, but I'm an old man now."

Rosy kissed him on the cheek. "You're still hot stuff," she said.

" 'Cept for my ulcers," the Negro said. " 'Cept for my ulcers, I'd live fo' ever."

"All great men live forever," Jess said.

"I sure hope so," Sam Juvenal said, smiling.

"You ought to know something about great men," Rosy said to me.

"I'll tell you when I'm as old as Mr. Juvenal," I said.

We went inside, down a narrow staircase on which I had to bend my head to avoid the irregular ceiling. We were in a *cave*. Jess and I stood at the bottom of the staircase while Sam Juvenal and Rosy advanced through the crowd to a small platform. "He's tops," Jess said. "He's lost a lot. Jesus! he's lost a lot, but he's still tops." The *cave* was crowded with French and American boys and girls who sat on small stools. It was smoke-filled and hot. Four men were on the stage: trumpet, bass-fiddle, drums and piano. Sam was the fifth man. He announced his number, was applauded, and began to play soft, hard, loud, and sweet. There was a fast pounding beat to everything in the room, and the audience shouted, "Go, boy, go!" Juvenal went through four numbers, accompanying Rosy on the last one.

"He's terrific," I said.

"Sure he's terrific," Jess said. "Just listen to a dying man play out what little's left of his guts. Forty years he's been playing and what do they do to him? They gave him jazz, and he played, but every time he plays, it's another slice out of his guts, so what happens? Jazz is dead and he's dying. He comes to Paris because in the States he's just another old time nigger . . ."

Jess was waiting for Rosy to be through for the night, and he had a couple of hours to kill. We went to the Café Select in Montparnasse. When we were seated, I said, "Hemingway used to come here, didn't he?"

"He still does, when he gets to Paris. They got myths about

him, about how much he can drink, about his strength. Whenever he comes to Paris they play him up big, they splatter his picture all over the front pages. *L'enfant terrible,* he's only about sixty. But they love the kids and the dogs here. You're not a Frenchman unless you love the kids and the dogs. They're human here. Shit on the States, on New York. They're not people there. They're refrigerated, laundromated, toasted, mass-made dummies. Do you see it? They got *pissoirs* here. They walk along the streets and if they gotta take a leak, they do it in a *pissoir,* right in the middle of the street, and they don't bother to button up their flies until they're back in the open. That's what they need in New York. Half the goddamn rush in New York comes from people who're running about looking for a place to take a leak. It's not funny," Jess said when I began to laugh. "My God! If I had to live there I'd kill myself. It's crazy; life isn't worth living. How can you live with such shits and stay sane! It's impossible!"

"It's a question of getting along," I said.

"Who wants to? Spit in their faces, pick their pockets, that's what I do."

"But they're your people," I protested. "They're your family and your race."

"Your race? Your race is the race of Seventh Avenue businessmen, my uncle Max, the rat race; they're not even human, yes, your uncle."

When Jess left me to meet Rosy, I walked on the Boulevard St. Germain. I walked with my hands behind me, clasping my new diary; I passed the focal point of that *quartier* and turned towards the Seine, walking down Boulevard St. Michel. Then I walked on the dark embankment of the Seine. I heard the noise of the water as it rippled around the blunt bows of tied-up barges, the noise of occasional cars on the street above me. I passed couples embracing, sitting on stone benches, and I heard the sad music of loneliness.

I would return, my clothes unpressed, enter the elaborate showroom of Larry Cohen, Incorporated, or Ben Cohen, Incorporated. The models and office girls would say hello and ask me about the French girls. My uncles would shake my hand and ask me about Paris, about Grisha and Olga. Larry would make some jokes and then go back to the telephone, or the buyer in the private showroom. There would be no embraces, though there might, in the evening when I would go to one of their homes, be some kissed cheeks. I did not know where I was walking, and I lost my sense of time. I walked through dirty streets and, finding myself blocked by blind alleys, I retraced my steps. I watched the whores as they sat in the bars, watched the *maquereaux* as they laughed among themselves. I walked the side streets, the small thin curving streets, and heard the noise of the juke boxes, and finally entered a small bar. I sat down on a stool and was immediately enveloped by the smoke, noise, pungent alcohol odors, and the people closing tightly about me. I drank beer and a Negro asked me, "You're American?"

"Yes."

"Me too. Haven't been back since the war."

I felt the pressure of a woman's body on my own and turning, looked into black, liquid eyes. "Buy me a drink, honey?"

I heard the whores argue and heard the Negro tell me the history of his sufferings and hates. He finished a beer and, his breath reeking, he leaned towards me and announced in fluent and nasalized French, "*Mes amis, attention.*" He continued in English when the several people standing around him turned towards him. The juke box was still playing and two whores were dancing together. The whores stopped dancing when, not understanding, but impressed by the Negro's heavy and powerful voice, he announced:

"ASH WEDNESDAY . . .
Because I do not hope to turn again
Because I do not hope
Parce que je n'espère pas
Because I do not hope to turn again . . .
Listen," and he repeated slowly, "Because I do not hope, I

do not hope. How that says everything. It's great. It's all life in one line. What do you think of that?" he asked me belligerently.

"It's fine," I said.

"Is that all you can say. You dumb white bastard, it's life . . ."

"Shit!" I said.

Outside it was almost light. I heard a dog barking. The sun had come out and the stores were opening as I walked back to the Seine. I watched the traffic increase and, later, the book sellers arranging cheap prints to hang from their stalls. There were people sitting on benches reading newspapers. I crossed the Seine and walked past official buildings, museums, department stores. I sat down at the Café de la Paix and ordered coffee. People passed me and, watching them, I opened my diary. There was an inscription on the first page: "To remember your trip by. With love, Grisha and Olga." I faced a book of blank pages. Borrowing a pencil from the waiter, I thought for a minute, arranging sentences in my mind. Then I wrote: "July 30, 1952. Sam Star is my name, and here and now I claim my heritage. My progenitors were the warriors and prophets of Israel, and my God is the God of Israel. When I speak or sing to God, my head is unbowed and uncovered. I look Him in the eye and, with love and anger, I'll say my piece. That's the way I am."

An old man, selling newspapers from table to table, asked, "*Herald Tribune,* mister?"

I answered in French: "*Je ne lis pas les journaux Américains, seulement les Russes.*"

The old man shrugged his shoulders in a familiar gesture and said, "*Shalom,*" as he walked away.

For a moment I wanted to laugh. It had been a long day. I believe he was too far away to hear when I called out, "*Shalom!*"